Pra

LUCKY TURTLE

A *New York Times Book Review* Editors' Choice

"An unforgettable love story." **—*People***

"Fans of Roorbach's prolific work will appreciate his signature lyricism and sense of place, his sweeping narrative, humor and romance. New readers are walking into the hands of a skilled storyteller who's not afraid to take on a big, messy tale of love, privilege and abuse." **—*The New York Times Book Review***

"Look out: Roorbach has created the sexiest man seen in literature in a good long time . . . An epic love story . . . No greater reading pleasure to be had anywhere." **—*Kirkus Reviews*, starred review**

"Nobody else could have written this gorgeous novel, full to the brim with tragedy but also fun, as well as the best kind of romance. *Lucky Turtle* is an ode and a love letter to our wounded, imperfect, and oh-so-beautiful world."
—Nina de Gramont, author of *The Christie Affair*

"A thrilling, blistering tale of young love and old hate and the steady endurance of both." **—Lily King, author of *Five Tuesdays in Winter***

"Roorbach's understated, luminescent novel beautifully evokes an idyllic world created when two hearts are braided together." **—*Booklist*, starred review**

"An engrossing novel with standout characters." **—*Library Journal*, starred review**

"A story of love and heartbreak in a world of breathtaking splendor and deep injustice, Bill Roorbach's *Lucky Turtle* is a novel of perseverance, brimming with entertaining dialogue and rich details of the flora and fauna of the West."
—*Shelf Awareness*

THE GIRL OF THE LAKE

"Each meticulously chiseled-down and polished tale contains enough plot, character development, and emotion to fill a novel . . . These stories, with their smart and funny dialogue, characters both wise and fallible, are sure to capture the reader's imagination, and heart. For fans of Richard Russo and Russell Banks." **—*Booklist*, starred review**

"Bill Roorbach knows so well how to break your heart, how to make you fall in love, how to see you well through both and feel so much the greater human being for it all. What a wonderful writer, what a beautiful book."
—Brad Watson, author of *Miss Jane*

"The ten generous, daring short stories in the new collection by the author of *Life Among Giants* range from tricky romance to dark comedy to breathtaking adventure . . . Roorbach's cunningly crafted stories start off ordinary, and then turn magically strange." **—*Publishers Weekly***

"Elegant, assured short stories . . . Roorbach writes in unadorned, vigorous language . . . Readable entertainments that have much to say about the world." **—*Kirkus Reviews*, starred review**

THE REMEDY FOR LOVE

Finalist for the Kirkus Prize for Fiction

"Snowbound in Maine, two strangers struggle to survive—fighting, flirting, baring secrets. Their sexy, snappy dialogue will keep you racing through." **—*People***

"[A] superbly grown-up love story . . . Lyrical, reserved and sometimes unsettling . . . Another expertly delivered portrait of the world from Roorbach, that poet of hopeless tangles." **—*Kirkus Reviews*, starred review**

"*The Remedy for Love* is not the remedy for sleep deprivation. You'll stay up all night . . . It is relentless and brilliant. Leave it to Roorbach to tease out the subtlest nuances in the progress of love while stoking a tale that is as gripping as any Everest expedition—and that is also tender and terrifying and funny and, in the end, so true it seems inevitable. I'm not sure there's another American writing today who can lay down a love story, or any story, with the depth and appeal and freshness of Bill Roorbach." **—Peter Heller, author of *The Guide***

LIFE AMONG GIANTS

"*Life Among Giants* is a larger-than-life production. Yet all of its wild characters feel genuine, their aches and flaws and desires wholly organic; and the plot they're tangled in moves forward at a breakneck speed. It's a dizzy romp. There's murder and intrigue and sex and terror, and Roorbach is generous with it all . . . These characters are not regular people, but they never feel like caricatures . . . Alive, electric and surprisingly dangerous." **—*The New York Times Book Review***

"Hilarious and heartbreaking, wild and wise, Bill Roorbach's *Life Among Giants*, which is earning comparisons to *The World According to Garp*, is a vivid chronicle of a life lived large." **—*Parade***

"A bighearted, big-boned story . . . *Life Among Giants* reads like something written by a kinder, gentler John Irving . . . Roorbach is a humane and entertaining storyteller with a smooth, graceful style." **—*The Washington Post***

"Consistently surprising and truly entertaining . . . Deliciously strange and deeply affecting." **—*The Boston Globe***

"A novel of extravagant imagination . . . Roorbach makes the novel a leisurely mystery as well as a bildungsgroman."
—*Shelf Awareness for Readers*, starred review

"[A] thrilling indulgence, a tale of opulence, love triangles, and madness, set against a sumptuous landscape of lust and feasts."
—*Publishers Weekly*, boxed review

BEEP

ALSO BY BILL ROORBACH

Nonfiction

Summers with Juliet

A Place on Water (with Robert Kimber and Wesley McNair)

Into Woods

Temple Stream: A Rural Odyssey

Fiction

Big Bend

The Smallest Color

Life Among Giants

The Remedy for Love

The Girl of the Lake

Lucky Turtle

Instruction

Writing Life Stories: How to Make Memories into Memoirs, Ideas into Essays and Life into Literature

Contemporary Creative Nonfiction: The Art of Truth

BEEP

a novel by

BILL ROORBACH

ALGONQUIN BOOKS
OF CHAPEL HILL
2024

Published by
ALGONQUIN BOOKS OF CHAPEL HILL
Post Office Box 2225
Chapel Hill, North Carolina 27515-2225

an imprint of Workman Publishing
a division of Hachette Book Group, Inc.
1290 Avenue of the Americas,
New York, NY 10104

Printed in the United States of America.
Design by Steve Godwin.

Library of Congress Cataloging-in-Publication Data

[TK]

10 9 8 7 6 5 4 3 2 1
First Edition

For All My Monkeys

BEEP

Chapter One

I AM BEEP, MONKEY.

I live in the world of monkeys near saltwater on the sunset side of the vast beyond. We have relations and ancestors all the way across to the sunrise side, so the old uncles say, impassable mountains in between. One of the mountains supposedly smokes, even spits fire! Legends, prophecy: somemonkey crossed over those fearsome peaks in some unexplained way to here, separating monkeydom. But, you see, a monkey one day will come along whose accidental courage will reunite us, even save the world and not only find him a mate—quest enough, we all agree. Anyway, it's all the stuff of long discussion while mutually grooming in deep shade these hot afternoons, well fed: how could it be, that monkeys got where we are? Babies believe the legends, the old uncles believe the prophecy, but I'm a grownup now, or nearly, and on to grownup things.

I like this river we live near partly because the goers don't come here much, except to look at the birds, our beautiful and distant cousins. I think the goers study them to perfect their own flight, which is messy, loud, and marks the sky with criss-crossing clouds. It's the goers that make the world need saving, the old uncles say, more and more of them all the time, more and more imposing. I have noticed this even in my mere short life.

But some you-mens seem okay. Many are pleasing to look at, with fabulous black cushions of hair, or golden hair long as orchid tendrils, others with tresses red as sunsets. Once on the beach a large male caused a sensation among us—he was nearly hairy as a howler, once the peel was removed. And many you-mens are pleasant, unthreatening, a certain burbling of spirit. Some you-mens even call forth food from the land: these we call growers and consider cousins, if cautiously. But many again, the goers, we call them, are pure terror: loud, careless, unaware of the lives their sudden movements end. My old cousin Pooop got his name for his aim as the worst of them walked under us oblivious. But Pooop is dead. He climbed in their terrible black vines, lightning vines, we call them, lightning that burned that monkey so badly he smoked on the goer-stone below, that hard black stuff the goers use to make their go-ways, hot as sun.

Chapter Two

LATELY I HAVE BEEN SO restless. The aunts observe me and say so: Beep restless. My mother, called Peep, all mine these three rainy seasons, has an infant at her breast suddenly, *my* breast, and on her back when we travel, *my* back. Mother-my-own pushes me away and for a joke calls me a punk-monkey and truly, I feel like one, ready to curse all the girl cousins aiming their rumps at me, insulting! The aunts, too, mean to me, like I'm not Swee-Beep anymore but one of the old uncles who spend their time in lonesome cogitation.

So, I go to the wise one with his many rainy seasons, one for each finger and each toe, imagine how old! I speak of my restlessness, my agitation, the busy mind.

And he holds my eye a long uncomfortable time, says, "At your age I left my inland troupe and climbed through the treetops entirely alone for ten sunsets, imagine how far, imagine how big this water when first I spotted it from the Windy Tree! I, your ancient own uncle, had never tasted the salty sea! And this troupe, now my own, came the very next morning for the Windy Tree days, and there was a particular lass that smelled like afterlife and haven't I stayed here among us since, and now around me my children and my grandchildren and my great-grandchildren and even great-great—you are one."

"I thought so."

"It's time to urinate as the grown ones do, urinate upon your hands and your feet and make your mark wherever you go—you've seen this practice—just don't do it here, for here is my place to mark, and your other old uncles, if I let them, and there are too many of us, and the mademoiselles too few, all of them claimed double and triple and some more than that. We uncles await any new females, and we know they will come. They will come from the other old troupes from far inland, and some may have seen the hills, or come from the river, that way, and one day one will come who has seen the smoking mountain, even the sunrise ocean, and the sprawling verticals of the goers, all right angles rising, which I call wrong angles, and she will be queen, for she will reunite the ancient troupes."

"Oh, uncle, those are myths, and we have no queen."

"Myths, eh? You've seen the you-men enclaves, all the boxes!"

"Enclaves?"

"Their dwellings, their gatherments!"

"Ah, you mean the billages?"

"Yes, the billages. They have further separated monkeydom! Even I have seen places where the you-mens are so numerous and their dwellings so packed together that no trees can grow, or none of consequence, and no monkey can cross. You've seen them kill the trees. You saw it at the turn of the water." He didn't point but only tilted his head, aimed his gaze that way.

I said, "They made the ground hard."

"And so hot."

"I've seen hills," I said.

"I remember. You were with us when the fruit wouldn't come and we ventured. And that's the way I would go if I were young again, back into the hills, as far as your arms and legs and the forest can take you, find one of the inland troupes, find one of the inland ladies tired of inland uncles and piss your way in, new troupe. And then perhaps your babies will continue toward the sunrise when it's their turn, and then their babies, and then many through generations, always toward morning, and finally our clan will once again unite. Because when we do, the great universe will change, you'll see. A queen, you'll see."

Such grand language. Meant to inspire. But I knew what my old wise great-great-grandfather was up to—he was trying to get rid of me as he would any young male coming of age.

"But when," I said. "When do I go."

"Today is always the right day."

Wisdom.

So back to my mother to say farewell, but she just scolded me—baby sleeping, the very breast upon which I once. And to my aunts, who were all up high in today's tree because of a flush of tasty pinkish bugs, and who turned their backs to me. And to my cousins, fewer today than yesterday, one-by-one gone out into the great forest and whatever lay beyond, which was more forest, from what I'd seen, or denser you-men gatherments, and after that nothing but impassable mountains, if you believed the legends, mountains full of the cries of all the scary things. Animals we didn't know. Birds that ate monkeys, Pooop said—and this a monkey believed, because one of our own old uncles had been carried off just a handful of seasons before, biting and kicking all the way, died when he was dropped, torn apart and eaten where he lay, savage beak. From high in the sky he'd cried out—they'd all heard it, the monkeys in that generation, many still with us—"I see the smoking mountain!"

Now the troupe intones that very thing when somemonkey is extremely sick: *He sees the smoking mountain.*

Maybe I will be the one to see the smoking mountain but also stay alive, return to tell the tale, a girl monkey on my arm! A queen, and why not?

Popular monkey Laugh hugged me tight. She would stay—a new monkey had claimed her, and his name was Blue. He dropped down from the very height of today's roost, a great mango tree in flower. "Do I scent urine on your hands?" he bellowed.

I laughed, but it was true, the urge had been unspeakable.

Laugh was the monkey I would most want to mate, very long tail, fine hands, neck long, eyes wide and amused, scent intoxicating, but my older sister.

"I'm going to find the smoking mountain," I said.

And they chided me, chided me, turned their backs. I climbed high as I could, high as the highest branch that could hold me, stood on it tall as it swayed, ocean that way, river this way, more ocean that way. But forest toward the sunrise, promise of hills, and so that direction I proceeded, the chiding of Laugh and Blue and all the cousins and my aunts and the old uncles and even my mother fading behind me, shadow of a predator bird to chase me back in under the canopy and back safe into monkey world.

I ran hand-and-foot down the longest branches and onward to branches interlaced, leaping any gaps, eye out for snakes, for cats on the ground, for bullet ants and scorpions, for poison frogs, for youmens (especially goers!), swung arm-to-arm and flew across the gaps, brachiating it's called, tail for balance, dropping, climbing, hands quick and fingers quicker for good things to eat: there's a kind of grasshopper I like, and always termites, and here and there a blue lizard, which are slow and best flavor. And in the pockets of branches sips of water, nothing wanting but rest.

And so I kept the afternoon sun on my back, traveled high up in the canopy as the boldest monkeys do, leapt and swung and dove and climbed and made my way toward the sunrise. "May it ever recede!" was one travel prayer of the uncles, not one I was saying. Five trees, five more, the ignoble constructions of the goers beneath me now, this box and that, silly things impossible to understand, their treeless expanses, that hot black rock, the machines going and going, coming and coming, or resting by a dwelling, often in pairs. The canids of the goers barked, co-opted into whatever life this was, silly overweight wolves.

Five more trees again, and then five and five and five and five till nothing in the world smelled the same, and there were no more you-men dwellings, just a hot black go-way, their machines awake and roaring, grunting, hissing, farting. I'd been this far as a small. So I knew there would be a crossing that way—a monkey never forgets the way—and five more trees and five and five and five and there it was, the bluevine, we called it, but we knew it was not a vine or branch but the work of a you-men, one of the rare ones who meant to help us, to keep us off their lightning vines, a grower, likely, who'd kindly tight-braided several blue strands of some non-monkey material to make one thick blue vine, pulled taut in some way across the go-way from this grand tree to that one, thus spanning the impossible gap where the branches of friendly leafies could no longer reach one another, and so very thoughtfully creating a monkey crossing.

I availed myself gratefully, crossed the bluevine over the danger-way and back into forest, sense of a new district. In a great strangler fig that had overtopped its host tree I paused a long time, finally got up the nerve to climb. So high, that one, and the ever-present danger of birds, snakes, howlers. I, Beep, saw into the next valley. And then past it, though a gap unimaginably far away, a kind of vision: the hills that the old ones said came before mountains. The great fig was the furthest place I'd ever been, the furthest I could go and still know how to get back to my troupe. I could still hear the chiding of my sisters and cousins, my mother cross and rejecting, the useless gossip of the old uncles, the insults of the new males, nattering fops and dandies arriving every day.

Well, goodbye to all that.

I lingered in the fig, watched the good world a long time, those hills so promising but so far away, a kind of haze that made it all seem to fade and fade again, the greens going lighter, the blue of the sky lighter, too, till it was all one thing: destiny.

If I would be a true monkey, it was time. I took deep breaths. I greeted the hills, turning my eyes to each. I chided all the things behind me. I honored all the things ahead. I pissed carefully on each foot, then each hand, patted my fur with it, sharp smell and wild, me and we, and continued on: all the territory forward was mine.

Chapter Three

HUNGRY MONKEY. EACH SEASON HAD its foods and the troupe knew where to go to find them in abundance, or where to go and what to do if abundance failed. But the troupe knowing and I, Beep, knowing were two different things. I found that I'd confused troupe and Beep. I was, though, something even on my own, and real enough, if diminished. But here were some leaves we monkeys have always liked the taste of. And here a hurry of ants, ugh, that formic flavor, but eat. Not so much fruit, not as yet. I heard a toucan and called to her: "Toucan help this monkey."

She said, "Nope, nope," but then there she was, that bill like a big crab claw, and colorful.

"What's to eat," I said.

And she looked me over, said, "Some fine termites that way. Caught a lizard. No fruit if that's your pleasure." Her bill clattered: "Nope, none. Nope, nope, nope, nope, nope, nope, nope."

Lizards aplenty, but not the good blue ones, just the big greenies, too squirmy for me, if I could even catch one. Termites though. I thanked the bird, and she clattered her bill. And had not lied. The termite mound was enormous, like a pillar of stone, unassailable, but the termite traffic was heavy and I just took a seat near one of their routes and plucked and ate them as they came and went, sharp little sweet things, oblivious of one another, so it seemed, crunchy.

"Fuck!" they'd cry when I bit them, an emotion that rippled through the entire colony. And then scarce.

I carried on traveling for an orange fistful of sunsets, slept in the protection of trees from kingdoms I knew well, the inner canopy comforting, the soft song of tree mind. In the day I got some rest, perhaps not enough, here and there a pause in a sunny break (but watch for falcons, Beep—none of the old uncles to stand sentry and sound the alarm, and this monkey jumpy—but it was only some shiny you-men roarbird the once, a large leaf falling the next), no sound or sign of monkeys like me—just the stubid howlers making their show, far away, and here and there the shit of the mean ones, which we called punks and the you-mens called spy-dirt monkeys, so the rumor went, why? Their eyes were not on the ground, and they weren't we: we were the monkeys.

Leaping a gap to a proper vine I spotted a squadron of peccaries in a wallow far below. I climbed down closer and watched them. Eventually they took notice of me, and we shouted insults back and forth (they are very funny, these fellows, and viewed from above flat as mango pits), traveled over them through my branches an afternoon, slow going and calm, laughing at their jokes, resting when they did, and surely enough they arrived at a place with sour plantains, short, thick ones like a grower's fingers. They'd shown me the way so I helped them, knocked bunches down from the trees, saving out the ripest for me, and gobbled the bitter things as the tayassuid did. In the heat of the midday then, well stuffed, I slept on a thick branch ignoring their shouts for more. Of course I'm a lazy monkey! And you are pigs! (Peccaries hate to be called pigs!) You call *those* insults? Try harder! They thought I'd throw down more if they managed to anger me. And truly, once I woke, it was fun to bean a couple of them with the hardest and most unripe fruits. They'd jump and shriek and all the others would laugh. Some say they're smart as monkeys, nope. We spent the whole afternoon unto evening at it, and then we all of us slept, each at our level: mud for them, mid-canopy me.

In the morning I fed them a little more, and beaned a couple of the loud ones, shat on a snoozer's head—don't sleep late in the woods!—ate a few more plantains myself, dropped as many bunches as I could to the forest floor for the peccaries, and then, well rested and well fed, also much amused, carried on, their comical shouts and laughter and fellowship behind me.

The landscape was climbing now. Ah, terrain! So, I'd made it to the hills! Nomonkey had ever been so far, I thought, only the Ancestor. I listened for our voices, but none, only the sobering cry of a forest eagle and somewhere a terrible, thundering bellow—one of the goers, no doubt, the constant cracks and pops and clangs and snarls and explosions of their handiwork.

Our trees, the mother trees of monkey life, climbed a hillside, and I climbed with them, flinging myself across the gaps, catching swinging branches as the wind rose, finally again to a crest and then the highest tree, and another view—a grower billage, but with many goers clattering their way through, so much commotion. But the trees inter-groped and without climbing too high (and thus into the open), I kept moving in the direction of sunrise, afternoon sun on my back that is, amused with all that went on below. Until I came to a place where the goers kept their rolling machines, just a vast black wasteland, as if fire had come and turned everything to rock. And the trees—few and far apart, mostly palms, which do monkeys little good, especially traveling monkeys, especially this one alone.

And hungry again.

I reversed course, found thicker forest, unpleasant wafts and whiffs of you-men, large numbers of their dwellings, those boxes. Curious, I examined more than one, no single color predominant, surrounded by unknown shrubbens all isolated and alone, a sorrowful keening. And lots of the black rock, which seemed bedding for the rolling machines. And crossed a brook, found a drink in a crook, came to a beautiful fig tree, rested a while. Down below, yet another dwelling of a goer family, fake pond, again the forced confinement of plants, it seemed, poor shrubbens.

Suddenly I noticed a pretty you-men tween sitting in a contraption eating something off a piece of tree chopped flat and set on stilts. I sniffed voluptuously: pineapple! One of the main reasons for the monkey fondness of growers. The lean tween ate like a monkey, hand to mouth very fast, and if a piece fell on the ground retrieved it, stuffed her mouth.

There'd be none left!

A scare tactic was in order. I jumped from my hiding branch and right onto the wood plane in front of her. It shook on its stilts. But instead of shrieking and knocking over the contraption and running away on rubber feet leaving the pineapple for me, she only laughed.

"Mr. Nilsson," she said clearly.

One thing everymonkey knows is that the goers and growers aren't too bright, and can make no sense of us. I pointed to my mouth: sign was the best way.

"Hungry?" she said.

Little remarking that I'd understood her, I gave all the positive signs I knew, even the you-men smile (which looks like war to monkeys), and surely enough she held up a piece of the fragrant fruit.

I crossed my arms over my chest, cocked my hip. That was one of our imitations of you-mens.

"Don't trust me, eh?"

Slowly, clearly, I said, "Just toss it over here."

"Ha-ha, chitter-chitter," she said, and gobbled my piece of fruit!

I stomped my foot, had a few words to say.

She only laughed, retrieved another chunk, held it out to me, fragrance. I took a step closer.

"Say please," she said.

I was not the best sharer, either. Memory unbidden of half my male cohort chasing me in and out of the vines at the rainy-day tree, I with a nice stolen grower fruit in hand.

"Please, some for me," I said.

"Coo-coo to you, too," she said.

I stepped closer, quick look at the trees to divert her, and when her green tween gaze followed mine I dove and grabbed and leapt back out of reach: pineapple chunk. Stuffed it in my mouth. Oooh, sweet! And a memory of we-the-troupe robbing the whitefurfaces of just such a prize. I jumped back into the welcoming fig.

And should have been on my way, but. Oh, gosh that fruit was good. The half-child had a clink-shiny sharp stick and cut more pineapple with it, slicing off all the parts you hate pineapple for, the tough skin, the slashing leaves—only crazy whitefurfaces had ambition enough to raid the grower farms for it, bash it open on beach rocks, where we smaller simians would dart in for fragments.

Tweenie held out another piece. Such an appealing oddity, this juvenile, her cheeks spotted prettily, her hair in fantastical ropes. She smelled like roses and chemicals. That was most goers—smelled like chemicals—not so most growers, who smelled like dirt. So, I'd identified her, goer: danger. Something about her, though, so peaceful, so lanky, a little tall, a little unformed, so proud of herself to have made my monkey acquaintance. I took the next piece of fruit, less urgency. Then the next. Fibrous ambrosia. The lanky one patted her hairless knee and so I stood on it and took sustenance, then took turns with her, my piece, hers, my piece, hers. I had never shared a thing with a female before, much less a goer female. She patted my head. Worth it. She scramched my neck, very nice. She tucked me in up against her belly like she was my mother and scramched my ears, patted my back. I couldn't help it, I fell asleep.

I woke to the voices of others of her kind. She put a finger to her lips. Monkeys do that, too: *be quiet*. And opened a kind of cage beside her, a cage full of pretend animals, very colorful, chemical fur, eyes perhaps real, giving the lie. She set me gently in there among them, fanciful creatures, brightly colored as birds. Finger to the lips again. And before I could jump away, a large goer was there, burly male.

"Inga," he said sharply, "remember pain-o practice."

"It's vacation," she said.

"Pain-o," he said. "And pick up all these stuffees. Mom will be home soon and we've got packing to do."

He didn't wait for her but picked up a pretend dogg and a pretend I-don't-know-what and a pretend whale that would just sink in the ocean, threw them all atop me in the box.

"Let's go!" he said.

I was mesmerized, hypnotized, you-men-ized. That's the only explanation. Because I didn't shriek and leap and steal the pineapple that was left and take it to the forest but just lay in the perfumed pile of fake fur, so comfortable, even as Inga closed the lid and latched it.

I was inzide. I was alive, not pretend, no stuffee. But already my loyalty had been excited and I didn't want the large male goer to be angry with my new friend, so skinny, so delicate.

The box was lifted. By her. I had seen her as feeble but she was far stronger than I. Strength can be either threat or protection to a monkey, so I remained calm waiting to see which. My little prizzon swung, bounced with her step, the light changing suddenly, noises unknown: clonks and sweeps and paddings.

The cage was dropped upon something that gave, my shock absorbed, a bounce.

"You just wait here," my pretty captor whispered.

I said, "What choice do I have?" Overwhelming urge to urinate into my orange hands and feet and declare this my space, but it was not my space, and I did not want to get this angel Inga in difficulty with the gruff male. I began a speech to that effect.

"Hoo-hoo, little monkey. Please quiet," she said. "I'll be back quick."

She was kindness, I was trust.

Plus I was comfortable, so comfortable, rose and chemicals, and *so* tired, had been *so* alone.

A cacophony arose from somewhere near, multiple tones, like the goer-loving whitefurfaces hitting rocks with rocks on the beach, plus infernal you-men wailing. Except there was a heart rhythm at the center of it, so regular, lullabye.

I snoozed.

Chapter Four

AND WOKE TO A BURST of light.

"Mr. Nilsson," said the girl, opening the cage, ropes of fur now piled on her head and tied with a bit of pink root.

I climbed out, stretched. "Actually, I am Beep," I said clearly.

"I adore pain-o," she said. "I act like I don't, but."

We were in a pink atmosphere, many objects, many straight lines, the interior, I slowly gathered, of one of the you-men dwellings, boxes within boxes. I scanned every object and spatial relationship, could find nowhere to shit that would not seem hostile. And I smelled like pretend roses—in the Home Tree I'd be pummeled for it by aunts and uncles both. But this was not the Home Tree, and I was on a quest. Yes, and already feeling strongly that this goer child was part of it.

Still.

I gave a speech, formal: "I'm on a quest to spread my genetic material beyond my Home Tree, but more than that to reach the lost troupe that live over the hills and mountains in the far trees where the sun rises. You yourself, big as you are, are probably not more than a season away from adulthood and that sort of consideration, genetic material and all that, but you'll know whereof I speak—else why hide me from the male, correct? You protect my quest, and so you are a quester as well. Further, I want to see the mountain that smokes. You laugh, you grin. We have our legends, I'm sure you, yours."

"Oh, precious monkey, quiet," she said. And lifted me up out of the cage by my armpits and brought me to her face and pressed her mouth on my cheek with a smack. Would she eat me? No, no, calm please, Beep. Every instinct to scramch out her eyes and leap from her grasp and do what? I could not see an opening in the pink foliage and sheer pink walls.

"Precious, precious monkey," she said.

"I must shit," I said, and wriggled from her grasp. She was so non-hostile I almost felt badly about it, leapt up to a crystal disk on the underside of the pink ceiling of the artificial cave. Cave, I suddenly realized—it was just a cave. The howlers used such places, deep hollows in cliffsides, not so dry as this one. What mysteries!

"I know I can't keep you," she said.

"Keep me?"

A commotion.

"Shh, shh," she said, this Inga. "My mom's home."

Light behind the great pink leaves hanging. I swung down to them, soft as baby fur, those leaves, and made of chemicals, that particular smell, and swung again to pull them aside, and the light grew brighter, an exit! But no—the view, clear as water, was hard as rock, more crystal? Like the stuff the whitefurfaces would knock on when they went begging in the grower yards? Ice, they called it, ancient lore. Out there a large creature had rolled in, made of what monkeys call *clink*, but the humans call *meddle*, all the meddle sounds, and a grown female goer, mouth red with blood, chest engorged in some way, belly flat as a crocodile rock, paying no attention to the sky—any eagle could nab her—climbed out and started pulling unknowns out of the meddle roller, and then a you-men infant, hunk of all-too-familiar beach rubbish wrapped around its waist.

Inga snapped the luxuriant pink leaves back in place, cut off the sunlight, said, "I know, you want outzide."

"It's just that I have to shit."

"But don't you think we're going to be friends?"

I did think so. I leapt straight beside her and upon her and took her enormous hands, squeezed the slender, long fingers. She pulled me in tight, closed her wrapping around me.

I admit I protested. Her mother's mouth, covered in blood!

"Quiet, quiet," Inga said.

She cracked open a pink plane, a *dar* she called it, and there was another space, this one more a sandy color, and carrying me hidden at her throat she ran us outzide, as she called it, back into monkey world, I called it, all green, all green, all blessed green. She put me on a pile of stones lined up so very straight, and I was free again, had always been, leapt to the nearest tree (a bitterbeanpod tree, not the ones to eat), and watching overhead for birds, for snakes, found a high branch, crouched and shat.

She laughed! I knew it was a laugh by the energy of it, a burble, a calling of waters. "You poooped!" she cried.

Yes, call it what you will, and then I peed, dampening my hands and feet against the pretend rose smell. Oh, that made her laugh.

"Come back visit," she said.

"On a quest," I said, thinking ruefully of pineapple.

She raced to the blank wall, opened a slit somehow that was a dar, and disappeared inzide the boxes that were her dwelling. Once again I was alone. I didn't want to carry on, but put the sun to my back, leapt to a high branch, then the next tree, and continued.

Chapter Five

I LISTENED FOR MONKEYS, BUT heard none, that part of the day when the wise things rest. I'd had my pink slumber, and so I forged ahead, more and more disoriented. Maybe I'd just never been so close to so many goers, their boxes everywhere under the spreading branches now, but also their blackly roasted go-ways, their cropped meadows, one each to go with every box. Boxes inzide boxes, remember, and pink inzide, and very cold. So much noise! And not just the usual male shouts and female wheedles (and all the everything in-between), but slams and screeches, roars and hisses, squeals and rattles, sudden bangs and unexplained splashes, hoots and explosions, the local trees not inured to it but shaking, gripping the ground in terror. I couldn't begin to fathom the goer vocalisations—which of them were joy? Which fear? You-mens! They marched about alone or in twos and threes. Was there no affinity among cousins here, no troupe to run with?

Go, Beep, go!

Branch to branch, tree to tree, that was the monkey way, sun on my back, sense of the ground climbing, views looking back: there was the ocean, which had never been so far from me. Ahead, plenty of green but also that wall of noise, and below so many boxes, so many meddle rollers. Suddenly I was at an edge sharp as a beach. But there was no beach, no water, just a break, one of the goer go-ways, the biggest and widest I'd ever seen, wide as the crocodile river, no blue pretend vines provided, yet sun at my back. The river-wide trail was right in my path to the smoking mountain and to the sunrise, and to my heritage, that lost troupe.

There was wisdom in the family about crossing goer trails: do not. Unless where branches touched or a vine extended, and not one of the lightning ones! The you-men bluelines were safe and much used. Some of the oldest uncles remembered their advent and considered them proof of the goodness of you-mens.

I ranged that way, ranged this way, but found no blueline, and no trees great enough to reach their branches all the way over—the meddle rollers roaring or sputtering or whistling past, some of them enormous like I'd never seen and smelling like fire had burned them.

My belly rumbled. I could locate none of the leaves we monkeys like. No fruit. The trees in this you-men forest were so much smaller than in the true forest and not so many kinds. Overhead great birds roared—I winced, I ducked, but they only roared and rumbled, glinting meddle roarbirds that left their straight lines of cloud, maybe farther away than I could tell, which would make them too big for the monkey imagination, which is vast, I tell you.

The pineapple called me. The scramch behind the ears. The goer tween, Inga. I slept in the biggest tree I could find, the farthest from any goer boxes. Nothing to eat but ants, and not the good ones.

In the morning, I peed my hands and feet and thanked—as monkeys do daily—thanked the clouds in both sky and in puddles, gave them thanks that I'd lived through the night, then retraced my route, returned to the sweet trees above Inga's box. I waited above the stone flats where she kept her sitting contraption, watched the side of the biggest box, the mysterious dar that had swung to allow our escape. And after a long time, the dar did open, and with a cry, here she came.

Inga!

"I won't!" she cried.

"Sweedie, our flight," the adult female called from inzide the box, almost begging.

"Inga," I said clearly.

Her ropes of hair flew, she searched the branches for me, found my eye. The adult female, clearly Inga's momma, was close behind her, bearing the small one. Inga put a finger to her lips. She made happy eyes and showed her teeth, burbled with that you-men laughter that even monkeys like.

"What is so funny," her mother said.

"There's a monkey," Inga said, and pointed her pink finger right at me.

"What on Aarth," her mother said.

"It is I, Beep!" I said. "Aarth is my cousin, if that's what you said."

Even the baby saw me.

"Squirrel monkey," the mother said warmly. "Ooooh. They aren't usually solo. Oooh, ooh. Keep your eyes peeled, there will be more."

Ugh, eyes peeled?

"I'd like some fruit," I said clearly.

"Oh, how charming," said the mother. "Hoo-hoo, monkey." She'd wiped most of yesterday's blood from her lips, but at the edges of the enormous mouth some remained (probably she'd caught and eaten a bird). Also part of her outer wrappings had come loose and her poor chest looked more distended than ever, wrapped in a bright banner of some kind. Somemonkey once said they look like us, but come on: they do not.

"I call him Mr. Nilsson," Inga said.

Her mother laughed, very much like the girl's laugh, bubbles popping in a tumble-brook. "Well, when we're back in Nyork we'll have to read *Pippi Longstocking* again," she said.

"'I am the strongest girl in the world,'" Inga said and lifted her arms like a male punk-monkey would do, why?

Because it was true, I supposed—she was the strongest girl in the world. Look how she had carried me in that box full of pretend animals, unimaginably heavy!

"I will attest to your offspring's strength," I said. "Also to her courage, which has emboldened me. Still, there is the question of some fruit, if you would oblige me."

"Oh, ha-ha!" the mother said. "Ooh-ooh-ooh, ahh-ahh-ahh! Well. He seems friendly enough, but please keep him away from Willie."

"But, Mom."

"It's your hour with Willie. I have my thing on Zooom. It's just till noon. Mommy's going to get you two a snack, then have a rest. Okay? You watch Willie out here on the paddy-o, I rest."

"Just as we do it," I called down.

Inga's mother ignored my pleasantry, put the baby down on the stones. He wailed. Momma disappeared behind that blue dar, which cracked just enough for her to enter the box dwelling. The baby stopped wailing. He reached from his sitting position, suddenly scooted himself bottom-wise to a pretend meddle goer. He pushed on the center of a circle thereon. It made a comical sound.

"Beep," the baby said clearly. "Beep."

"Yes, Beep," I shouted down. "I am Beep, Monkey."

"Beep-beep," the baby said.

"Beep-beep," the girl said.

The baby pushed the button. I understood the onomatopoetic nature of the boy's locution, that it was not my name—but.

I made some noise myself. "I am Beep," I said clearly.

But Inga only laughed.

Could I make the sound they were making? Imitate the toy? Sort of. And patted my chest.

"Beep-beep," the little boy said.

And I didn't say Beep, my name, but made the sound the toy made as best I could, patted my chest.

"Beep," the girl said, looking up at me.

I beeped. I patted my chest. Patience, she was no monkey.

"Beep-beep," the little one said.

"I am Beep, Monkey," I said. But that did no good. I made the toy noise, pointed at my chest the way the girl had pointed when she called herself Inga.

"You are Beep," she said. Joy, it is visible even upon the you-mens.

I gave a congratulatory and self-introductory speech, formal locution, I'm afraid, the level of this social moment eluding me, but Inga laughing all the while, the little boy noticing me, too.

"Beep," the girl said pointing at me.

I made the noise and pointed at me, too.

"Beep," the baby said.

Inga pointed at herself. "Inga," she said.

"Yes, Inga," I said.

"Ooh-ooh-ooh," she said, mocking me as her mother had.

"Beep-beep," the baby said.

"You are Beep," Inga said.

I was exhausted. I was mocked. But I was understood. I was unpanicked, only cautious. This was the strongest girl in the world and also very bright.

The dumb adult female returned with a pink flat sort of shiny rock, round as the sun and covered with clever foods. She'd forgotten me entirely. "Time for my Zooom," she said, incomprehensible. "Please feed Willie his snack." And she hurried back into the boxes that were this troupe's dwelling.

"Beep-beep," said the baby. He was only making a sound.

"Beep," said Inga. She, by contrast, was saying my name: "Beep, Beep, Beep."

I swung down a little closer. I did not want to be back inzide that dwelling. My freedom had tasted good. But so had the pineapple. On the crystal disk I saw only one familiar food, a redsharp, we called it, often stolen from the growers, this one torn into pieces with the neatest straight lines, how? Otherwise the only things on offer were white squares of spongey matter with purple innards leaking out, and brown gook. Also orange sticks that I took to be injured carrots.

"You want samweedge," the girl said to the baby.

He and I made similar assenting noises.

She laughed at that—that I could imitate the wee-bee—handed him a white square.

And she held a fat piece of the redsharp up to me. "Pebber?" she said. "You like red pebber? These are my fayb-fayborite."

I was wary and must have looked it—not about Inga, just all the noise, the adult female apparently near, the gruff male unaccounted for, this strange understanding. Inga tossed the redsharp piece, pebber, as she called it, to the stones of the paddy-o. There it glistened, beckoned. Okay, so I bounced down and grabbed the redsharp fragment and brought it back up to my branch, used my two orange hands, now pleasantly pissed upon, to politely feed the morsel into my teeth.

And Inga picked up her own piece. Giggling, she ate it the same way.

Yes, mocked!

So I mocked her, patting at my not-hair the way she patted at her long ropes of hair. And she wasn't as sensitive to the teasing as the aunts might have been but brought me over a samweedge, she'd called it, the white square oozing its purple blood. I took it straight from her hand—we could both be brave—unexpectedly soft, both hand and so-called samweedge. I sniffed the samweedge, to her apparent delight. I licked the blood—not salt as I'd expected, but sweeter than sweet. The brown ooze was the salty stuff, and I licked that, too, mysterious substance, but deep and delicious. Now the white square, soft, like textured air. She just bit her samweedge, so I bit mine, and the flavors in combination were. They were.

They were *afterlife*.

The goop got all stuck in my mouth, and the purple blood sticky in my hands—it was honey, purple honey, and tasted like fruit. These goers, maybe smarter than a monkey gave them credit for.

No, they were only fortunate.

Pointing seemed to work. I pointed at the next samweedge. Inga lifted it, handed it to baby, who smeared it mostly on his face. So babies were babies. I pointed at the next samweedge, this you-men plenty. Inga picked it up, folded it in some way, stuffed it all in her mouth, laughing around it. But picked up the next samweedge and held it up to me. I grabbed it summarily and ate it same. And more redsharp—nothing like what I'd ever tasted. And the orange sticks, hard as nuts and crunchy, no name forthcoming. I licked the purple from my hands, ecstatic:

I'd found a friend, one who'd maybe help a monkey cross the goer's go-way.

Chapter Six

MUCH ACTIVITY IN INGA'S HOWZZ, as she called it, a difficult concept, but more than a cave dwelling, for objects were stored there. I could suss every sound her sadly small troupe made, lazed on my branch, awaited my moment. At one point the blue wall split open (dar, dar) and Inga leapt out into the sun, sat in her contraption, arms folded hard across her chest, lips pushed out big (sign of unhappiness universal), then flowed water from her eyes, wailed. Curious. After a long interval her mother came out, patted her comfortingly—and I remembered: when there's a new one, the first child must go. Inga was being pushed out of the troupe! But no, after a while the gruff male appeared, not so gruff now, also patted her back.

"All goothings come to an end," he said.

Ha-ha, hopeless you-men. The trees did not come to an end. The ocean did not come to an end. Monkeys did not come to an end.

But surprise, Inga liked this big male and let him lift her up in his (proportionately very short) arms like a tiny one and rock her. He made his wind-voice so sweet and said some long thing to her, high voice, higher, low voice, lower, all smooth as water pouring, and gentle. And she stopped her wailing and snuggled to him and he said something more, that wind voice of theirs.

"Promeez?" she said.

"Yes, we come back for E-stir. We wub it here. Pura Vida."

"Pura vida," Inga repeated soulfully.

And he left her, the blue wall closing behind him.

"Inga," I hissed from my branch.

Nothing.

"Inga, Inga, Inga, Inga, Inga," I said.

Still nothing.

I crept down my branch, shook it.

Inga startled, looked up, found me there. "Oh, monkey!" she said. Then, gratifyingly, "Beeeeeep!"

But just then the adult male popped out. His name, apparently, was Dabby. He had a blue-crystal disc for her, covered with more foods, more samweedges, small squares. Not many uncles will share. Maybe affection, or then again maybe competition with the adult female. I began to feel some respect for him. He put the foods on the tree piece in front of Inga. She made her lip big again. Perhaps she'd had enough food.

Not I.

"Sweedie," said Dabby. "Sweedie please."

"I'm not going," she said.

But Dabby just grunted and clucked, some kind of private knowing. And heaved himself back into their dwelling through the dar, which seemed to open magically at his touch, a turning of his thick wrist.

"Food," I said from on high.

Inga understood! She held up a curious item, long and white, perhaps a mushrooom stem, but drooping. "Cheeeestick?" she said, offering it.

Ugh. I said, "Is there pineapple? I think I'd prefer that. I was most pleased by the pineapple. And you've taught me to look beneath the exterior of that estimable fruit next time they are happened upon by troupe or just I, Beep, and not count on the whitefurfaces to supply it. Sweet, delicious, toothsome."

"Hoo hoo hoo," she said, like a tinybaby learning monkey. "Ah, ah, ah, ahhhh!"

I took the cheeeestick, texture like a slug but no life in it. I expected it to pop open the way a lizard does when bitten, yum, but it only severed and a dense piece sat upon my tongue, clammy. Well, when on adventure, be adventurous. I bit into the thick excrescence, chewed, swallowed. Sweet, very salty, mostly salt, unctuous. That last comes from animals, usually, but this was no animal and never had been. Mystery upon mystery! To please her, I finished it. It sat hard in my stomach.

The girl forgot me, made that big lip again, wailed, shoved the disc of foods away from her onto the stones of the paddy-o. It was pineapple in those magical cubes! Offered thus! I dropped from my perch, retrieved a chunk, stuck it in my monkey mouth, then quickly retrieved as many more as I could, couldn't leap carrying them so stuffed my maw till my cheeks bulged, lunged for my branch. But I needn't have mistrusted Inga. She was delighted once again. In fact, she leapt up off her contraption and fell comically to all fours—no tail! Or was it hidden in her wrappings? And on all fours like a you-know-what (a monkey!), she picked up pineapple chunks and stuffed her mouth.

Capable of learning.

And she laughed and I laughed and she tossed me up a round fruit I didn't recognize, sharp taste, hot as a rock in sun.

"You don't like rabbish?"

I, Beep, did not like rabbish, spat it out dramatically.

Inga burbled with you-men mirth, tossed up the last chunk of pineapple. I gobbled that. Then she threw another cheeeestick. I tossed it back, hard, beaned her. Good companion, she shrieked with delight, shied the next rabbish at me, hard red little thing. I caught it easily—my game, after all, just substitute pooop—waited for her to pick up the next one and while she was bent, beaned her.

She rubbed her head, then laughed like a javelina, *ee-see-ee-see!* And a compliment, monkey style: "Good one!"

I jumped down, grabbed part of the white cake the samweedge was made in, glob of purple, but just as I got it in my mouth the blue wall cracked and the wall of the howzz swung open, dar. I leapt sideways and climbed a meddle tube to the hot top of the straight lines they lived among, and from there into my tree. Because through the door came the abandoning you-men mother, baby on her hip.

"What on Aarth!" she said. "Inga, what on Aarth! You'll clean this ubb. You'll clean this ubb immediately!"

"It's that monkey!" Inga said. And pointed right at me.

"Yes, it was I," I said. "I, Beep. I take full responsibility, and can explain. I leapt down in search of pineapple and ubbset that precarious disc of foods so that it fell to the stones there, the paddy-o, if I might." Monkey mendacity would have been hopeless: my hands were dripping purple, crumbs of the white cake still decorated my chest.

"Awww, monkey. So cute!" the mother said. "But such a mess. Hoo-hoo-hoo!"

"Beeeeep," said the baby. "Beep-beep!"

"Inga, take the baby," Momma said, suddenly remembering him, as suddenly forgetting me.

And just like that, Inga took the baby, bounced him, and he was all happy again.

Meanwhile Momma disappeared through the dar, which was a crack in the wall one took advantage of at will, it seemed, that quick and twisty hand gesture.

Inga scanned the canopy, found me on my branch, and stuck her long tongue out at me. "Eee-eee-eee," she said.

Her monkeytalk was poor.

"Let's try that again," I said. "If you're making fun, you say, Monkey is a slug. Try that. Monkey is a slug."

"Hoo-hoo, hee-hee, ahh-ahh!" Inga said. That tongue again. Well, she could say *slug*, at least.

The mother popped back out with a bright blue piece of beach refuse, perfect rectangle, used it to wipe up the purple honey, placed rabbishes back on the disc, stray pieces of pineapple, several cheeeesticks.

"Now sweedie," she said. "Don't feed the monkey. And come inzide if he's a bother. They're cute but they are wild animals and unbredictable.

Still, the baby will like to watch him. Just careful. I am inzide packing. We're almost done. Your father is on his work Zooom now. We'll be on our way in two hours."

And with that, she disappeared through the blue wall once again, Dabby's food in hand, confiscated, yes: clearly an intratroupe competition.

Inga was leaving! I had to communicate. I called her name, impossible to vocalize, but I tried: "Eeee-ah."

"Beeee-eeep."

Formal mode: "Eeee-ah, dear female, I journeyed many a day and many a night from here in the direction of sunrise unfailing, but came to the blighted path your meddle rollers trample so constantly, six deep, such roaring. I need your help in effecting a crossing. Is there a way for a monkey to effect a crossing? That is my question."

"Hoo-hoo-hoo, slug-slug," she said. And indicated I should come down and join her.

Cautiously, aware of the grown humans behind the blue wall and the suddenness of the dar, I approached.

"Beep-beep," the baby said, smug little thing, waving his hands wildly.

"You'll be abandoned, too, one day," I told him.

Under another of the sitting contraptions I spotted a forgotten piece of pineapple, leapt and feinted, scurried crabwise, got it, couldn't stop myself, plunked it in my mouth, leapt to the stiff-legged slab of wood directly in front of baby and girl.

"Good monkey!" she said.

"Yes, I try," I said, could not have said it more clearly. "But Eeee-ah, I need your help. I need your help to cross the goer go-trail."

"Cutest monkey," Inga said. I let her scramch my ear. The baby held out its little swollen hand. I had meant to let him scramch my ear, instead endured a mild pummeling, then a tugging of fur.

But I, Beep, could endure anything if it would help me communicate.

I pondered. I inspected. The baby—he had his toy vehicle in hand and then mouth.

"Trugg," his sister said fondly.

Several more truggs lay tossed on the ground by the meddle fire receptacle (these horrors of you-men ingenuity always smell of incinerated animals—and in that moment, perfect clarity, I recalled one of the old uncles saying the you-mens raised enormous animals, gave these animals to their gods in fire, incomprehensible). I picked up the toy rollers, brought them to the slab in front of girl and baby.

"Trugg," she said to me, also fond.

I rolled the little trugg, rolled the little other.

"Carr," she said.

I made trugg and carr pass each other. I did it again and again. I pointed to myself. I pointed to the vehicles, to the go-way I'd implied.

Inga took sudden interest—I was no baby. "Monkey, what are you saying?"

"I need help crossing the big trail, could I say it any plainer?"

Blank you-men look. I pointed to myself. I pointed to the toy rollers. I rolled them this way and that. I repeated my phrase: "I need help to cross the big trail. Do you know the big trail? It stands between me and my quest." Pointing, rolling, implying the go-way with eyes back and forth, narrating need.

"You want to come with us?" Inga said. "Oooh! You want to come with?"

I showed so much happiness at that that even Inga understood: "You do want to come with!" she cried.

"Yes, with you through the forest a ways, not far, and then with your help over the furious black trail, where once having crossed I can push on toward the sunrise, resume my quest."

"Okay," she said, finger to her lips. "I'll get my stuffee carrier."

That cage I'd been in. She hefted the baby onto her hip, went inzide the you-men living box through the blue wall. I raced back to my branch, peed till there wasn't another drop, just casting it to the breeze. I didn't pee my hands and feet because I'd be in her territory, and a monkey has manners. I shat, just whatever would come out. A monkey prepares.

Shortly she was back with the carrier, as she'd called it.

She put it on the wood plane, tavle, it was called. Inzide the carrier were several pretend animals. I climbed in with them. Inga arranged them around me, a warm, agreeable bunch, all those pretend eyes seeming to see, all those pretend hands so useless. But who was I to judge? I'd played with a stick as a child, even given it a name: Stickens.

"Just be very quiet," she said. Finger to her lips.

I put my own finger to my own lips.

I was pleased I'd cheered her up.

Not long and every bite of her snack shared, the baby sleeping, I among my pretend brethren nearly so, Dabby appeared. "All loaded," he said so loudly, yet somehow gently. And then, "Oh, jeez your stuffees, sweedie."

"They go on my lap," Inga said.

"On your lap it is," said Dabby, who, I saw, was still of vital age. He scooped up the baby careless of its waking, but it did not wake, just grabbed a fistful of the gruff male's wrapping like anymonkey might. I felt a queer wave of affinity, all of us with our fists in one another's fur.

Inga, strongest girl in the world, picked up the stuffee carrier and she and I were a we, sense of sympathetic communication flowing between us silent. She swung me and my fake compatriots off the tavle and (wonderful swooping sensation!) swung us into their dwelling, through its now lifeless rectilinear spaces, finally down a long interior trail and through a tall dar and back outzide, where a rolling machine—a grown-up carr—stood up high, a certain shine and animation. The baby was now shrieking, having been pressed through an opening behind one of the vehicle's squeaking wings (four, like a dragonfly), and tied brutally into a sitting contraption mounted inzide. The baby stopped his caterwauling when Inga got into the machine beside him, total change of weather, the powerful Inga effect, kindest girl in the world, swinging me and the other stuffees onto her lap, strabbing us to her in some way, then clamping down her arms protectively.

Soon the adults were onboard, and soon there was a roar and strange howling, then movement, a lurching and swinging, all of us being freighted along, Dabby somehow in charge.

"Turn off the mewzzik," Momma said.

And Dabby made a fast gesture, snapped the strange howling silent, and we were rolling.

I, Beep, was a goer!

Through the maybe mica underwings of the carr I could see the blessed tops of trees moving by, then whizzing by, then nothing but a blur of green. My stomach rolled this way, rolled that. I concentrated on Inga's face. Poor thing, all pink-skinned and covered in spots and not a hair except over her eyes and on her head. Her wrapping was also covered in spots, bigger ones green and blue and orange and red. She hadn't forgotten me but stuck a you-men finger through a slot in my convenient prizzon. I held that finger, suddenly exhausted. She, too, I saw. Anyway, like the baby she slept, then I.

Chapter Seven

I WOKE TO CHAOS—LOUD ECHOING shouts, air like too close to goers, rapid you-men speech, a sense of panic, much rushing hither and yon. Momma was freeing her baby from the monstrous contraption, Dabby unstrabbing dear Inga, who slung her legs sideways, swung herself out into the stinking air, never letting go of me and the other stuffees in our special conveyance, wouldn't let Dabby touch it.

We hadn't crossed the infernal trail at all but seemed to be in the middle of it.

In the back end of the carr under a kind of caudal flap, Dabby had sequestered a number of colorful boxes, which he called soupcases. Another male you-men approached, his wrappings all red and spangles, clearly a chieftain, clearly dangerous. But there was no altercation, just a tribal touch of knuckles, Dabby secretly passing something to the other Alpha—an offering of some kind, a crinkling as of old leaves. And then, more mysteries, the chieftain helped Dabby wrestle all of the colorful soupcases from the machine, rolled them away on their clever whilzz to a small but waterless river, upon which they floated into a voracious meddle mouth. Offerings! Of course! Even the gods were automated in this world! What could I be but *next*, some kind of coin. Had I been duped?

But no—I smelled stress on Dabby, too—for the sake of his tiny troupe he must pretend, but this crossing terrified him. Inga lifted the carrier with me and my fellow stuffees—no effort at all, stronger even than the enormous males. Her mother, another power, lifted the large baby, who was as happy as my hateful own baby sister had been.

"I'll return the carr," Dabby said clearly. "You all go cheggin. You're going to be alright, Christima?" He meant the adult female.

"If he's all right, I'm all right," Christima said, meaning the baby, who was agog at all the action, his idea of a good time.

I'd begun to imagine some kind of reality among my carrier mates—particularly the whale, biggest and softest, and very quietly I hugged my arms around him, pulled him close, little sigh from inzide him—yes, yes, there was some kind of life! I hugged him all the harder. Yes, a sigh, a sigh: life! My fellow prizzoners? My fellow questers? Whatever the explanation, they were very passive, apparently a successful strategy, and one I'd best emulate.

We were not fed into the maw.

And then suddenly we were inzide an enormous you-man space, pretend atmosphere, strange mechanical whistling and bizzing, you-men hubbub, shiny inventions of every description, long lines of submissive you-mens handing over their stuffee carriers to still more royalty behind meddle barriers, many you-men words said, crinkling sheets of thinnest wood shavings exchanged, why? I smelled canid. I smelled feline. I smelled gecko, yucko. Ubb in the artificial heights (as if the very sky had been imprizzoned!), a few birds flew. I couldn't call to them for advice lest I blow my cover and the cover of my mates. I noted other you-men juveniles and that many of them hugged stuffees to their chests, and further, that many carried fake you-men juveniles, squeezed so tight their heads flopped. Momma exchanged fistfuls of shavings with the mild male royal behind his counter, and though he seemed satisfied, we waited interminably. A monkey is not used to holding his pee! But I did, as did my you-men troupe, except the baby, judging from the sudden scent, the only one keeping himself marked. I was in Inga's hands. There was a trail to cross, a mission, and we shared it.

"Bathrooom?" Mommy Christima said.

Ritual baths?

But we only walked, and walked some more, then into an echoing chamber with walls of shining stone and reflections, that pernicious chemical smell of not-quite flowers and not-quite fruits, also filth, a broken old female in the corner, a sad elder left to die with her bales of what smelled like the wrappings humans wore, all folded onto a meddle cart, jars filled with fluids, pretend lemon sniff competing with flowers unknown. In front of reflective walls female you-mens rubbed old clay on their faces, smeared blood on their lips, charcoal on their eyes, ran ritual water over their hands. Some had small birds in their ears that sang. I was beginning to understand: you-mens brought companions with them, pets and talismans and effigies to help effect the awful crossing, assuage fear.

I, Beep, saw that I had a job and not only a quest.

The chamber was divided into smaller chambers and Inga brought me into one, dead end, small bathing pool, more real water. She flipped ubb her bright general wrapping and tugged a smaller wrapping off her bottom, sat on the very lip of the pool! In the next chamber we heard mother cooing to baby, the splashing of urine. And Inga followed suit: peed. Then pulled a receipt or ticket from a dispenser and with brilliant contempt wiped it across her nether parts, dumped it in the water! I felt fear: those royals would be angry, would they not? Treating their scrip like that? But no one was there to see. Brave Inga! She fixed her wrappings, then bid me pee, too, with hand gestures, and so with relief I did, standing on the lip of the bowl and assiduously keeping the urine off myself as this was not my territory but that of the royal you-mens. Let Inga be the radical!

She lifted me under the arms when I was done, put her lips to my forehead, ritual, ritual, then slipped me back into the carrier with my whale friend and a torpid wolf, both lost like sloths in hypo-metabolic states, wise.

"You're so good," Inga said to me before closing me in.
I put a finger to my lips.
Then she to hers.
We were communicating as animals.
Plus, poor whale, another sigh.

Chapter Eight

AND BACK OUT OF THE water room into the greater cacophony. You-men voices so loud I shuddered to consider how big their mouths must be—but no giants evident, only images of them, images everywhere, some in movement, enormous beyond measure, many showing their teeth, but never naked, none of them, only almost naked, those poor swollen females. Voices from all directions, you-men juveniles multitudinous, smaller voices, crazy trajectories, various speeds, shouts and cries, floral smells and foul, food smells and chemical, ahead, behind, above, below, movement, movement, you-mens quietly riding zigzag meddle grates like moving teeth that compacted the large crowds, delivered them higher, while meanwhile an equal number came down, some sort of exchange, impossible to understand, these fungible parts.

Momma, an extremely happy baby Willie strabbed into a kind of pouch upon her chest (no fur to grab onto!), led the way now that Dabby had disappeared, mystifying passages, great structures made of light, as far as I could tell, other structures made of *nothing*, and a new kind of noise, you-mens wailing and beating on hollow trees and making various tones with wind, one of them fingering a pain-o, Momma called it—so this was the dreadful instrument!—and bid us stop and listen, stout you-men female grinning at us and shouting: clearly a display for their insane gods; two noblemen in their red suits stood listening, tapping their feet menacingly, shouting imprecations. The stout female pointed at them, shouted back, clearly terrified, her whole troupe banging and blowing all the louder, the pain-o tinkling in fear.

Mewzzik, Momma called it: that noise in the carr.

Wolf squeaked disconsolately.

I understood. In the mayhem we stuffees might safely breach our silence, if only for one another.

Momma took up Inga's hand and led us to a shiny wall, where we stood interminably until suddenly the wall gaped, exposing another boxy enclosure, size small. We stepped in, the stuffee case banging on the bright-meddle walls, which closed behind us, the view and all the noise suddenly cut off, another shiny wall to stare upon, different mewzzik: the other world was gone. Good riddance. But then my stomach dropped, my body lifted, sagged, and the shiny wall gaped once more. We stepped out into a different place! But yet the same place, all the same sounds, smells, just the view rearranged, the inhabitants, a miracle, material transubstantiation, all the rites in the other world apparently having succeeded.

I rode inzide the swinging carrier, whale sighing in my arms, beneath us Wolf, who at times of greatest bumping stress squeaked piteously. The other animals seemed sacks of gravel to me—perhaps their bones had been broken, no animal scent, none, souls departed.

Comfortingly, Inga's wrappings swished against the case.

We came to a crossroads where the great magical sheets of nothing held up the rooof, separated us from wind and any natural sound, though sunlight poured in upon us as if in-here were out-there, an out-there where meddle roarbirds the size of monkey territories languished or fidgeted, some with their ears to what looked like sagging you-men dwellings. Here and there magicians of some kind waved wands bright as flowers, calling the birds out, a little frantic I thought, some kind of rite.

"What a view," Momma said. "I quite adore these enormous wimdoes."

The male called Dabby hustled up to us all pretend jolly.

"Well!" he said. "We've made it."

Momma leaned at him, suddenly put her mouth on his mouth, a wetness. Some of the blood on her lips stayed on his. She wiped at it.

"Ew," Inga said.

Agreed!

"Let's get snacks," Momma said.

I shuddered. I'd been smelling food—you-mens here as everywhere insisted on burning nearly everything.

"Me want chiggen!" Dabby said.

"No meat!" Inga cried.

"They have salabs," Dabby said. "We go to Pollo Loco."

Codetalk.

Pollo Loco was a rooomish open to the greater expanse. I smelled fire-ruined plantains. Burned animals. Perhaps disaster had struck. But no, my humans took seats in contraptions around a tavle made of pretend wood. Inga carefully placed my stuffee carrier on her lap—this could not have been comfortable—Momma noticed but noticeably decided to say nothing. The male got ubb after much talk and marched to a counter staffed by young nobles, special brooches and caps. They hardly noticed Dabby's alpha status, made him stand there a ritual amount of time, a humiliation he accepted passively. There was talk then, a sudden exchange of crinkling leaves and bits of meddle. And more waiting, why?

One of the nobles took pity at last, handed Dabby a parcel. And in it, remarkably, was food. Which came wrapped in paber, it was called, a kind of pretend rind that crinkled like leaves, an outer layer, then many inner layers, noisy, fragrant, burned. Dabby pulled out smaller paber bundles from the big one, passed these around to our small troupe. Inga opened hers first: leaves and fruits, my kind of monkey.

"Famished," she said.

Okay, yes, this was a disaster, and here I'd thought only of myself while my you-mens were facing starvation!

No, it was just an expression.

And soon my own hunger was abated: Inga slipped bites through the vents on the carrier, subtle girl, slivers of fire-tasting plantain, something else oily, all of it salty as the sea, all in a zero-flavor range, hot as beach sand at high sun, satisfyingish.

A lot of urping and burping and rapid talk, clearly covering for fear (which poured from Dabby—Momma was only tense, I, Beep, of course, more sanguine, deadly mission aside): the trail crossing must be near.

Dabby suddenly smashed all the wrappings into a ball, tried to seem nonchalant on his way to an altar I'd failed to notice, offered the anointed ball with a slight bow to a passive but gleaming meddle goddess who opened her mouth to receive it. And dear monkeys, I tell you, she chomped down on that stuff with a clang. Trazch, Dabby had called her. Many others worshipped Trazch, I noted, a constant stream of you-mens stuffing that insatiable gape, paber, bits of food, water vessels, unknowns.

I remembered something an old uncle was said to have said: "Cheap gods tempt fate."

I do not know what that means.

And suddenly again we were on the move, Dabby's all-alpha pace, bellies full, no sunny branch to nap upon.

Just as suddenly we were stalled again—a queue at the long-awaited end of which royalty stood at tavles demanding bribes, a pinch point I could have breached in a second, all sorts of zignals and commands, priests guarding the portal to a new realm.

As if to confirm my theory, Dabby and Momma took the tough coverings off their feet upon a disembodied command, something about shoozz. And they pulled all the meddle things out of pouches in their wrappings, poggetz as the voice said, and put these items into binzz, they were called, binzz, binzz, binzz, poggetz, poggetz, poggetz, shoozz, shoozz, shoozz, jaggetz, jaggetz, jaggetz, the disembodied voice explaining it all without patience but no detectable malice, either.

Dabby folded the baby wilzz up in some ingenious way, *strawler*, it was called, put it onto one of the continuous rivers we'd been seeing. What demanding gods! And what demanding priests! First, Dabby went through a portal, arms in the air, some kind of stoic obeisance. Then Momma and baby Willie, making a game of it.

"Please put your carry-on on the belt, here," a bored priest said.

"No, no, my animals won't like it!" Inga cried.

Whale sighed.

The priest reached to take us from her, more efficient than unkindly.

But just then, my sacrifice to this fresh god imminent, Inga crying false tears, a different priest stepped up, said, "Now-now, Cutie, we'll skip ahead for your menagerie!"

And taking Inga's free hand, this sensitive soul led us all around all the equipment to a shiny steel platform. Inga put our carrier up there, tears still flowing. Mommy had stepped over, baby in arms. "Her stuffees," she said.

The priest winked, suddenly popped the carrier open, secret knowledge.

"No!" Inga said.

Plan: bite any hand that got near, leap out and into the canopy, join that solitary pigeon up there in the criss-cross you-men sky.

But the priest reached his hand in gingerly, petted my whale friend, made Wolf squeak with a friendly squeeze, petted me one pat back of the head. "Beep," I said, following Wolfie's brilliant lead.

"All in order here," said the priest. "A very nice crew!"

We weren't to be sacrificed!

Inga closed the carrier with a snap, practically on the priest's retreating fingers. And just like that, my prizzon swinging, Whale sighing with relief, we rejoined the troupe, ahh.

Inga seemed oblivious of danger, then, dancing, twirling, swinging us stuffees, a merry hum: she had a secret, and the secret was I, Beep, monkey. We trekked to a waiting area overseen by a priestess at a podium, and there we waited, then waited some more.

For what?

Suddenly the wall opened, a queue formed, and we jumped up to join it, Dabby in the lead, I in the swinging carrier. Dabby showed our priestess some paber, and our obeisance paid, we proceeded down a drooping passage—jet britch, the priestess called it—plodded until we were inzide a roarbird! Inga hummed soothingly, bumping our carrier along the rows of sitting contraptions the roarbird had swallowed, full of you-mens.

We'd been eaten!

But no, we were only seated three abreast, baby on Mommy's lap, Momma between Dabby and Inga, who slid a flap in the skin of the wall. Sunlight roared in, blinding. Inga lifted my carrier just so, and through the brilliant oval of light I perceived a flock of giant roarbirds in a line.

Soon we were flying.

Flying!

I watched the world below, all the human boxes giving way to the bounteous lost forest, and we were rising, rising, through a cloud into the blue. And shortly, over there, I saw it.

I saw the smoking mountain.

I was one dead monkey.

Chapter Nine

I WOKE TO INGA POKING food at me—some spongy substance with little flavor, but also a chunk of crisp fruit, toothsome. Beside her, Momma had nodded off, baby, too. Dabby was deeply involved in a plane of light he held on his lap.

"Okay," Inga said, a whisper, my only *we*, her lips at the edge of the stuffee carrier, a little beautiful those lips, a little grotesque, teeth white as coconut pulp. She said, "Beepie-Beep. You're doing so well. *We're* doing so well! Just one more *annoying* inspector or whatever they are. But don't worry, they never even look! And just a few hours to go. Shall we watch tee-bee?"

Tee-bee? She was so outsize and took in so much so calmly—I just kept forgetting she was a juvenile. And unlike all the other you-mens, she I could understand, communication on the animal level, interspecies trans-association, like moodling with a fruit-drunk kinkajou or a bored old tapir or a frustrated frogg, a think that only happened under the right conditions, usually someanimal stressed in some way, even by an excess of joy, like the little fast-legged beach birds poking at the sand, their thoughts for everyone to hear: delight. And through Inga, I understood much of what was said and done around us, this quest so like emergency. She punched her fingers at the back of the sitting contraption in front of us and a kind of curtain snapped open to brightness and soon there were recognizable you-mens visible, some tiny, tiny species—tinier even than my own—apparently trapped behind crystal, apparently living in the seat cushion but trying to stay positive.

From a slit in her coverings, Inga produced a pair of smoothest white shells on a fine white vine, tucked one in her ear and one through the mesh of the carrier, pointed at head, made a couple of provocative hisses, kept pointing and hissing till I poked my half of the talisman into my own ear. Immediately, you-men hubbub: voices, mewzzix, loud noises, a magical mix.

Inga offered her fingers to the tiny people, poking, poking, but the various brave creatures ran from that touch. A single you-men appeared, in raiment like I'd never seen, a male. Behind him a proportionately enormous fire seemed to burn, trees snapping to light. I smelled no smoke. The male spoke and because of his good heart and Inga's attention I understood him precisely, call it sub-moodling: "If humankind doesn't act, these fires will only get worse. One million ache-grrs now burned."

Inga poked at the speaker's face, and suddenly a new image appeared, some kind of pretend human made of bright colors, then switched again, and again, and at her every touch new you-mens, priests and many nobles and lots of busy goers (but not a single grower), all of them going, going, going in every conceivable direction, some bigger, some smaller, some so tiny they were like mites. And with a monkey gasp I realized the plane of light, this tee-bee, was a portal to another world, a world of multiples and magic. There were no creatures in the seat-backs, not really! That was an illusion! And it was conjured by Inga's digits, perhaps by her longing. I cast my eyes away.

"Don't like it?" she whispered.

Whale sighed at the tightness of my embrace.

"Don't like it," I mooded.

And it seemed Inga felt me, because she tapped the you-men currently declaiming, and the plane of light winked off. Reality returned, this moment around us, no less unsettling: the flying tube. I cast my eyes at the oval of sky the wimdoe allowed, for it was a wimdoe, small size regardless: clouds, moving at storm speed.

"When Mommy wakes we'll go to the bathrooom," Inga whispered.

"Sweedie," Momma said, her eyes still closed. "Are you talking to your babies?"

Shortly, a rustle and much verbiage from another disembodied priestess voice. Dabby snapped his lightboard closed, unstrabbed himself, and lumbered ubb the trail between the rows of contraptions. Momma said something about changing the baby—was she unsatisfied with him?—unstrabbed herself and rearranged the little chubby bundle over her shoulder. He caught my eye, held it, that wise baby gaze, and then with Momma was gone. Or no, Inga and I were following them, Inga balancing the carrier on her head, apparently amusing, many you-men smiles as we made our way ubbhill along the incongruity and into a tiny booth where Inga peed (they must have bladders like small lakes, these you-mens). "I won't look," she said. And opened the carrier.

And glad for the moment to be so, there in the midst of our monumental mission. "Dear friend," I said so clearly. "I understand my debt to you. This passage across the great trail is so much more difficult than I'd envisioned, and yet you continue to serve me."

"Hoo, hoo, Beep," she said. "Hoo, hoo, sweedie. Please be super quiet." And put that finger to her lips. She gave me a stick of the limp slug meat, which I ate, that hungry. She then produced—from a clever crinkling purse, bright yellow—a blue object like a pebble, offered it to my lips. I accepted, trusting her. The object was sweet beyond imagining, and with a nut inzide, and something more, vague brown rain-forest flavor. Then a green pebble, exactly the same flavor. Then orange, exactly the same, ecstatic monotony.

"That's enough!" she said. "You'll get a tummy ache." From a hole in the meddle wall she extracted a paber cone that turned out to be a drinking vessel, pure magic, filled it with chemical-laced water, bless her, and handed it to me, not delicious, not at all, only necessary.

"Now I'm going to give you this," she said. "I stole it from Momma. It will make you sleep. So we don't get in trobble. Still a long way to go." A tiny white object, bit of seashell, perhaps, pinkish white. She held it out. Touched her own tongue with it when I wouldn't take it, tried again—ah, comprehension: It was something to eat.

"This will help you sleep through it all," she said again.

"All what?" I moodled.

And fairly clearly, proto-moodle, she compassioned back her great hope that I would just eat it.

So I did. In honor of her near leap to the mood. Gaggingly sour, this pebble, but trust her. More of the bad water. I knew a phrase that a thousand monkeys had long ago invented, I supposed in the boredom of the old times: "To sleep, perchance to dream."

"Hoo-hoo," she said. Then eased me back into the carrier, which was not a cage, I told myself.

I climbed in without protest. My fellow stuffees were stiff with indignation that I'd been chosen. I said, "You guys don't have to pee?"

But nothing from Whale, less from Wolf, poor, poor things, so close to death, I suddenly realized, sacrificed for me, or perhaps we.

The smoking mountain had been the shape of a cone and very tall, and the plume that drifted from it a little gray and a little black, and all around it seeming devastation.

Inga, an angel.

Chapter Ten

How to describe it. A broken world. I woke groggy like after the time cousin Tink and I crashed heads, he leaping this way under the assault of an eagle, I leaping that, meeting accidentally in the middle, head to head, waking to silence on the rain-forest floor, just a chachalaca kicking up the leaf litter around us after insects.

But here in this waking the world was all noise, goers galore it sounded, some kind of non-animal screaming and hooting, also aggressively non-Beep beeping, non-bird honking, also some displaced you-men pleading his case from a tee-bee.

"We'll be right back," he said giving up—but not forever.

When next I woke, it was to sumptuous luxury, I suppose, all sorts of hot you-men bedding smelling of bird. I felt I'd been transported back to the pink cubicle Inga had inhabited back in monkey world, but this chamber was doubly rooomy, quintuply filled with deceased stuffees, but here including pretend you-mens, as well, a couple of dozen girl creatures dressed well in wrappings of great variety, nonfunctional bodies, two small teeth showing in placid, slightly stubid smiles. I'd carried a coconut around when little and called it my baby, so no judgment!

And no Inga.

The stuffee-carrier was in a corner, and I could see that Whale was upside down, dead, Wolf smothered below him. Where was Inga?

Calm, monkey. You've lived.

I shoved off the heavy coverings, stood wobbly on the soft surface, tail to support me, legs aching, head pounding. I smelled water and knew its direction, leapt from the bed to an open darway, hung from the top edge of it, a wooden border. And swing, and I was inzide the water room, hanging onto a branch draped with pink wrappings, from there to the pretend sun hanging from the ceiling, a far taller see-ling than I'd found in Inga's rain-forest home. Below me now were the expected grottoes, one the dry kind, the other a place to pee, if I had their customs right. And so I did pee, pictured the forehead of a querulous coatimundi to sharpen my aim, and heard in my heart all the subsequent coatimundi swearing, those cross animals, a happy splashing. From there if I swung I could pooop as well, and I did, I poooped, expelled a tight turd at the crucial moment of the arc, satisfying splash.

Thirsty, though, and I'd fouled the water source. The dry basin—how had that worked? I jumped down, slippery surfaces, monkeyed with the gleaming meddle outcroppings, and after a twist of the wrist (like freeing a mango from its branch), the waterfall commenced. Why not a bath? Well, because the water poured away down a perfect round leak in the basin, that's why. On a shelf were some fragrant kind of cylinders the right size and I forced one into the hole, presto, pond. I do like to sit in water. The waterfall was brisk and wonderful till suddenly it was warm, then hot, then too hot, and leap out of there! Very pleasant sound of the water flowing, however, and continuing, wetting the floor, a glorious splashing.

Monkey bored!

Monkey hungry!

I'd smelled fruit in the bathrooom but none was real.

A conch shell, though, carried here from there, it seemed, and set carefully on a kind of ledge, sweet reminder of monkey world.

Inga rushed in. "Beepie!" she cried. "You're up! I'm so sorry! I had to join the fam for breakfast!"

I moodled hard, trying the troupe mood, the affinity mood, the we.

"The sink!" my friend cried, and rushed to halt the waterfall.

"I took a bath," I mooded.

"You poooped?" she said. "What a good monkey."

"All monkeys are good," I said. "And while what you say is true, what I'm trying to communicate is the bath."

She threw the large cloth hangings on the floor, contained the water. Brought one small one out to me, rubbed me with it, why? She only said, "Hoo-hoo!" And then, "Naughty wet monkey!"

Ah, that was it: they were big on being dry. She petted my head, she patted my face. Her courage was great, no sign of fear at our captivity. That made me brave, too.

I concentrated very hard on her glimmer of consciousness, moodled my mood, formal: "I'd like to continue on past the monstrous trail. I fear it's far wider than I surmised. I'm sure you're anxious to get going, too."

She only cooed and said, "I brought you a banana."

"Monstrous trail?" I mooded. "Anxious to get going?"

But nothing. I took the banana, very real. As from the gardens of the growers, large, sweeter than plantain. I bit it in the middle, yanked off its covering, ate it all, big bites—but Inga was no cousin, no uncle, she didn't make a single move to take it away. Soon I was fat with it.

My dear host pulled off her own wrappings, or some of them, replaced them with heavier ones, said, "It's almost like spring out there! We can go to the park. Daddy just left for work. He's a lie-yer. Mommy's got a Zooom. She's a judch, partial maternity leaf. I don't have sss-coola till tomorrow! It's still springbreagh. The howzz-kipper is with Willie."

I'm doing my best here, but it was mostly all incomprehensible.

"Will you be good? If I take you to the pargh? We can use my Bitty Twins strawler. Oh! And you can wear Bitty Twin cloze!"

She didn't make sense, but she hadn't forgotten the quest, good: we were on the move.

Shortly the boy Bitty Twin was stripped to his naked nonbody, and I was tucked into a smart pea-coad (she called it) and pamps. These went on your legs.

My subjugation was complete!

Chapter Eleven

A Bitty Twins strawler turned out to be a conveyance much like baby-brother Willie's, only flimsier, nothing but a kind of sling for me to sit in. Whale had recovered somewhat and lay across my lap, sighing when I hugged him. Wolf was not dead either, just wordless beside me. And beside him in the other sling was the girl Bitty Twin herself, pink ruffles, head covering shape of a coconut shell. Silence from her. I saw Inga's wisdom—the outward effect of our cavalcade was a sweet girl with her toy babies. She herself wore a thick wrapping seemingly fashioned from the bed coverings, also smelling of bird, and brightest possible red. This was a puffy, and also a coad. She stuffed her braids into a thick cowl of some kind, also braided, I saw, and colorful, vague redolence of the animals growers liked to keep prizzoner.

Inga rolled me out of her pink space through the magical dar and into a greater space, much light. Across that rooom in one of the ubiquitous you-men resting contraptions, Momma sat taking in light from that folding plane of theirs, whatever nourishment coming hard today—she looked consternated.

Inga said, "I'm taking the Bitty Twins for a walk."

"Okay, Sweepea," Momma said, not so much as a glance at me. "You have your phome?"

"*Mom*, of course."

Baby Willie was in the food rooom in a tall chair being fed by a you-men new to me, a small female darker than the others in this troupe, all in white wrappings, striking.

"Taking Bitty Twins for a walk," Inga told her.

"Oh, that's good, Sugar. I'll be out with Willie very soon then."

The lingering smell of dearly departed Dabby became stronger as we approached a blank wall, then stronger still as Inga opened a crack in the wall, which was not called "a" dar but "*the*" dar, then in a tiny space we waited, staring down the blank wall, which slid open—an even more magical dar—to reveal a small interior like the one at the airport, El Vator, she called it, sudden Español.

And after a stomach flight, the booth wall slid open to another reality, this one made of polished stone. A very jolly nobleman in his fancy uniform opened the enormous transparent wall for us, a moving wimdoe, but grand indeed, befitting a portal to the next world on my quest.

"Dear Inga," he said. "Dear, dear, dear Inga. How was your trip?"

"Divine, Ollie," Inga said. "Simply divine."

"Pura Vida!" he said.

And Inga sighed.

Outzide the air was cold, cold as brooks from springs high in the hills, or colder. I'd never felt such a thing. My eyes watered, nostrils, too. I was glad for the pea-coad, which, according to Inga, was precious. The pamps were another thing, cramped and silly. The goers were going hard in their carrs and truggs, thundering and clanging past us, but then on an urge they suddenly stopped as one. Subvocal communication? Whatever, there was an opening. Bravely, Inga pushed our conveyance out across the mad black you-men bedrock and right in front of the clicking and whirring and rumbling machines, their big shiny eyes looking at us hard. And then across a stretch of rougher stone and between towers of stone, and suddenly we were in an airy and pampered forest. Inga sighed and swept her arm to present this new vista: "Cendrall Pargh," she said.

Ah, trees.

We'd done it.

"May I emerge?" I said.

"Hoo-hoo monkey," Inga said. She meant, Be quiet. And it was true, there were agents of the goers all around us. And now a further trail to cross. And then trees, glorious trees. And proper animals! A squirrel above. I climbed out of the strawler, permission or no, stood atop the little canopy of the thing, freemonkey.

"Squirrel," I called. "I say! Squirrel!"

Squirrels are chatterers, unreliable. Sharers of the mid-canopy, and when it comes to food, liars. This one was foreign, though, all gray, fat. He regarded me rather coldly, surprised me with true moodle, clear as a raindrop: "Now the dress-up dolls are talking?"

I switched to true moodle, too: "But I'm not a doll. I am Beep, monkey."

And the animal moodled back. "I am Squirrel, squirrel."

"Beep!" Inga cried—she didn't like me out in the open like that.

I climbed back down into the strawler—many you-men go-machines all around, not quite carrs, not quite truggs, and many you-mens on foot, smell of their bad food, and shouts not distant. At least there was a breeze high in the great trees, and it carried their stressed messages. Was this Cendrall Pargh merely a flawed oasis? Another waystation in the terrible crossing? Or were we close to success?

"Do what the girl says," Squirrel urged, accompanying our progress on high, aiming a lot of energy my way, unusual force, possibly a god: we'd been through many portals, come to think of it.

I challenged him anyway: "Why should I accept your rhythm?"

"Greenhorn, feel the truth. We are here to help. We've a heard a rumor, a burgeoning in the communal mind. I see I've lost you. Well, start with this: there be doggs coming. You are at risk. Doggs, doggs, doggs, doggs. You know doggs?"

"Like wolves?"

"Worse, to our minds! And to them the you-mens throw these objects, flying circles, little moons, and horseshoes, what the fudge, ask the horses—I hear one now. The horses drag conveyances and live in tall buildings just to the west, miserable slavery, humiliation. Dyed feathers attached to their heads! Pooop catchers at their butts!"

The trees around us shivered at that, a compassion that hurried out through the pargh beyond, perhaps around the world. "Slavery," the squirrel said again.

At length I said, "You speak excellent monkey."

"You speak bad squirrel, and I would have expected better of you, since—get this—you're a *squirrel monkey.*"

"A what?"

"A *squirrel monkey.*"

"Fresh off the monkey boat," another squirrel said.

And then they all started chattering, wind voices: "Monkey, monkey, monkey boat, squirrel, squirrel, squirrel monkey."

I found I could understand. "I'm no such thing."

Squirrel moodled away: "You'll learn. We entertained one a few lifetimes ago—name of Paul—escaped from a private menagerie, the former prizzoners so conspicuous with their you-mee names."

"You-mee?"

"The you-mens. Named him Paul. We all got fond. He was all over this park for months, this monkey, a full summer and into fall. He knew what he was: squirrel monkey. His captors had told him. Brave lad. They hadn't mentioned winter, not exactly."

And the chorus chimed in, emanations far and near: "Squirrel, squirrel, squirrel, monkey, monkey, monkey, prizzoner monkey, wearing you-mee garmends, pamps and jagget, legs and arms in shaggles, shaggles!"

Squirrel twitched his tail: "Hate to tell you what became of Paul."

"Tell me."

Inga said, "Beep, back in the carriage." Her voice sounded so low and protracted, her speed so much slower than that of the squirrels, all this moodly communication more or less instantaneous, leaving the overbusy you-mens to seem near frozen.

The chorus: "Survival demands we tell you, yes. Your survival, that is, yes."

The descant: "Electric, Electric, electric fenz."

And Squirrel himself: "Got electro-cutied."

"What does that even mean?"

"Tried to visit the Japanese monkeys in the zzoo, right here in Centrall Pargh."

"There are monkeys? Is a pargh like a reserbe? Like where the sloths live, back home?"

Squirrel went all warm: "Oh, bubby. Your home is far away."

I said, "Let's get back to what you said earlier. There are monkeys?"

"Japanese monkeys. Can't hardly understand a word they hoot."

"And electro-cutied? What's that?"

"Cooked. It means like, like: lightning-gotcha."

The chorus chimed in: "Burned up, burned up, burned up!"

"Black vines," I said. "Even here!"

"What's wrong with these squirrels?" Inga said. Yes, her time was different from squirrel time, her legs and long braids swinging slow as moon arc.

"Fried—it means burned up, and yes, black vines, here, too. But these ones are bare shiny and no other purpose—he touches one tendril of the thing and he's fine, and then he touches another and he's fine, but then he grabs 'em both and lights up like a Times Square billboard, he does. Squirrels see it. A few generations now, but we all remember it, being squirrels, and always it's today."

"What is a Times Square billboard," I said.

A barking.

"Fudge!" My interlocutor hissed. "Here come doggs!"

A great chattering went up: "The doggs, the doggs, the doggs."

Squirrel warned me: "Don't talk to the doggs!"

And all around us: "The doggs, the doggs, the doggs!"

"And don't eat the peanuts," squirrel said. "The you-mee peanuts, those are mine."

"Mine, mine mine!"

A peanut, what was that?

I climbed back in the Bitty Twins strawler. Squirrels, so many, nearly as connected as bees, the many all but one. And here came a pair of domesticated wolves. Doggs. Extremely curly things, now that I looked at them, orangey-brown fur the color of my own.

"Go away!" Inga shouted.

I was glad to be under her protection.

"Max! Minnie!" a you-men voice called, female. "They don't bite! Maxie!"

One of the doggs stuck a muzzle straight under the canopy of the strawler, tried to nab Whale, but I held on tight, brief tug-of-war. Then, though, a sharp word from brave Inga and the dogg creature let go, those enormous teeth, crocodilian. Then the other dogg, this Maxie, stuck his head in and gave me a long, voluptuous sniff, began to bark, barely intelligible. But let me translate: "Heavens to Betsy, it's some kind of small person!"

"Stop, stop!" Inga cried.

Minnie shout-barked, "Oh, poo, small person. Baby alert! Maxie, *no touch!* Trobble."

And Maxie shout-barked: "No, no. I sniff some kind of animal fur and rank urine."

And Minnie, so loud in my face, sniffing Whale: "It's a doll, dummy. Get out of there before the Queen sees you."

The Queen!

The Queen, the actual you-men Queen! Her Majesty! She called so firmly yet so gently, tone of disappointment: "Maxie!"

And Maxie froze like a snake-struck anteater. *Click-click*, hardware and leashes were attached to collars I'd assumed decorative, but no, the Queen yanked both doggs away easily, superpowers.

"It's okay," Inga said.

The Queen, the you-men queen herself, said, "I'm so sorry, young lady."

"They're cute," Inga said. "No worries."

"Just don't let them near your stuffees!"

Inga only laughed. Strongest girl in the world, and bravest.

"Doggs, doggs, doggs, stubid doggs," the squirrels above us cried in near unison.

And then Squirrel said, "Good luck with the zzoo."

The Queen was still retreating, doggs leading her to further dogg encounters, lots of wolfish yelling.

"Let's get a prezzel," Inga said, relieved. "For a good monkey."

"And while you're at it, grab us that pack of peanuts," Squirrel mooded after us. "Don't eat, just chuck 'em on the ground."

The squirrel chorus, too, every tree, gleeful, using their wind voices: "Don't eat, don't eat, don't eat! Just chuck 'em on the ground!"

Centrall Pargh was vast ahead of us. Inga's pace returned me to you-men time, hurried us on, the wilzz of my conveyance clattering joyously, sparse green forest all around.

Chapter Twelve

There were rocky gradients, there were structures, there were meddle poles, there were bodies of water. There were dozens, scores, maybe hundreds of you-mens, all tottering foolishly, too proud to put their hands to the ground, swaying this foot to that, some slapping past on rubber platforms called snikkers, huffing comically.

I tried to mood my Inga: Were we questing, or simply circling?

Nothing in reply: we weren't on that level, not yet.

Goer juveniles kicked a bladder of some kind. Fragrance of nonmonkey food, Inga hurrying toward the scent—I'd not seen her olfactory sharpness till then. But perhaps not definitive; perhaps, in fact, she knew right where the food was to be found, was not properly foraging but recalling satisfaction. So, to those uncles who claimed the you-mens had no memory (proof being their constantly making the same errors), I say this: You were wrong. Inga gave the man chits of paber and he gave her a curious growth, looked like, some kind of root, heavily dotted with salt. Inga smeared the thing with yellow mud the man gave her from a squeezable, then effortlessly, mightily, she tore the thing into parts. One of which she offered me, sticking it into my face under the canopy of my strawler, merriment.

"Prezzel," she said.

The yellow mud smelled so strongly of seeds, the salt heavy as upon a stick from the ocean, the mushrooom, or root, or whatever it was, tasting like the white part of samweedge, but dense. Not a root. And not quite food, not quite not.

"The squirrels mentioned peanuts," I slow-moodled.

But Inga only gave a push, and the strawler leapt ahead, cold breeze in my monkey face. I took the opportunity to jettison the prezzel, and oblivious, Inga raced onward.

Everymonkey knows that all things are in moodly communication at all times, and not only like with like. And though this natural law seemed at best barely true for most you-mens, when I shrieked it seemed to mean to Inga just what it meant to my troupe back home: Stop! I see food!

She stopped. She'd understood.

I jumped from the conveyance still holding Whale (who'd provide some cover, I felt), plucked the fat slug from where it had slimed its way onto the treacherous black pavements of the you-mens and gotten stalled.

I offered it to Inga, of course, and oh my, the face she made, priceless. I was beginning to find her beautiful in the manner of all friends, which is to say most things alive, the naked you-men ugliness breaking as she burbled with mirth and pretended to retch.

The slug took no notice of her but mooded, "Bless you monkey for ending my misery on that sidewalk," and then I said the universal thanks, which amounted to enjoyment of the snack, appreciation of the gastropodic sacrifice. I waggled the slug and popped it in my mouth, that delicious muddy-soft and moist delectation.

"Off to the next incarnation," moodled the food.

Famous last words.

I was delighted as well that Inga hadn't become unhinged by my leaving the strawler but remained just as cheerful as ever. Clearly the quest continued. And therefore I leapt right back onboard, carrying Whale, who was not real, I had come to understand, but who'd been imbued with the stuff of life by Inga's adulation, imagination, mood.

And the mood was compassion, nothing less, and thus esteemed, Whaley lived.

Japanese simians in the park apparently. But you couldn't believe a squirrel—they kept chattering overhead, all one voice, one conversation, such that you felt you were being accompanied by Squirrel One, but Squirrel One was all squirrels, and all squirrels were one, uncommonly connected, the plural squirrel.

"Is that a monkey?" a passerby exclaimed.

"Bitty Twin," Inga said soberly, jolting the strawler to speed, and we hurried along.

I suppressed protest. I, Beep, was a monkey, no Bitty Twin, and no squirrel!

O, dear Inga, learn this: trees are connected, more than mere forest, their roots entangled, their thoughts carried by the mycelium of fungi, every fallen leaf mourned, all the knowledge of the web of life carried in calm concentration through time so deep that memory only glances from it. To speak with the leafies you didn't mood or wind-talk but only awarenessed among them, and I asked if the claim that there were simians in the park were true, and further that, if so, we be guided through Inga's empathy to their location.

And there arose a vibration, a thought moving through not only the trees but all things green, and all things. The forest always knows you're coming, and that's how the rocks know, and so the lichens, the mosses. First, I was led to understand something: many of the trees were still asleep from the cold season. The acidic ones were wide awake, though, and needled me: "You're a squirrel monkey. We've known your kind. Tiny and trusting." They knew, too, that I was on a quest. "You've taken the detour that is yet your path" was the message, typical tree stuff.

"I'm no squirrel," I said.

"There's a zzoo," Inga said suddenly, reading the mood unbeknownst. "Do you want to go? We can see the seals from the fenz!"

Seals were wet doggs, that much I knew. Fenz, that was foreign.

But simians were there, too, Japanese or no.

Inga laughed, oblivious in the you-men way of nearly everything. But not of the current message. The wilzz of the Bitty conveyance sang, and Inga sang, too, her movements hyperspeed, at least as observed in relation to tree time.

Chapter Thirteen

We proceeded east, the original direction of my quest, so heartening. But then there it was, reality—we'd simply crossed the eye of a vast storm of you-men-ity. Ahead of us, rather than the continuing and deepening canopy I'd envisioned, were canyons that even in their mountainous height I understood to be the dwellings of the you-mens—why so tall, so many, so ongoing?

Inga turned south, ran us toward the biggest of the cliffs and toward a roar of goer noise, the snorting and clopping of horses, rattle of wilzz, shouts and imprecations, smell of burning animals, chopping sounds from the sky, and cries and moans louder than a thousand eagles. "I hate those sigh-rings!" Inga said, and covered my ears.

If that ringing be sighs, cover my eyes, too! I'll see no evil, even if I hear it all around, and, monkeys, I'll say what I want!

She hurried us along the black stone way, under a dry grotto, and then over some go-stone terrain and into what seemed a trap—the very corner of the grid I'd begun to notice, a grid being the refusal of curves, and then gaytz to pass through, she called them, a kind of airy dar, gaytz at the far end, too, but wide open, you-mens coursing this way and that, unaware that at any moment their captors, some even more horrible breed, could close the gaytz at both ends, dinner.

My soul did not darken with fear: a monkey could fit through the steel interstices. As for the you-mens, good night.

I realized only slowly that these thoughts were being shared to my psyche by the Japanese monkeys, imprizzonment the vibe, dark depression: the group consciousness having sensed me was warning me, but so vaguely, and layered somehow with a strangely exuberant pinniped consciousness, a kind of vision of swimming in circles in scant sun, but prizzoners nevertheless. Heedless, fearless, Inga pushed the Bitty conveyance through the gaytz under a kind of portico with stiff, clonging bears dancing on top, and other animals unknown, no detectable soul to them even when they whacked their odd belongings and twirled. Immediately in the new area, which was a space defined by the bars of a black-meddle barrier, I smelled the cousins I'd been mooding. And dirty ocean water, also a confusing welter of other stenches, some of it foodlike, some of it chemical, that constant you-men burning, odd birds, large mammals, a tortoise even, maybe a tapir, shades of the home forest. And in fact there was splashing, and just a branch-length away a small ocean, not so small that it did not have an island in it, and around the island, a sense of burgeoning under the water, then a splash, yes, seals, as mooded. I popped out of the Bitty Twin strawler leaving Whale behind, leaving Inga shouting, one leap to the top of a kind of bower out of all you-men reach, its spring-wakened vines urging me on sleepily, thence to a convenient branch, strong swing, then along a bird-smelling rooof, unerringly drawn to the simian emanations and the simian scent and now a muttering: cousins. Sitting to their necks in steaming water.

Inga voice-shouted my name, a consternated conjugation: "Beep! Beepie! Beep-monkey! Hoo-hoo!" Then a rumble deep and I felt her, that nascent mood.

"Just looking," I said.

She was pressed to the high black-meddle barrier, gripping the bars like a captive, watching my every move, sudden big grin as my message hit. "Beep, good careful," she moodled, clear as air.

The Japanese simians seemed oddly content, a little embarrassed, quite disconnected—their vague, depressed moodling continuing though they didn't spot me poised just above them.

I was distracted by a crazy huge white animal emerging from some neighboring rock, shifting from paw to paw, groaning and muttering: "I am Polar Bear, once great, once fearsome. I am Polar Bear, miles did I roam. I am Polar Bear, once great, once fearsome." And repeat, gone mad.

Unfamiliar birds calling, unfamiliar phrases, then some refreshingly wild crow speak, something about liberated hotdogg buns on the Ubber West Side. I leapt higher, tree branch, careful of the fire vines overhead. Simians below, huddled in the warm water. And around the unmonkeys, finer, shinier vines, the same meddle material: those lightning shockers. But I found I could slither close above their steaming pool.

"Simians," I called, using sound—their depression was too deep to crack moodwise. "Simians, hear my voice."

A couple of them found me with sad eyes.

"Eh, kusogaki," a big uncle said clearly.

And the others muttered it, too: "Kusogaki."

I said, "You call me a brat, you soggy simians? You Japanese tub junkies? I'm not a brat," I said. "I'm full-grown emissary from the far world. I am Beep, Monkey. I'm on a quest."

"You are Beep, pet," another moodled strongly. "Dressed in cheap doll garmends."

"Jeepers, Beepers," a youngster said.

"Come touch the wires," an old uncle said. "You wouldn't be the first. We could use a little entertainment. Tragedy would surely suit. We've seen enough of your comedy."

"Are you so jaded?"

"Phht. Jaded. We are prizzoners, how else should we be?"

They'd seemed free, to me, then I saw that the pool and rocks around it were ingeniously constructed to keep even prizzoners as big as they contained, and not by shocks alone. Why would you-mens do this?

"I will work to free you," I said.

"Free us? And where will we go? To the Apple Store for iPhones? See a movie at the Paris Cinema? Maybe tea with Eloise at the Plaza? Go looking for the man in the yellow hat?"

I emanated puzzlement, also judgment: simians learn a lot of strange filth in such proximity to you-mens. Nothing came back, however, not so much as an insult. Their mood was not so fluid.

"The pool is nice," a young simian voice-spoke. I was able barely to understand. "Life is good here at the zzoo."

The older simians all muttered bitterly.

"This one is a born-here," one of them said, knocking the youngster over the head, much chattering.

"Beep!" Inga called from the distant barrier, wind-voice so plaintive. "Beep, come back."

"And the you-mens begin their incursion," one of the chorus of them garble-mooded.

To that one I mooded, "May I talk to an elder?"

"Hmf," said an old monkey I hadn't spotted, prime spot in the steaming water.

"Uncle," I said.

"He is Great-Grandfather," my mood-interlocutor said.

"You'll have to shout," another voice-spoke.

"Great Grandfather," I did shout, in voice. The you-mens milling all around us looked up. I'd been noticed, not good. Juveniles pointed. A parent hurried away. Likely you-men royalty would arrive any moment. And look what they'd done to these unmonkeys! They'd do the same to me. "Great Grandfather, where may I find my kind?"

The eldermonkey turned slowly, fixed clouded eyes upon me. "And what kind are you?" he said, a sort of growl, but moodled—he'd not lost the knack.

"I am Beep, monkey."

"He's the same as the one who fried on the scream wires," one of the bitter ones said.

The elder blew through his lips till they fluttered. "Squirrel monkey, then. South American, or Central, by the stench of him. We learned that by listening in. We are great listeners-in. Once upon a time some of your monkeys lived here—up there, where the raptors are caged now—but too clever, they were, and several escaped, which we cheered, we Japanese. We cheered those efforts, unable to mount our own. We never learned what became of these creatures."

"Dead," Squirrel said from above, but not the original Squirrel—they all had the same name, same thoughts.

"Dead, dead, dead" came the squirrel chorus.

"Bug off, rodents," the elder said.

A great chatter arose, shower of acorns.

"*Freenuts*," a young unmonkey said, jubilant, gathering them in a flotilla.

Great-Grandfather thought a moment, made a decision, good, clear moodle-growl: "Yes acorns. And give them credit, they do tell us things, know things instantaneously, our connection to the outzide world, mostly to torment us. More of your kind live to the east. A child you-men told us so, mooded so, during the visitation, before the electrocution. Simians in the Bronzoo, she said. Lots of simians, big and small. Afriggan, we think, but you South Americans, too. Though the one who died was not a redhead like you, but brownette, the you-mens call it, meaning brown-haired."

"How does one get to there, this Bronzoo?"

"Tunnels through the Aarth."

"Tunnels through the Aarth? You are twitting me!"

Just then two you-men royals came clopping in great boots out of the seal enclosure, pointing and shouting.

I shouted right back: "I am here! Beep, monkey!"

I saw Inga racing away, saw her turn, saw her running uphill pushing the Bitty strawler ahead of her, then lost to eyesight, but not to mind and mood: she was coming around outzide the great black-meddle barrier and positioning herself behind the zzoo itself, tactical. More of the royal guards appeared, one with a large net, another with a shooting stick, the Japanese grandfather called it, alarmed.

"Darttz," he intoned.

Briefly I felt Inga's mood: worry. Not my intention.

"Flee monkey, flee," the Japanese called. So, they did care.

I swung myself over a railing and then onto the rooof over the crazy polar bear. "Flee!" even he cried. "For as I was once free you must remain."

And so, via a series of branches, all while avoiding death-tendrils, I made it to the top of the bird enclosure. "I'll be back," I shouted down from there. "We will free you one and all."

And the zzoo burst into squawks and roars and chittering.

I leapt then into the trees among the squirrels, who all pointed with their eyes even as something banged and a careening dartt, that thing with feathers, whistled past my head, stuck into the bark of an unfamiliar sort of tree, bare of its leaves yet still sensate: tree mood is all thrum. No time to slow to that speed. One leap, two, then a mighty blind swing-and-release, which landed me exactly in my seat in the Bitty strawler, Inga already racing full speed up the hill and away from all the sorrow.

"Bad monkey!" she cried when we were safely far from the bright throngs.

"Are there really secret tunnels?" I said evenly.

"Hoo-hoo," she repeated, "*bad* monkey!"

"Inga, dear. Monkeys are neither bad nor good—we do what monkeys do."

"Say you're sorry!"

"I'm sorry dear Inga. I'm sorry for all I've done, but not for meeting you."

And her mouth fell open: she'd understood.

"I wubboo," she said.

I'd understood as well, and felt the same: wub.

Chapter Fourteen

LATER, IN HER PINK BOUDOIR among my new inanimate friends, we lounged. On her phome, which was a kind of box of light, we watched various patterns repeat themselves in rhythm to Inga's fingertaps, and mine when she let me, but she didn't let me much, apparently jealous of the sensations it brought her, and something about my scramching it.

"I'll have to cut your nails," she said.

No comprendo, friend-o!

Something I touched made the phome cry out in obvious distress. What sort of life was this?

"Inga, I heard that," her mother called.

"I'm doing sigh-ence," Inga called back.

Now one of the patterns resolved itself in a way that nearly made me shriek: it was a you-men male made of light and talking in a deep voice, incomprehensible, and slowly I saw that the patterns when he disappeared (his voice still going) were objects, and that he was naming these. One of these, a tall roarbirdish caught in a vertical cage, was a rogget, and the rogget smoked, shuddered, suddenly crawled into the sky letting go of the ground in some way, escaped, then went faster, long white tail like any roarbird, then not like any. Next a round blue object in blackness, and the rogget flying into and out of view in front of it.

Okay, sigh-ence.

Later, waiting for Inga to be back from her dinner with scraps for mine, my eyes fell on the sphere she kept on her writing tavle. It was blue, somewhat green, none of the white swirls, but it was clearly the same object the rogget had escaped. The man talking in the light had been on the ground like any you-men. The rogget had plainly started there. The rogget had taken to the sky, you see. And then flown away, shown us its view. And the rogget's view was *us*, I realized, something bigger than monkey world. Our *collective* world. And our collective world once you flew above the canopy of the canopy was curvaceous—that much I'd noted from the the windows of the roarbird that had delivered us here. But, if you went higher, it seemed (and sensibly) that curving aspect resolved into a sphere, a sphere like the moon, a sphere like the sun. And this was not only our shared home but our smoking mountain, do you see?

The object on Inga's tavle was our home in simulacrum.

It spun at my slightest touch. I put my face close to it, moved slowly away playing rogget. I was still spinning the thing, my thoughts also spinning, still trying to absorb the hard lesson, when Inga returned. She had something called beetza. Beetza's provenance was very mysterious, though there was animal involved, and the general echo of samweedge and prezzel. The thing called zzalad was more familiar. Zzalad was leaves, ripped up as if for an infant. Upon the zzalad I focused my attention.

"You're looking at the glope?" Inga said, but to some degree truly moodled, such that I understood. "Let me show you where we are." She turned the thing slowly-slowly, put her broad fingernail on a spot at the edge of the blue. "We are on this island," she said. "It's called Madhattan. It's in the citty of Nyork, all of this." Poke, poke. And then she traced a line right along a blue edge. "Florrriba," she said. "Florrriba is where we changed playnz, although, dear monkey, you were sound asleep."

Playnz were the meddle roarbirds.

"See? It's not hard." Her pink finger with its profound nail continued across a smudge of blue. Water, I suddenly understood. And continued till it hit the green. "Mezzico," she said. Her finger followed the bulge of the glope, landed on a narrow strip of green. "Cozza Rica," she said.

I, Beep, had heard that phrase before, often spoken by goers back home, often reported by old uncles with theories. That it was youmen for monkey world, for example, preposterous. Because a monkey couldn't even make that sound. But I tried vocalizing, a piteous shriek.

"Chee-chee, monkey," Inga said, poking the glope. "Cozza Rica. Your home, silly."

"Nyork," I said, understandingishly. "You roam, zilly."

Quizzical Inga—she'd felt me mood, shivered with it. "You *understand*," she said. And pointed again, more aggressively, colored spots on her glope, saying these words: Nyork, Cozza Rica. Did I really understand? I did not. I was lost, not home at all. I'd never felt lost before, even when I was truly lost—that time following a spotted deer all day back home in the forest—because when I'd been truly lost I'd been lost among monkey things in monkey world, and here there were no monkey things, and no monkeys, unless you counted the Japanese troupe, who were prizzoners, deeply depressed, and yet for whom prizzon had become home, had become ancestral even: ask that happy young fellow among them.

The dar popped opened and Momma appeared, pushed it open wider, luckily backing into the space to accommodate baby Willie, who all but dangled from her hands, blubbering. I froze, but Momma was oblivious, carried a disc of blue crystal covered in apple slices smeared with the brownish samweedge goop.

"Back to ssscoola tomorrow," she said brightly. "Spring break is done! What excitement! Do you need anything washed?"

Inga rose, flung her wrapping over me, too warm. "Ugh and uck," Inga said. "Ssscoola!"

"Do you want me to lay out cloze for you?"

Inga was moody: "I will do it myself. I'm not a little girl anymore."

"Oh, Sweedie, I know. So ancient! You're eleven! And so I know you'll also take a bath and wash your harr!"

"Ugh and uck," Inga repeated.

Mother was so understanding, so warm, that interloping infant crushed against her chest and yet so kindly: "Have you any homework?"

"Just that boog."

"And what about your boog report?"

Daughter reached out to mother, embraced her awkwardly around the new infant. Half smothered, she said, "I finished it on our trip. It's so interesting, Momma. And scary, too. Fozzil fuels, sea-level rise, melting everything! I want to be like her."

"Greta is a hero, Sweedie. And it *is* scary. But not insurmountable. We all must do what we can."

"There's time to change, she says. And we kibs are the ones to make it happen. I'm supposed to let you know. There's time to save the world."

The world was the glope!

Momma was very warm: "I do believe she's right. And I'm glad you've let me know. And I'm glad she's visiting Nyork this week."

"She travels by zailboat."

Momma did not sound fully glad: "And you'll get to see her speak! Still, Hunny, she's a pribileged soul from a pribileged nation, and that should be taken into consiberation."

Momma a poet!

"Okay, I will take a bath."

"Yes, perfect. And don't forget to wash your harr. And rinse the bathtup after. And then dinner. And then early to bed for all of us."

Bath, dinner, reading time, Inga speaking it, half-mooding it—glopal warming, zailboat, fozzil fuels—so much for a monkey to absorb. Likely I'd need to understandish all of it to get across this vast crossing and complete my quest, perhaps even get myself back to the world of monkeys, which was part of a greater world, so it seemed.

The bathtup was a bigger tiny pond than the thing you-mens must piss in. It had given its name to the rooom though: *bath.* A bath, I already knew, was a cleaning in deepwater. Learning curve high, but not too high. Inga removed her coverings so easily—I'd thought it might be difficult (I'd seen a snake during the process, so arduous, so vulnerable throughout!), but it was just a matter of ducking out of each item, and there she stood naked. The only fur upon her was on her head, and it wasn't fur at all. Saddest sight: the you-mens really were monkeys, just no fur, except for a male or two, and the horripilant flesh, Inga pale and pathetic as a plucked bird (another whose covering comes off hard, those stout feathers!). But seemingly unharmed, even cheerful, she tested the water with her cute you-men hand (so like a monkey's) and, at last satisfied, climbed in, face shifting red.

"Come in, Snow Monkey," she said, cheery little insult. "You can sit on my knees."

And so I did, sat upon her knees, which she rather wryly lowered, first my legs dunking, then my trunk, the water warmer than the home forest after rain—warm as a floodpuddle heated by hours of sun—finally up to my shoulders. I settled in, set about imitating Inga's nutty behavior, this perfectly clean sleek thing scrubbing like she'd come through battle, bubbles arising from a fragrant kind of shell or stone she rubbed upon herself, very slippery stuff. She rubbed me with it, raising me up on her knees, and soon I was a fragrant puff of foam. She dunked me lower, and the foam floated all around like islands, fun to sink.

"I'm sad about ssscoola," she said, just a hint of unconscious submoodle, which helped me understand. "Becky is such a beach. We used to be such easy friends, but."

Confiding in me!

Big sigh: "Now she only cares about crob tops and stubid bras and stubid, stubid things like, ugh."

And suddenly hot tears ran down her face.

"Monkey," I moodled softly. "Monkey, my little monkey."

She blubbered: "Will I ever be happy again?"

"Happy is our natural state," I said. "I'm happy in this bath, for example. And happy to be with you on this mission, so harrowing. Always there's something to be happy about. A monkey dies, at least there's food to be found. A friend is stubid, but at least there is another."

"Oh, dear monkey. You're making so much noise!"

And she laughed, and Becky was forgotten, this you-men kib growing up too slow and too fast at once, and she laughed some more, unraveled her braided tresses laboriously, then lathered them ferociously and dunked herself multiply and it became apparent this was harr, the color brighter red than on our monkey heads.

Honestly, to bathe was fun, my fur whipped again into foamy peaks by her busy hands, her knees comically collapsing under me then rising me up again from the drink, my face carefully wiped with a limply comforting kind of pink leaf rough as a tongue, everything pink as I have noted, and now her laughter, then big pink wraps called talzz and a lot of ruffling of my ears, a lot of you-men mirth-burbling, little clicking thing stuck atop my head to match the big harrclib atop her own: equal torments between friends. I adopted my warmest slow-blinking gaze, gave a garrulous peep or two. She wrapped her mane in one of the big talzz and spun harr and tal both into a miraculous kind of helmet, that bright face shining pink and polka-dot. She lifted me, a monkey wrapped in a tal, danced me into her rooom, spun us twice, bounced me hilariously on the sleeping platform, bounced down beside me. Her sadness over that big beach Becky had fled.

The old uncles say there are many kinds of wub and a new one befell me in that moment, suffused me: buddies.

Shortly Momma came in, baby Willie likely left on a safe branch somewhere with aunts. And Momma watched so fondly as Inga took the wrap off her head, threw it wholly over me, my one eye peeping out, helped her stroke that burnished harr into straight lines, so much harr, no more ropes, and then did lay out wrappings for the next day as, upon her command, Inga put on bajamazz, they were called, especially soft wrappings, pink again.

"Dinner is ready," Momma said.

My tummy spoke.

Momma gave a sharp look my direction.

But Inga leapt on her, hugged her, kizzed her face, made her forget, and the two of them left the rooom.

Which was hotter than the home tree on a windless afternoon! I climbed free of the ferocious bedwrappings, waited, examining first the glope, then the images she'd hung on the wall behind it, squareish items with white borders in wooden cases, a certain glossy mediation that kept monkey fingers away, but you-mens flattened in there, lifeless incarnations, effigies. Momma, and Dabby, and of course the foolish baby. But there was Inga, too, in various sizes. How slowly the you-mees grew! I felt tenderness toward her and toward her tiny troupe. I studied the representations, the forced you-men grins, the awkward postures. How hard it must be to live in the middle of the crossing and pretend such happiness lest their gods find them ungrateful!

One case was face down on the floor. I righted it, focused till four of the magical images resolved. Small Inga with another young you-men female, arms about each other, faces painted bright colors, big smiles and laughter. And then the same girls a little bigger, sitting like monkeys in a small tree. And then bigger girls yet, holding up paber shapes in red, arms about each other, cheeks smashed together in jolly affection. The last was Inga, all right, but Becky (for I slowly then suddenly realized it was she), looked puffed, her chest distended in the manner of some of the grown you-men females, the great grin of friendship replaced with a scowl. I put it back face down on the floor: there'd been intention, and the wood had retained it.

Forever and Inga was back, that pink disk covered with fruits and what? Dead bird chunks! And lots of ripped leaves, once again, these greasy with strange flavors but satisfying. When I was done, Inga finished the animal bits I'd left, collected the disk, trotted back out. Then reappeared, the dar swinging wide open.

"I'll tugg you in," she said. And placed me delicately under her coverings, my head on a corner of billow, gave me kizzes, put Whale and Wolf strategically atop me, several other creatures all around. I tried not to sigh with happiness. But the mission was still intact. Nothing wrong with hiatus.

"Momma's coming to read to us," Inga said. "No burping!"

Ugh, to share my Inga!

Shortly Momma arrived. "The baby will not go down," she said cryptically.

Momma and daughter mirth-burbled and ignored me, jealous red pang, the two of them paging through a boog, Mommy interpreting the mood it offered. Inga clutched a stuffee I hadn't met, a stiff kind of bear thing, no animal spirit detectable.

Sounds of baby Willie crying, somewhere not distant.

At last, Momma put her lips to her first offspring's forehead and said soft you-men blessings, dug among the other stuffees, found a tattered square of woven fabric in worn pink.

"Your blankie," she said.

Inga took it, folded it a certain way, held it to her cheek.

"Night Sweedie," Momma said.

"Nigh-nigh," Inga told her.

And Momma was gone, leaving the boog to my girl, who held her blankie to her cheek and continued to page through the boog—I swear I heard some passages rising from the paber, the undermood unbidden. I climbed out from among my colleagues, snuggled my you-men, who, gauging from the sighs, needed a friend. And was snuggled back. Who needed a snuggle. And my new buddy read from the boog, incomprehensible, but mooded so much wub and satisfaction and the occasional phrase of intuition that we were one mood.

Then, surprise, the grown male was there, Dabby, and bold as

Momma he lay down beside Inga. She jammed me in among the stuffees, and I played inanimate, a tough game, while he read impatiently from the boog, very fast patter I could not grasp.

Inga snuggled him. Inga put a pretend you-men child atop me, heavy. But soon Dabby was satisfied with the atmosphere he'd wrought and stood up out of the bed with much groaning and yawning, bent and placed his lips on Inga's forehead as Momma had, affection, then slipped out through the dar. The wall sealed itself and my buddy and I were alone. I disentangled myself once more, tore Bear from Inga's grip, tossed him shelfwards—comically, I hoped.

Inga tugged me in once more. I was so warm after the cold adventuring of the afternoon, too warm. Night had been in the sky outdoors a long time. My eyes drooped. My monkey thoughts went universal. All was well with the world, Becky be damned.

"Oh, Beep, how I wubboo," Inga said. Then mooded it very clearly, perhaps unconsciously.

I'm not one for breath-words, but I imagine my own wub was felt all the way to the corner of the pargh where the Japanese snow monkeys were imprizzoned, and I felt they took their share.

Chapter Fifteen

MONKEYS SLEEP FROM WHEN IT'S dark until it's light, but Inga slept from Dabby to Momma, dark at both ends.

And, perforce, I.

The voluble Momma: "Good morning Starshine!"

Her name is Inga, first thought. It is not morning, second.

Inga agreed, slept on.

I realized with a terrible start, third thought, that I'd failed to move off Inga's arm and back among the stuffees in the night—my one hand was under the girl's shoulder, the other atop it, her unbelievably luxuriant hair covering me redly and near completely, Momma leaning in close. I froze unblinking, held my breath, waited as the older female put her lips once again on the forehead of the younger, who stirred not one bit. And so Momma pushed me aside—me and Whale and Wolf plus a long baby seal, pushed us away as she pushed away the covers, lifted the girl by the shoulders and into an embrace.

Momma sang another of her poems: "Inga Sweedie, Inga girl, Inga Sweedie, Inga pearl!"

"Leave me be!"

My heart settled a little. The baby seal was inert, possibly dead, that brusque mother like my own: tender toward issue, rough on the distant, even if cousins.

I was buddy, one step up from stuffee.

And in the dark, this buddy was awake.

And then Inga, too—yawn, stretch, then with a start remembering her secret, and so leapt from that sweet nest.

Thus, Momma was free to go, and did.

There was a frenzy, then, Inga wildly rebraiding all that harr into ropes, and the wrappings momma had arranged rejected in fabor of first one, then two, then three alternates of various bright colors and thicknesses, all of it subject to elated narration: "This is a hoodie I got in the East Billage but I have to tuck the hood part inzide, see, because they are against the dress code. And these stockings are not striped like Pippi's. O, Beepie. I've been wondering what Mr. Nilsson did with himself when she was at ssscoola and what I should do with you." And at length, dressed, she said, "I'll be right back with some snacks to tide you over and when I'm home we can go outzide."

"But you *are* home," I said.

"Hoo-hoo, little pritty monkey."

So much for the moodle. So much for buddies. Now I was nothing but a pritty, and to be left behind!

And she cracked open the dar in some way, using, I realized, a glass ball that waited there, a crystal ball you turned. And then like a crystal ball, I waited. Soon in a flurry my Inga was back, Momma shouting behind her, crucial numbers it seemed, eight and fifteem repeated over and over. Onto her sleeping platform beside me, Inga flung two bananas and a red fruit, also cheese strings, ugh.

"You know where to pooop," she said.

And after stuffing a load of boogs into her noopsook, she poked my tummy a little pointedly, pet my head. I tried to climb up upon her shoulder and ride but no, she felt she must leave me, no explanation. And turning the crystal ball to open the gape in the wall that was a dar, she left, the dar closing behind her. I heard a click at the precise location of the ball: mechanism, you-men ingenuity: always a way to make things more difficult.

She'd turned it. She'd turned it to the south. I gave it a try. It was slippery, immovable. And so I returned to the warmth of the sleeping platform, carefully peeled a banana, removed the strings, ate it in bites, studied the problem, sounds of Momma out in the other roooms, which I could picture with precision, also the next wall I'd have to breach, the dar that led to the dars of the magic box, El Vator, which in turn, if magic was consistent, would lead me to the bright place and portal where the nobleman Ollie held court, and from there a scurry outdoors. I leapt to the wimdoe. On the blackstone trail below, untold numbers of you-mens passed this way and that—the eastward group should tell the westward group that there be nothing satisfying where they're going, and vice versa! The happiest you-mens seemed to be going into the artificial forest where the snow monkeys were held, some of them even running, barely dressed.

And then down there—unmistakably, wonderfully, stirringly, frustratingly—walked Inga, forward-leaning under the weight of her load. Ssscoola it was called, the place she was going. Ssscoola did not make her happy. And still it was night! Her ropes of hair bounced. She walked west. Anymonkey could figure this out.

But the crystal ball on the dar, the darnooob. I thought if I could bash a notch in it I could get a grip. And so, with apologies to the conch shell (far from its home in any case!), I clobbered that noob, once, twice, thrice.

"What the hell?" Momma's voice.

"I, Beep the hell!" I didn't say but mooded, lay back silent among the stuffees.

Because here she came, the dar opening so slowly, her face peeking in—frightened? No, only curious. She was outfitted in a thick wrapping that reached the floor—how hot that wrapping must be, thick as the coverings on the bed.

"What the?" she said again, and picked up the conch shell, inspected it, then crossed the rooom all tentative and into the water rooom, which she also inspected. The wall remained cracked, dar open. I bolted while her back was turned, leapt into the next rooom, straight down the passageway to the great dar that led further, but sad to say, noob of steel, not slippery but only immovable. Seconds to think! Behind me the fragrance of Momma was strong. I turned, spied her supply pouch, enormous thing, capacious. I climbed in, burrowed down among the objects and jingles and softness and jabs, lay still, occluded view.

"Oddest thing," she said to no one.

Suddenly the aunt from the previous afternoon appeared, carrying the baby. Willie's true mother? Anyway, she emerged into my field of vision holding him. "All the banging," this woman said, jouncing the delighted cherubim. I felt her pure heart, this close to moodling. "Likely duppies, but if it's not duppies it's the heating pibes."

Willie knew right where to look, held my eye, pointed in the baby way, directly at me. I found he had power, couldn't look away.

"Yes, of course, Jama, it's the water pibes," Momma went on, oblivious. "There are no ghosts in here!" Aunt of lower status, that accounted for the curious tone. "Now just you feed Willie his grapes and he'll be quiet a while before lunch. Please don't drop him in front of the tee-bee till after nap, okay?"

"Oh, ha. He begs for it, mum."

"Just don't give in."

"Beep," Willie said distinctly, still pointing. "Beep-beep."

"It's not as easy as all that," the auntie said.

"He's just a baby," Momma said.

And suddenly a jolt and a jounce and the supply pouch with me in it was lifted in the air. The main dar opened and we stood a moment in front of the magical wall, El Vator—I could hear its song and shortly the whispering of its opening, felt the stomach-drop after it closed. Same drop when a monkey fell from a tree. So that was it! We were falling, all together, rooom and all, falling to the level of go-way and vehicles, the portal from this you-men dwelling to the other world, my own.

Noblemen in the rooom of lights greeted Momma, calling her Missus so-and-so, and she greeted them back, good morning, good morning, very formal. Ollie practically groveled. So, she was very high status. Ten long you-mee-mommy strides and we were outzide, rush of sound and movement, mayhem. I popped up through the important detritus of Momma's go-pouch, clambered up her garmend to her broad shoulder even as it convulsed, leapt into a citty-toughened tree just there and climbed as she shrieked and spun, threw her bag to the ground, stepped back from it.

The biggest of the noblemen hurried out to help her.

"Someone," she cried. "Somehow."

"It's okay, missus."

"Tried to take my bag. At least I think. And jumped into that tree?"

"No, missus. That's not possible, missus."

She pointed. The tree, being leafless, offered no cover.

"That's a squirrel, missus."

"Let me explain," I began, using wind-voice.

"That's a monkey!" Momma cried.

The nobleman laughed heartily at that, but then at my next expostulation looked surprised as an old uncle, said, "Well, I'll be switched."

"I'm off to find Inga," I cried.

"Monkey!" Someone shouted.

And a you-men chorus to rival the squirrels: "Monkey, monkey!"

And then the squirrels themselves, omnipresent: "Run, monkey, run! Run, monkey, run! Run, monkey, run!"

I leapt from the tree to a taut membrane in front of the portal, the very mouth of Inga's cliffside dwelling—a y'awning, she'd called it—made it to a ledge and from there around the corner and down to the next tree, and then the next and the next and the next, all these naked torpid trees all in a row over all these resting goer vehicles: west.

Only at the next corner did I realize how cold I was. I'd eschewed the Bitty Twin pea coad and pamps, and not only for their ill fit. The next goer trail wasn't sleepy at all, meddle machinery all going someplace, the same place by the look of it, all in the same direction, and the old problem rearing its head: how to cross a you-men trail? Plus a new problem: Where had Inga gone? I couldn't spot her, but from the safety of my perch I watched the coursing you-men-ity. Many things seemed to be burning, some slightly familiar, the cooking of the goers, the stench of their machines, but something else, as well, the very air, and a tang of ocean, which gave me hope. I needed Inga. I studied all the you-mens. The walkers among them weren't like the goers in their carrs. The walkers proceeded in every direction at once, like monkeys who'd heard disparate rumors of food and picked different rumors to believe. But I, Beep, detected a pattern—younger you-mens carrying those noopsooks (stuffed with ssscoola tribute of some particularly heavy kind) all walking bent as Inga had, as if falling forward, direction aligned with Inga's last known. West, as I've said, and verified by the rising light across the limited forest of Centrall Pargh far behind but visible down the canyon of dwellings. Yes, friends, the sun, here as everywhere, coming to warm us and light our way. The thousands of false suns or perhaps moons of Nyork began to blink out. I'd have to cross the go-way. No bluevine to ease the way, but cold meddle poles that reached to the middle of the wide trail bearing boxes of everchanging light, red, orange, green, back again. From the tip of the thing I could leap to the next bare tree and continue.

But out there with the goer carrs and truggs rushing below, a kind of panic overwhelmed me. A little like what a monkey felt swimming the crocodile river, but I knew what crocodiles were like—this unknown was scarier. And worse, the tree was farther away than it had seemed from my perch. Worse yet, the busybodies had all caught up and were standing pointing up at me: "Monkey! Monkeeeee!"

Suddenly, magically, the traffic stopped, and these you-mens rushed out into the trail just below me pointing and shouting. It was time. I urinated on my hands and feet for moxie, poooped onto the head of the shrillest lady down there, very satisfying, and thus girded and unburdened leapt at the tree, barely caught a branch, which snapped! But my momentum brought me down on a purple y'awning that bounced me high and safely out of reach of the growing mob. I leapt to a ledge of stone and ran along it, then an easy leap to the next tree, and onward, west, west, and west.

At the next corner, the juveniles with the noopsooks, even more of them now, none Inga, fell northwards. There were fewer trees but a good ledge, then a little pargh, bigger trees, and into them I was able to climb quite high (eyes on the sky for eagles, none, just the thudding you-men sky machines like prepossessing dragonflies, oblivious of monkeys). The shouters were left behind, a tale to tell: Monkey in Madhattan!

The little pargh came to a point and at that point I made a decision, climbed to the far tip of a drooping branch and dropped onto the top of a kind of trugg called a buzz, I would later learn, and the buzz lurched and crossed the trail just where the noopsook juveniles were staggering. It picked up speed, but at the corner I was able to grab the next tree (this one clinging to its own dead leaves like a monkey momma mourning her clawed child).

I adopted the pace of the young you-mens below, they on the ground, I up high.

A long barrier made of clangy black-meddle lances, pointy as tusks, ran along an equally long you-mee structure made of nothing but wimdoes, like hardened air, and there at an opening the noopsook crowd all turned and hurried up a drystone waterfall—stars, they were called—to a great bank of dars: this was ssscoola.

Inga was in there!

Chapter Sixteen

A LOT OF TREES OUT front, and among their bare branches and their sleepy but wily springtime intimations about the best route, I made my way till I was positioned just over the river of young you-mees as they made their way up the stars to the dars. If I just leapt down and darted through one of the open dars, I'd be in, but everyone would know it and the shouts begin. Nothing foreign in that—when any interloper comes into troupe territory, we monkeys all scream. It's about safety, in that case. In this case, though, it would be about delight.

And I'd be caught.

But then I spied a male juvenile rolling up the go-stone solo, not on foot like the rest but seated in a contraption, hugged by its arms, a kind of personal carr, very small wilzz in front, huge wilzz in back, purr of whatever quiet machine powered its momentum. The rider tilted his neck, wriggled his fingers among the stubby controls of his conveyance, and in that manner seemed to guide himself. Past the stars and to an inclined plane likely installed for the purpose, he rolled himself to a special door at the top, pressed a blue plate to open it, rolled into the ssscoola as willingly as the others.

So I dropped unseen into some dense shrubbery alongside the ramp. Soon, sure enough, another rider approached, this one less silently, a whirring and beeping. As he passed, I clambered unseen into the little basket beneath his seat, rode cramped in there, felt the tilt of the plane, heard the special door swish open.

Inzide the building, cacophony: that meddle-ish clanging, and juveniles hurrying faster, all of them shouting, "Bel! Bel!"

I flinched, I shivered, I did not belong. I gripped the rim of the basket, peered out, the lowdown view.

The stream of you-mee juveniles flowed upward on more stone zigzag stars, which of course my driver could not negotiate—and so I rode with him down the long hallway among the wee-est wee-bees to yet another magical dar, El Vator III, rolled inzide, and shortly my oblivious benefactor and I emerged from that soothing silence into a fresh but very similar universe: cacophony, narrow hallway, narrower dars.

Ssscoola, ssscoola, a kind of storage place for juveniles, who, I saw, were self-herded in groups of similar size through these dars and into pens.

Always thinking of my own quest, selfish monkey, I'd thought perhaps ssscoola was a place the troupe sent juveniles to escape to the other side, but no. It was as much a cage as the one the bathing monkeys lived in—just more inmates here, some morose, most too young to know they should be, no hot-tub.

But there was Inga! Coming up behind us! Laughing with a boy half her height and a girl twice. The tall one turned suddenly and fell through a dar into one of the pens and Inga carried on, gaining on my conveyance fast. As she passed I tugged her pamps leg, climbed quick up inzide her coad, warm at last, and, self-possession of a spider, she didn't even startle but hugged me tight inzide there as we ducked into the next pen, where we and the others were treated to a cheerful speech by a stout female you-men, called, as I would learn, Miz Britt, also Teecha (which was the name of one of my cousins—poor Teecha, who fell from a high branch into the river, what we monkeys call the Crocodile Goodbye).

"Coads, coads!" Miz Britt called.

And the juveniles, still mirth-bubbling and blabbering, stripped off the thick outer layers they were all wearing. Inga, not a word, stripped out of her coad and stuffed me in the arm of it, hung it on a meddle stub meant for the purpose. She lingered as the other kibs got their coads hung, then arranged things so I could see out, breathe.

"Why all the excitement?" Miz Britt said.

"There was a monkey on Columbus!" a plumpish female said.

"Just a squirrel, Becky," said a dull voice.

"You're half right, halfwit," Becky said. "It was a squirrel *monkey*."

Becky! I studied her: definitely the you-men juvenile from the magical image back in Inga's pink swelter.

"On Columbus," Miz Britt intoned.

"In the trees," someone else said, very excited.

"You, one and all, were hallucinating," Inga said coolly.

The class erupted, jeers and cheers, sides already picked.

Becky rose, insulted. "I tell you it was a monkey!"

"I saw it, too," Inga said. "It was a kinkajou."

Another eruption.

"I did a report on kinkajous, remember?" someone called.

Here's Beep's report: Kinkajous, perfectly boring, named after their one utterance, and yet here, so far from any rainforest, the you-men juveniles knew all about them.

"I remember," Miz Britt said. "But I'm inclined to go with squirrel." How she commanded the rooom! "And so shall we all. Please open your Integrated Mathemabics to page one hundred one."

Becky said something under her breath.

Inga, temporarily victorious, held her chin high.

Slowly, very slowly, the holding pen quieted down.

Chapter Seventeen

Apparently a god was coming to ssscoola. "In person," Miz Britt said, meaning, I guessed, that the god would be taking you-men form. Monkey gods are said to do the same, form simian. Teecha suggested the kibs (she called them, bigger than wee-bees) write down a question to ask the god. Remarkably, every kib in the holding pen took the suggestion, scramched on colored carrds with colored sticks, passed them forward. The god's name, apparently, was Greta, the very same invoked by Inga at bedtime the night before!

I dozed to the hum of Miz Britt reading from the cardds, which made it sound very much like it were she asking the questions—perhaps the kibs helped her moodle in this rudimentary way, shared thoughts via colors and squiggles.

"Will there always be maple trees?" one cardd spoke.

And Miz Britt nodded. "That's a good question. No name on this one. Frank?"

Everyone roared. I did not get the joke, but the jollity was amusing in itself, and pushed into my dreams: Beep swinging down to the forest floor among urgent peccaries, some kind of warning that wouldn't come through. And Beep surfacing to the laughter of the kibs, another question entering their minds via the interaction of its cardd with Miz Britt's mind: "Will Nyork Citty be under how much water?"

"That's kind of two questions," Miz Britt said. She'd gotten more gentle as the morning wore on. "But two good ones! Will Nyork Citty be under water? And if so, how much?"

"I would add, When?" Inga said.

"Yes good," Miz Britt said. "If inevitable, then when? Who can tell me what *inevitable* means?"

"Gonna be!" shouted a male.

"I have a question," bulbish Becky said suddenly.

"Yes, Becky?" said Miz Britt skeptically.

"When will Inga get how much boobs?"

The class fell into raucous laughter.

Inga sagged into her dezzk.

Miz Britt looked stern, then cross, and the hilarity died. She said, "We all develob at our own paces, Becky Crankbrood. And you have just develobed a week's demention."

"I'm serious, though!"

"Two weeks, Becky Crankbrood. Last straw. One more peep and I'll put you up for discipline board and probable susbension."

Susbension meant hanging, some stray thought informed me, possibly arising from one of the big boogs behind Teecha's station.

"Not fair!" Becky cried. "I'm just telling the truth!"

"That's it," Miz Britt said evenly. "You're to see Brincibal Markette."

Sent away! And good. My Inga had not recovered, head on her dezzk.

Becky was only defiant, this Brincipal no punishment to her. She needed some monkey mediation. Earlier I'd seen her unload her orange noopsook just in front of my closet, and while the class tittered and clamoured and Miz Britt wrote on a paber for Becky to take to this chieftain called Brincibal, I managed to creep down and unzib the thing. Silently, I removed every item in that noopsook, boogs and gumm and paber and samweedges in blastic, and finally something even a monkey knew was secret: a blankie, sweet soft thing adored to tatters and smelling of hot tears. And put everything back but the blankie, zibbed the noopsook closed but nipping the sweet weaving so that it hung from the gape, then leapt back to my hiding place.

Sullen Becky said, "You're not the boss of me!"

Firmly unperturbed, Miz Britt said, "Just get your things and march yourself to the offizz!"

"Gladly!" And like a storm she blew back to the clozzet, ducked dramatically to grab her noopsook, threw an angry arm through a strabb, stomped among the dezzks of the room toward the door, her blankie bouncing unmistakable.

"It's *pinkie!*" some no-doubt wounded former intimate shouted.

"*Pinkie! Pinkie!*" half the class began to chant. They'd known one another from momma-riding days.

Exquisite.

Becky gave a shriek, rushed to the dar, waited for Miz Britt to let her out, some device in the noob she fiddled with as the class hooted their derision.

"*Stop!*" someone cried suddenly. "Just stop it, *now!*"

Inga!

She surveyed the class, the rooom suddenly silent. At last she said, "Let she without a Pinkie throw the first stone. Becky is our, our, our *friend!*"

Becky wailed, pushed at the unyielding dar. At last Miz Britt got it open, stepped away, poor Becky rushing through.

And now this monkey felt terrible.

The class erupted in chatter, Inga the lone atom at the center, chin once again held high.

Miz Britt only managed to quiet the kiblets down, but only after a long interval, gave a little lecture about kindness, bless her. And then, efficient woman, it was back to class.

A good if not uncomplicated day's work already accomplished, this monkey let his eyes droop, fell asleep in the capacious warm embrace of the arm of Inga's jagget.

Chapter Eighteen

HOWEVER LONG LATER, A TUMULTUOUS stirring. The class, getting ready to go in search of Greta, when here I'd thought she was coming to them, to us.

Before I could get my bearings, Inga was lifting her coad off the hook, pretending to struggle with it, slinging her strategically unzibbed noopsook over a shoulder. With a sweeping drop she popped I, Beep, inzide, so smooth. Of course I knew to play stuffee, even though no one in their excitement was paying attention. Out in the air, so cold, we marched along in a group like gossiping prizzoners (Becky and Pinkie were apparently sitting in a tree, K-I-S-S-I-N-G) till we reached a stopping place, goers roaring past in their various goer machines, many of them bright yellow, why?

"Wait for the zignal!" Miz Britt called.

And I had a revelation: the crossing of these crazy you-men byways was by agreement, something to do with the brights I'd climbed on escaping Inga's building. And far across, a red bright that I suddenly saw was shaped like a hand, and everymonkey knows what that means: Stop! And then, magically, the red bright changed to white bright, unmistakable image of a you-men male running from one crime or another. And reminded thus of danger and in a sudden herd we crossed the byway, simple as that, a vanguard of the yellow goer machines securing our path, some honking like great, protective geese: heaven's defenders.

And so I understood that we were going to this special you-mee

Greta's howzz, and that there we'd get the news we needed to solve all the problems we still had in front of us, my quest no different from all quests.

We proceeded. The you-men structures were cliffs, the dull colors relieved by flappings like you-men wrappings and by reflections of sky and cloud, long lines of structures divided by blackened go-ways, the roar and hooting and wails outrageous. On the corners, growers burned meat. I saw prezzels, too, and wished I could eat. The line of us pulled up short in front of a palace, fountains of water squirting in preternatural plumes, magnificent you-men magic. A somnolent nobleman at a steel tavle looked through noopsooks, stuck his hand into Inga's beside me. My instinct was to bite those thick fingers but instead when he squeezed at me I peed a little, just so, enough that I could find him again if necessary, but more so that I'd be with him in spirit for days. He didn't even notice, just passed the noopsook back across the tavle to Inga.

Indoors once again, the smells of you-mens, their life of chemicals and perfumes and rot, we came to a cavern containing ranks and rows of sitting contraptions filled mostly with the young, who emitted a hum and vibration and buzz loud as any monkey tree. Inga chose a sitting contraption, fell into it, settled her noopsook on her lap, and arranged the open flap so I could see over the young you-men heads in front of us. The brights dimmed. A female adult, square as a you-men building, stood at a pobium, and very gradually the young you-mens quieted.

"Hello, hello," she said.

Some of the kibs said hello right back to her, cheerful shouts and cries.

Her wind voice boomed: power. "Hello! And welcome to this exciting event! Our guest will take questions after, and remember that today's afternoon lecture is just for you! Greta wanted to speak directly to ssscoola kibs! Tonight she'll speak at the U.N. to the grownups—and I expect some fire!"

The kibs cheered. Fire? Would they be burning their adults?

"And now, Labies and Genitalmen, boys and girls, I give you *Greta Thunberg.*"

Greta Thunberg popped onto the stage, no show of teeth, just a wave, a brisk march to the pobium, brisk grasp of the boss woman's big hand, which must have burned—the woman rushed away, her face a gracious rictus. Greta was barely visible behind the podium, diminutive god. I felt her as a fellow being, just something about her, a certain wisdom, and full undermood.

"Hello everyone," she said at last, pure authority. "I'm glad they brought all you kibs here. Because soon I will call for all of you to go on strike. Against the further degradation of the plamet, and of our lives. The grownups have caused all this. It's our job to speak truth to their power, to save the world despite them."

Cheers and shouts, a revelation: these little ones all together there were like a wave I once saw that scoured the beach of all you-men sign, and then a next wave came, and a next, magnificent storm like we monkeys had never seen. The uncles showed us where to ride it out, in the old grand trees in the high river end, the wind roaring imprecations. For days afterward the you-mens were quiet—you saw them blinking and walking among the sticks and flags of wrappings and bashed vehicles and cement slabs where their dwellings had been. Then in a dark antiwave those things were all built back—all their buildings, all their trails and blackened go-ways—louder, greedier, grosser, more goers, fewer growers. Or if I hadn't seen it I'd heard about it, monkey memory being shared in large part. But not this moment, this stirring Greta Thunberg. She had a giant plane of brightness behind her, a kind of magic-image case like those at Inga's dwelling but much, much larger. It produced moving images in some way, smoking you-men cities, burning forests, roarbirds leaving trails, and then an image of monkey world, so I thought, familiar mango trees and a sloth I thought I knew—Colin, his name was—but sloths look much alike to the monkeys among us.

And then to my mind's eye leapt the sphere, the glope, Inga had called it: Greta was *mooding*. Powerfully so. And from her mood I understood something—this plamet was home to every one of us. This plamet was the bal the you-men kibs kicked among themselves, and we rolled at their whim. Rain forests, Greta Thunberg said. And described my home! Were being destroyed, she said, at unprecedented rates. Never happened before, she said, defining her own terms. Inga booed with the rest of the kibs, not so much angel as I'd thought.

"So what do we do? How do kibs find more power?"

"Strike!" the audience said.

"Now-now," one of the teechas called out.

"Strike!" the audience said.

The enormous Greta-ish face glowing on the cavern wall remained impassive, then slowly brightened. Impish, eyes so alive, and I suddenly saw it: she was a monkey. Greta was a monkey!

"Strike," she said.

"She means it figuratively," another of the teechas called.

"Strike!" the kibs cried. They meant as a snake strikes, perhaps, or as an uncle whacks a coconut from a tree with a stick. "Strike!" And as the young ones in turn bash the nut with sticks and rocks till it breaks and leaks a meal. "Strike, strike, strike!"

And Greta went on to say all the things that were going wrong, and how little those responsible—adult you-mens all—were doing about any of it, how kibs had to rise up. Rise up! That made sense, too: that to take action, you-mens, like monkeys, must be on their feet.

I repeat: Greta was a monkey!

And more: I'd come all this way to meet her.

I shivered in Inga's grasp—Inga had been my ally, had facilitated my quest, and now the job was done. I listened closely to the goddess: The goers, it seemed, were destroying our only home, this plamet, this sphere, this glope, this blueness, this swirling of clouds, this draped-in-sky, this floating-in-a-void, the Sun somewhere far and yet near enough, the moon somewhere closer and yet helpless. But we should not blame sun or moon, cousin Greta seemed to be saying, but the goers. And wait, the growers, too, who when careless contributed to the problem. And the meat eaters, as well—not counting monkeys, I assumed, who only eat insects, maybe here and there a songbird, which I'd tasted so seldom that in any case surely I was absolved, and of course lizards, no biggie: Lizards were snacks.

"Strike! Strike! Strike!"

A kind of hilarity took over the proceedings, kibs of various sizes and so many shapes and shades, so wild in their wrappings, laughing and shouting, the teachers inexplicably singling out certain of them for condemnation even as the Monkey Goddess imprecated:

"Right here, right now, is where we draw the line. We children of the damned! Change is coming whether grownups like it or not."

The kibs cheered.

And Goddess Greta took strength from that mood and carried on, mostly incomprehensible to a monkey, but mooding the while and here and there moodling unmistakably, and definitely moodling her last line, even as she also wind-spoke it. She raised a fist, widened her eyes as monkeys do, spoke directly to me, to Beep, the undermood: "I have learned you are never too small to make a difference."

The kibs cheered at that. They all wanted to make a difference! Whatever that meant to them.

The female you-men in charge climbed wooden zigzags to stand beside the goddess. You could tell not even alpha status kept her heart from pounding, so close to celestial power. "Now," she said, "we have some questions on index cardds but will be able to take a few questions as well directly from the audience, as Miz Thunberg has requested." And she examined a blue rectangle of paber, caught its mood, recreated the voice of one of the assembled stupents, as they were called, the incarcerated ones: "Hi Greta. This is Mindy from Nyork. I feel bad because the citty is so bad for the enfironment. Should I move away?"

From! Inga had said I was *from* the rain forest. So to be *from* was to explain home, and home not the same for everymonkey or even every you-men child. And all the hot black go-stone, all the mindless goers, all the meddle machinery, all of the everything—that was Nyork. This obstacle on my quest, which had simply been to get to the other side of the terrible go-way, was their *home.* My heart sank: perhaps this *was* the other side, my quest greater than I'd thought.

Greta, goddess, screwed up her face in gentle intelligence, even more monkeylike. The question was pleasing to her, I could see. She answered very succinctly: "Citties are actually great in many ways but could be better, and as centers of wealth likely will be. Suburbs are worse—all the energy required for each howzzhold duplicated repeatedly, while in the citty these things are consolibated. You might ask: Greta, how could cities be better? I answer, Conserfation! Difestment from fozzil fuels!"

The head you-men said, "Would it be possible, Greta—for those among us who don't know—to define the term 'fozzil fuels'?"

"Of course. These are ancient plant materials that captured enormous amounts of carbon millions of years ago and protected our atmosphere from the danger. When we burn them, we spend from that bank account. Renewable fuels like wind and sun and even moving water, even the tides, are infinite and produce no carbon in their usage."

I'm sure I did not understand that, but many of the you-men children did, and cheered. My sense was this: all the citty noise around us, the roaring, the going, the pounding, all of that required sustenance, and not monkey sustenance but this stored carbon in some mysterious way that involved burning, which explained the foul smoke around all you-men gatherments.

I had a question, but of course couldn't ask, not with my wind voice, nor with a blue rectangle of paber. I mooded hard, moodled the question carefully, hoping the sensitive goddess would glean it from all the turbulent you-men kib cacophony.

"One from the audience," the head you-men female said very loudly.

A you-men child leapt to his feet near the front, shouted: "Where did the climate come from?"

The others all laughed, but Greta gave her chastening monkey stare, said, "That's a very good question!" And then she answered: billions of years, star dust, all sorts of things a mortal monkey was hard pressed to understand in these you-men phrases, yet very familiar: the climate is also the world we live in. Next question.

Inga leapt to her feet, as did others, but the lady somehow knew to call on her.

Inga said (very loud wind-voice), "My family travels to Cozza Rica every winter and spring and fall and we all wub the rain forest. What effects does climate change have on the rain forest, and the animals of the rain forest?"

"Such as monkeys!" I cried.

Inga stuffed me back down in her bag. The assembled children laughed and did sound like monkeys—the monitor teachers hushed several of their number—none the wiser about me, true monkey, too small to be noticed.

Greta, monkey of the world, said, "This is an important question. Cozza Rica in fact has done very well, and has entirely difested from fozzil fuels, far ahead of backwards nations like the USA."

The children laughed, the teachers hushed, one large male in short pamps and muscles clucking loudly.

Was Cozza Rica my home? Certainly the rain forest was—sudden pang.

"The trees of the rain forest process and store enormous amounts of carbon and give back oxygen, which all creatures must breathe. You have studied the carbon cycle, yes?"

The children cheered and shouted both yes and no.

"Then ask your teechas tomorrow! Because it is very, very important. The animals, the trees, the cycles of nature, all are blameless. The monkeys in the trees? The sloths up there with them? The anteaters on the ground? The fish in the sea? They are blameless, and yet it will be all of them that pay. Can the birds and the bees and the monkeys in the trees rise up? No! It is we who must do so, we the young, we who will inherit this fouled plamet!"

I'd understood every word. Because she'd moodled. Cousin Greta had moodled even while she wind-spoke! And her message, I realized, was the message I'd been launched on my mission to receive. And like all monkeys, she mistrusted all you-mens. All but these children, in whom the future lay, so she said, none of them too little for the burden. She'd missed something, though: the animals could indeed rise up, the plants, too, the fungi, even the minerals, rise up!

The world was bigger than we animals and plants and fungi and minerals knew. And the world, even as vast, was in trobble. I had to get back to the rain forest, they called it, get back home to warn everymonkey, and to mount a plan: we'd have to stop the goers. Stop the growers, even. Enlist the sensitives to help if we could, sensitives like Inga, the moodlers, the knowers, perhaps even their gods, this Greta. And alert the animals of the forest. Yes, the monkeys in the trees could rise up. And yes, all the animals of the world could rise up, too, and the plants, and the fungi, and the minerals.

Yes, indeed we could!

The stupents launched a rhythmic chanting and a cheering: "Save the world, kibs rule! Save the world, kibs rule!"

I climbed out of Inga's noopsook flush with revelation, leapt off her shoulder to the rail of the balgony just a few rows in front of us, stood high over the stage down there, chanted with the children, mood style. Greta's pinpoint eyes picked me out: we two monkeys were moodling.

"Yes, Freemonkey, you," she urged, holding my eye even at that great indoor distance, pure mood. "Yes, Freemonkey, you."

Inga, meanwhile, clambered over seatbacks and noopsooks and frowzy heads, dove at me, lifted me under my arms, the kibs all around us cheering, the mood so strong that my you-men girl let me climb up into her raised palms, and along with the Goddess Greta, who both moodled and voice-spoke, I moodled the chant, heard it mood-echoed back from just a handful of stupents—the sensitives!—rising up, powerful indeed, and even Inga, mood and moodle: "Rise up! Rise up! Rise up!"

Heads all around turned to stare: whose voice was that?

It was mine, Beep, monkey.

"Hoo-hoo," the kibs around us chanted, then the whole rooom: "Hoo-hoo-hoo!"

Goddess Greta kept my eye. How satisfied that sweet cousin looked, far down there in her jumbo image made of brightness itself: we'd found our answer.

"Hoo-hoo!" The crowd of kibs roared. "Hoo-hoo!"

The teechas in the aisles tried to tamp down the exuberance, but the exuberance only grew. Greta looked out over all she'd wrought.

Inga stood, held me high, let me roar along.

"Hoo-hoo, monkey," she said. "Hoo-hoo-hoo-hoo-hoo-hoo-hoo!"

The big magic-image went blank, but the roar did not subside. And Inga and I were getting an awful lot of attention, even as the chant continued.

"Good day!" Greta shouted. "Until we meet again! Thank you, and thank you."

The kibs leapt like monkeys from their seats and made for the portals beneath tiny red-glowing fires even as the indoor suns of that cavernous place lit bright. A teecha was heading toward Inga and me from one direction, shoving her way down the row of children and seats, and another teecha—that clucking male—from the other side, so Inga stuffed me in her noopsook, vaulted the rows, joined the ocean of chanting kibs, and out into the actual day, where she continued to trot, and not toward ssscoola.

Chapter Nineteen

INGA ON THE GROUND WAS as fast as I in the treetops, quieter. The other you-men kibs coursed back toward their prizzon, but we were making a break, Inga breathless, narrating: "We gotta get you home!"

We did not retrace my steps and swings and leaps from the morning but hurried down yet another perfectly straight trail with carrs resting peaceably in lines at the edges all the way along. The trees were ahead, Centrall Pargh.

A squirrel shouted down: "Monkey girl!"

And then of course all the squirrels knew. The trees sent a zignal, too, slower flow, and you saw the shiver proceed down the block in front of us and into the forest-ish of Centrall Pargh ahead. We waited for the brights, and when the goers in their machines finally thought to stop for us, Inga trotted across, I, Beep, bouncing on her back.

"Trobble, trobble," the squirrels were chittering overhead, but squirrels know little—they just spread the word, and quickly. The trees knew more, Centrall Pargh ashiver.

A wall of stones very tidily interlokked gave us cover as Inga ran us to her home, another cliff. And there I recognized the y'awning over the entry portal, the big meaningless numeral upon it, the fancy you-men lettering, the large-scale nobleman at the door talking to—Miz Britt!

Inga froze. The squirrel message through me had reached her. The trees all around us leaned in with their deep senses, reported back: Teecha was furious. Teecha was howling mad. Ollie was fending her off. Dar-man, Inga called him. Islandman, the trees called him, he having come from the rainforest like me, trees respectful of him, man who mooded, a sensitive.

And then there was Momma. The teacher used hands and vocalizations to express to her the whole story, plus emotion, Momma the same, she who'd seen me first among the grown ones.

Inga gulped. I gulped.

The trees passed the message along: Gulp.

"She's over here, she's over here," the squirrels sang, loving drama, but of course none of the you-mens spoke squirrel. The trees did, though, and fond of Inga, began to shake the squirrels off their branches, practically a squirrel storm, so many had gathered.

"What on Aarth!" the leader of a group of you-men females said.

"Oh, Jeez," Inga said to me, or didn't say but moodled. "We. Are. So. Busted."

She edged back along the wide and busy trail, the squirrels chattering our location all the way, the great trees protecting. Then my girl, and bless her for it, broke into a run. I bounced hard in the noopsook, jollity. She ran back toward the north where night lived, where the cold lived, a long way north through the pargh and then west and out of the pargh toward the gathering sunset, these short you-men days, darted into a shop that smelled of prezzel and salt and unknown things.

"Inga, ragazza, you're early," the friendly behind the counter said. "I getta you a slice."

But she ignored him, his great avuncular respect for her, and wub, too, the things a monkey feels first, and raced back into the dimness, into a water rooom. I stuck my head out of her bag.

"Don't look!' Inga cried, and sat to urinate, loud splashing.

She flushed that monster mouth and wiped everything down, scrubbed her hands, very quickly turned her big red coad inzide out, now blue. She gathered her bright braided harr into a knot atop her head.

Back in the shop, the friendly said it again. "I getta you a slice?"

"No slice but can I have your hat?"

"Haha! No, little woman."

"I'm in trobble," she said, and lifted me from her bag.

The friendly's eyes grew large as his beetzas. "Oh, big trobble, I see," he said. "I heard the rumors already! So you're the monkey girl! Of course you are!"

"Oh, Super Mario. Do you know where the Bronzoo is?" she said. "How to get there?"

"It's inna da Bronzz, gagootz. Take the Argh trayn to the Toot and Fife. Get off at a station called—get this—Bronzoo!"

And Inga giggled. And Mario gave her his hat, blue as her coad, beetza image on the brow of it, orangey-red disc with a wedge of the weird food only somewhat removed.

"Kib, take this." And he handed her a yellow chit, black stripe on the back of it.

"Ah, Mario, thanks."

"Ah, Mario thanks, she says. Pay me back, that's the thanks. Care for this monkey, for the monkeys are the future of-a the world. Think I didn't a-hear? Mayhem at the climate thing. Nothing make-a me happier."

"Well, you don't know it was me!"

"I know it was him!"

I gave a little bow.

"Oh, Super, don't tell."

"I would never. This monkey is-a my hero!"

"You're kind," I said, sensitive to sensitive.

Outzide again, the squirrels were excited—the blue coads, they said, those lesser nobles, had arrived at Inga's building with their brights-whirling vehicles and silver brooches, and I was glad she'd flipped her coad. She looked full grown in the big thing. She pulled the beetza hat down over her eyes, stuffed me deeper in her bag, and oh, how I bounced in there down whatever trail we were on, then more violently, *clang-clang*, roar of you-men machination. She opened the bag again, let me stick my head up: dark tunnel. The underground passage the Japanese bath monkeys had spoken of—it was true! My own monkeys were at Bronzoo! I'd been slow to put it together, but here it was: the quest continued.

Jubilation!

And rat chatter, almost all about food, from what I could understand (their inflections are extreme, but great stammering senses of humor: *p-prezzel, p-poison, p-paber, p-potatochibs, p-proteinbar*, and some violent infighting, every rat for itself, none of the squirrel communication, all muttering and chomping and hurrying this way and that). We'd met many back home, though seldom in the forest, more often in the rubbish tips of the growers and goers and all along the beaches—every shib disgorged them, world accents.

Suddenly a wind and a whine and roar and dinging and a silver rogget barely fitting the tunnel flew in—the trayn—magic dars sliding open, grim you-mens piling out, grimmer ones piling in, the eternal exchange. But not Inga. "We wait for the Argh," she said.

Several more arrivals, then at last the Monkey Line, the Argh, and we climbed in it and roared out of there, *clickety-clackety*, you-mens swaying, Inga swaying, a communal dance, somehow powering the machine—they were all in on it.

And stop, and dars open, and the exchange of fresh new you-mens for fresh power, and the *ding-ding*, and the dars closing, a muttery god's bored voice offering warnings and cryptic phrases till at last it spoke the right locution, and Inga ran us across the blatform and into a new trayn, the Toot and Fife! More rumbling and banging and dings and stops, more fresh you-mens, and finally the great voice spoke our destiny, spoke it twice: "Bronzoo-Bronzoo."

Inga raced off the trayn, up into daylight, trotted along a tall black-meddle barrier that she could not climb or crawl through, trotted until an opening appeared, not exactly a dar, definitely a portal, and blocked by a you-men female in a tigget booth, Inga called it. "This is it," she moodled clearly. Then used her wind voice: "One child," she said, revealing her face.

"Twenty-one dollars," the woman said.

"I'm with the ssscoola group," Inga said.

"What ssscoola group?" The female said.

"Catholic," Inga said, wily.

"South Catholic?" the female said, checking a raft of crinklings.

"That's right."

"Oh, hunny," the female said. "How'd you get so late?"

"I got lost," Inga said.

"Oh, hunny," the female said again. "You're paid. You'll need to hurry right along."

And we were buzzed in, told to wait (so much for hurry), didn't wait much at all until a young male you-men came, a tall one, lanky, confident, dressed all in green. He led us in a hurry (again) to a large crowd of kibs ambling.

"Thank you, thank you," Inga said.

"Da nada," the man said.

Deception! My Inga! She pretended to join the group.

Suddenly, I smelled danger: large cats. And unknown mammals, along with the floral-chemical smell of the you-mens. I smelled turgles and uglies and wild pigs and things you'd never want to meet at midnight, also rodents, injured avians, crocodilians. And somewhere faint, direction unknown: monkey, sweet monkey.

Chapter Twenty

What is a zzoo? One of the wisest oldest uncles (long deceased but oft quoted) apparently once said that we monkeys are little more than zzoo captives, that the goers and growers had made a garden of our wilderness and that we lived at their discretion, not that they had any discretion to speak of, being monsters. According to that uncle, I mean, who had never met Inga. Uncles say things like this and use words like "zzoo" that nomonkey can define, so it all comes out sounding philosophical, a form a beauty, not advice for the true world.

But the Bronzoo, as far as I could make out, was a prizzon for animals across the genera, including (more or less) the you-mens who worked there. The horrible smells were produced by prizzoners so sick they'd gone mad. But Inga was charmed, calmed by a striped horse called a zzebra who'd rubbed all the hair off his rump circling his overly small enclosure (in the wild, there'd be miles!).

"Hello striped horse," I said.

"Who speaks?" he said.

"I, Beep," I said. "Monkey."

"Freemonkey?" he said, suddenly interested, unable to find me, eyeing Inga with suspicion.

"And this is my friend Inga," I said, climbing out of her capacious bag.

"Ah, Freemonkey! It is thee. I am Lord Cucucucutootoo, Zzebra," he said. "Your pet you-mee is charming—most smell so poisonous, but she sweet as grass, and what a mane, so red, so nicely knotted."

"She's a good one," I said. "She brought me here."

"I've heard the prophecy unfolding onwardly," Lord C said.

"Beep wubs Zzebra," Inga said unmoodingly. "Hoo-hoo! Bray-bray!"

"What is she saying," Lord C said.

"She is surprised we're communicating and mistakes it for romantical, perhaps? It's her age, excuse her."

"Has she got jingle-jangle keeze to the hay?"

"Keeze? What are these? And excuse me, but much more important: what prophecy?"

"The herd believes a freemonkey will come and set us free to join him."

"What herd?"

"I'm what's left. We were four, but last season we died back by three, moldy provisions. I was sick a month."

"I'm sorry to hear that."

"Keeze free the feed. At least that's what I'm told."

Inga, oblivious, was walking now, bouncing me along. Lord C kept up, bumping the wooden barrier neurotically.

And then, due to a sudden turn in the path and a hard corner in Lord C's wee paddock, we were leaving him behind. "The jingle-jangle keeze," he called after us, repeated more and more plaintively till we were out of moodshot.

Prophecy, my monkeybutt. He just wanted to eat.

There were meerkats, Inga called them, chattering so fast I couldn't comprehend them, standing up like begging doggs. And near them, tapirs—to the tapirs I said hello, familiar folk. At home they're aloof, but spoke as had the zzebra: "Freemonkey!"

Squirrels, apparently, had spread the word. And if not squirrels, trees, and of course those great translators, the fungi.

"Tapirs in the cold?" I said.

"In the cold," they said. "The very cold. Tapirs with no mud, yet happy at last for spring and the outzide air."

Prizzoners.

Inga hurried along, devoted, wanting to find my species.

Next area was tall cages with birds I knew from home, raptors who couldn't get at me: blessed wire, woven into a screen.

"Freeeeeemonkeeeeee," one of them wheezed.

The other looked over its shoulder. "Deliciousssss."

"Use your words," I said.

It leapt, I flinched.

"Bad bird!" Inga said.

"I eyes eat," the bird said. "I eyes eat, no looking!"

"I shit on you," I said formally.

"Nahhhh-nahhhh-nahhhh!" Bird cried, and I saw that she, too, had gone crazy. Anyway, first time a knife-beak had ever answered any monkey insult, usually delivered from the talon view, and high above the trees.

"I see the smoking mountain!" I said.

It seemed they hadn't laughed in many years, but they laughed now, and long, Uncle's story famous even among these raptors so far from monkey world.

Inga pulled me along.

And now I smelled monkey, sweet monkey. Monkey very strongly.

How to communicate with my friend? The mood had faded in her. I touched my chest, mimed a wilting: sad.

"Sad?" Inga said, glimmer of mood.

I touched my nose, breathed in luxuriantly, looked all around.

"You smell something?"

And then I did a jig, pointing at I, Beep, myself.

"You smell monkey!" she cried.

And again I looked all around.

"Yes, where?" she said. I felt the mood rising in her. She pointed at a board hung high with many symbols carved into it. "Oh, my gosh! It says Monkey Howzz," she said. "The air-o points this way!"

And off she raced, monkey on her back. Ahead, a nobleman, one of the angry ones, wrinkled matching pamps and jagget, suicidal striped noose knotted tight at his neck, stood with hands on hips. Behind, two of the plumper type of blue guards were trotting after us, grunting, all sorts of guard gear bouncing around their waists.

"Catholic ssscoola group, eh?" the strangled man said.

"I meant Jewish?" Inga said.

No comprendo mi, but the nobleman didn't like her giggling, that I could discern.

"If you'll follow me," he said, pulling back his chin, turning briskly, marching fast.

And Inga made as if to follow, the blue men behind us struggling to keep up.

"Beep, Monkey," Inga moodled, truly moodled, the fresh emergency restoring her nascent powers. "Am going to shove you down in here because no think these men . . ."

And with that truncation, she pushed me down into her noopsook, hand strong as any aunt's.

To follow the nobleman, who walked at a good clip, would not have been my approach. But mine was still available, if need be: flee. I mooded that concept hard. Inga yawned, a sign that she was allowing in the thought, also that she was an animal like any other, and exhausted. She slowed, slowed some more, and then, in an unnatural dip in the unnatural terrain, a dip that put us momentarily out of sight of the grunters behind us, she very suddenly darted east, brilliant child graced with instinct (which, in a way, is mood), ran us down the most obscure of three paved paths, past more birds in very high cages.

"Skaw, skawwww!" they shrieked, "Freemonkeeeeee!"

Oblivious, my beautiful friend sprinted past a number of lazy-paced you-mee mommas pushing strawlers, that you-men baby smell, past various imprizzoned ungulates all burping gasses, finally up a climbing zigzag starway and into a moon-o-rail, Inga called it, a kind of trayn without wheels, a giant caterpillar-ish. The disembodied god voices were getting familiar: "Please find a seat and stay seated. Dars are closing now." And we did find seats, and the dars did close (speaking of prophecy), very comical view of the strangled noble meeting his guards at a dead end on the wrong path, pointing up at us. Each of the large guards had that brooch of silver on his chest. They ate well, these ones, and were not the fastest in the jungle, clearly.

They talked into their collars as we sped away, afraid to look at one another.

From the moon-o-rail Inga pointed out deer or maybe horses with freakishly long necks and prettily patterned fur—how I wanted to climb them and ride atop!

"Freemonkey!" one of them moodled freely, then her herd of five as well, deep neck bows.

"Chiraffes," Inga said. "From Afrigga."

"Haha, chiraffes," one of them said. "We are High Looks, and look out for us, for we see you up there!"

The High Looks turned back to plucking stray leaves, heads in the highest branches they could reach, which of course they'd picked clean. Only slowly I saw that their freedom was contained—barriers of meddle and shocks, half hidden, defined a finite veldt, the illusion of freedom if you weren't the one contained.

Around a mudless pond three giants loomed, gray and wrinkled with madly extended anteater noses.

"Elephumps!" Inga cried as the moon-o-rail slowed.

"Freemonkey," they trumpeted, feeling my girl, gazing up.

Inga held me tight, didn't want me jumping.

I gave a magnamimous wave, just being ironic, but the elephumps didn't seem to take it that way, bowed to us, scraped the dry stone with tree-stump feet. The biggest, moodheart clear female, rose, stepped forward, tears in her eyelashes, suddenly, runnels of tears down her dusty cheeks, following wrinkles, leaving trails.

"We are the Gray Walkers," she sobbed. "And, Freemonkey, if you set us free, free as thee, we have the strength to free others, and will march where the battle leads."

"Soon," I said, starting to feel my own moodheart grow, my sense of mission expanding with it, overtaking me—Inga, too, she gasping with it, her own blooming mood. The ripples of sympathy all around us grew to waves, waves to tides, tides to great world currents, voices from the everywhere, a kind of singing, the multimood, the world in chorus, no chaos.

But something more intimate, too: "They've taken my baby," the Gray Walker matriarch moodled, so gentle, so soft, she in her onlyness. "The you-mens. They speak in kind tones, wind from their lungs, they even bring melons, and wash us with hozes, which are sad you-men trunks, cool splash, warm splash, then this: they've taken my baby."

The others mood-muttered, all sorrow.

The moon-o-rail started up again all on its own, moved us slowly along.

"Sorrow," I said to the gray ones. Then, surprising myself: "Be ready."

A small spotted herd of leapers raced up to see us. Again I waved, again creatures bowed, scraped at the hard earth.

"Anteloop," Inga said.

"Leapers, caught in a canyon," they said in unison, beautiful moodle, a song: these ones had stayed sane. "We await," they said, then leapt away.

The moon-o-rail picked up speed. No one else was aboard, or at least not aboard our vertebra of the caterpillar. And below, speeding now, the Bronzoo floor, which was the commandeered surface of the plamet, just a few groups of you-men visitors, not their fault, well dispersed, in fact themselves on display, then a large group of ssscoola kibs, likely the Catholics, whacking each other with colorful sticks. Wolfpack in an enclosure, awful doggish things, screeching at one another and, as I now saw, electro-separated, the you-mens protecting their prizzoners from one another, thrwarting the order.

At last the undulating conveyance came to a stop, the dars swishing open—a different place than we'd embarked, as if the moon-o-rail were a sideways El Vator. Bronzoo was big as the world had once been, but so degraded, a kind of garbled quotation. No time for such thoughts, as Inga leapt from the trayn and hurried down a starway to a path, no one following. She pulled up at another carved board, more weatherbeaten than the first, equally friendly mood.

"Monkey Howzz!" she cried, pointing at the carving, words dug from old wood. A kind of moodling from trees departed. But something else, when you looked: face of a monkey, also carved, hard to decipher at first, then obvious: monkey, male, its expression meaning this: *Stay out.* Plus an air-o, as Inga called it. She hurried us in the direction it foretold.

Chapter Twenty-One

THE OLD UNCLES OFTEN SAID the you-mens were once part of the intuitive concatenation, the interbraided hitherto—the monkey chain, we smalls liked to call it, the fulsome communication of all things living—make that all *things*, since all things live, background vibrations in normal times, foreground in times of emergency, then life itself during disaster: being is all one. It was the goers that separated themselves from all the rest of the world, a false elevation that came in curious antiwaves, these overachieving stagger-clowns separating themselves from not only the true world but from themselves as well, creating the two kinds of you-mens, goers and growers; or maybe three, one old aunt liked to say.

The third she called the sensitives, and these were those who still had monkey sense, which was the same as lizard sense, and the same as rock sense and clam sense and mosquito sense and tree sense and tapir sense and mushrooom sense and trogon sense and plankton sense, that thrum that keeps us all connected and behaving, even while eating one another (as the eagles like to say)(and I, too, say it, Beep, who ate a lizard once named Jack, and didn't Jack yell and curse as I bit him!)(but I only ate Jack, didn't threaten every lizard on the glope!).

Hungry, hungry monkey, speaking of Jack.

Inga, surely a sensitive, relearning her moodle in our small emergency, hid in an alcove formed by a black-meddle barrier and a go-stone wall and peeled me a banana, took half herself, which we monkeys call monkey share. My you-men friend and I ate. As always I was beguiled by Inga's blue eyes, this you-men child so much larger than I, who had begun to know my thoughts. We heard a shout, the crackle of a woggie-toggie, Inga called it.

"Monkey," the dear calm girl said, "I believe we are in trobble."

From two directions came the huffing blue guards, the strangled nobleman, several younger nobles, and now a rank of adolescent-seeming you-mens dressed in green like our initial guide, perhaps footmen, finally a woman, pure alpha, marching in heavy footwear, the better to kick butts. They approached Inga as if she were an injured animal on the forest floor: cautiously, slowly.

"Don't move, young lady," one of them said tersely, the big man in blue with the glittering brooch on his chest, total goer.

"You didn't pay," one of the Greenies said kindly, obvious grower. "You lied and slipped under the gayt. Then you ran from these officers."

"Is that all?" Inga said. "You think a ssscoola-girl snuck in? Don't worry, my parents will re-imburst you."

"And, apparently, you have a monkey," the officious one with the brooch said.

"I was gonna say," the Greenie said. He didn't like the blue ones, either.

Impossible to read the power structure—all betas but with alpha acts? The female, dressed in carefully matching gray wrappings and eye-wimdoes, an aunt if ever there was one, stepped straight to Inga, stern but kindly. "Don't be afraid, young lady. We're here to help."

"I have no monkey," Inga said. She pulled her noopsook from her back and opened it for them: no monkey.

Because I'd pulled myself up and out of the bag she'd cleverly slung over her shoulder at their approach such that I could climb unseen down her back and over the spikes and spears of the black-meddle barrier she leaned on, through a hedge, then upply into the trees. The nice aunt, we could both see and feel, wasn't nice. The male you-men in blue with the brooch was deeply bored and thus dangerous. The mild male Greenie was my best bet. I crept out on a long branch and over them, crouched and expelled a turd, which fell end-over-end and landed neatly on the woman's head. My urine hit the one in blue straight in the face as he looked up.

And I was right, in the confusion the man in green simply let Inga leap the black-meddle barrier and shove herself through the hedge, little athlete.

"East!" I cried. "East, east, east!"

"Hoo-hoo," Inga shouted back. "Hoo-hoo east!" Distinctly, she'd moodled *east*!

The alpha aunt pawed poo from her 'do, the brooch fellow wiped his eyes, swearing and apologizing for swearing at the same time: auntie poo, she was the power person.

The male Greenie, that sweet you-mee, said, "She's like a monkey herself!" Meaning Inga's leap, but also covering for having let her go.

They searched the tree branches and building rooofs as if Inga might be up there.

I remembered what Goddess Greta Thunberg had said: "It's up to the kibs!"

From my vantage it was easy to see where the girl had gone: she'd followed a minor go-stone path that the Greenies must use, a way for those jailed jailers and their tools (carts and hozes and diggers and climbers and colorful coils of vine) to lurk unseen behind the structures they'd stuffed with sad animals. From there she'd climbed a gate and found her way east indeed, waited now among you-men ssscoola kibs and several teechas, suffer-consumers listening to a noblewoman, who pointed blithely into a compound full of miserable dog-things called dingoes.

"Freemonkey is here," a chipmunk chipped, then repeated. Her fellow rodents picked up the chant, wee mouse voices and the stammering of and then even the chittering of the closest squirrels, then all of the squirrels, the dingoes raising their heads in hope, the rodent message, they who could never be prizzoners, not in this zzoo, *the message* going round the local forests, carried by all the least animals, carried by the trees themselves, echoing then, out through every forest and into the distant world, also around Bronzoo, and you heard it spread among the species: "Freemonkey!"

C'est moi!

"What the hell is happening," one of the Greenies said.

"This zzoo is going nuts," one of the blue guards said.

"Nonsense," said their aunt. "They're only stimulated by the change in routine."

Haha! But in the excitement I'd lost sight of Inga.

The squirrels, loving an escape, reported her progress. "Girl, girl!" they cried, passing the word back. "Girl, girl, girl!" From the pitch and travel of their chatter I gleaned Inga's direction, and while the squirrels disturbed the branches over the officials for me, keeping their attention, I raced through the canopy after her.

Not far and I spotted her amid a ssscoola group. She'd turned her jagget back to red, smart girl, wore her beetza hat backwardly, those fiery braids a giveaway, even if her powerful energy hadn't been an easy beacon. I leapt to a bale of dried grasses in front of her, leapt onto her shoulder.

She wasn't even surprised. "Beepie," she said.

Startled by my own emotion, I pressed my forehead to hers, and we held that pose a moment.

"Where," she moodled clearly, said it in wind-voice, too: this was urgent, no time to nuzzle.

I could smell the way and pointed: Monkeys ho!

The kib in front of us turned to make a face at something boring the noblewoman was saying, shrieked at the sight of me.

Inga bolted, speed of a warrior, and I was her rider, braids for reins.

The monkey spoor weakened, dissipated, the way no longer clear. Worse, I smelled cat, uh-oh. Then heard cat, not like the cats of the

Corcovado but something bigger, bolder, a roar, and not just a roar, but my new moniker: "Freemonkey!"

Inga pulled up sharply before the cat's awful stone pound, a kind of pit and moat, fire vines easy to spot, and black-meddle bars strategically placed. The enormous lazy cat sauntered close as he could.

"If I may," he said, rumbling basso-profundo, toss of the once-glorious mane.

"Oh!" Inga cried.

"I am Lion," said the cat, still proud.

Inga stood back at all the roaring, only so much she could understand. "I am girl," she said. And then she repeated it, wind voice and moodle both, garbling-ish but sensible: "Inga!"

"And the famous monkey," said the big vain cat.

"Lion, far more famous," I said, "though none where I come from."

"Can you help us?" Inga said. "We're here in search of what are called squirrel monkeys."

"We are not natural friends," Lion said. "You you-mens, not at all, you monkeys, maybe in a pinch."

I said, "You would eat us if you could, I understand."

"Yes, 'twould be ill-advised to leap down in here. Ill-advised and delicious, my wee scrumptions. But today though you'd defecate upon this abject head given the slightest opportunity, we are friends. Today, Freemonkey, I beseech thee, it's time for a plan. We must all rise together: the you-mens, this one included, suicidally greedy, pathologically cruel, inexplicably self-entitled, will take us with them to their hell."

"Calm," Inga said. "Calm Rex!" So that's what the carved sigh'n said, more symbols, beyond the need of sensitives, a monkey might think, but Inga quite fond of her own expertise: "Sweet Rex."

"The name is Lion!" Lion roared.

I, too, hate when my name is got wrong. I could see his tonsils down in there, the uvula, the pulsating tissues of his throat, not particularly scary, given the circumstances, that diabolical barrier between us.

"Bad Lion," Inga said. And thought she'd reached him: he did stop.

I said: "Do you know where the monkeys are?"

And then a purr: "Free me, Freemonkey, and I'll walk thee there."

I gave a deferential bow, said, "And how I'm I supposed to free you, in the first part, and trust you, in the second?"

Lion was not offended. He only said, "I've a thought been burgeoning since we first felt thy presence, thy coming, the glory of thine arrival, long prophesied, even we prizzoners aware, that voice in the wind, heralded not only by tree rodents (our friends who can't be imprizzoned!): there's an entrance in back of my crypt here that the keepers use. They call themselves keepers, such hubris! We do not call ourselves kept!"

"Calm, Rex," Inga said, the brave one.

"She calls me Rex," Lion roared.

"The sigh'n says Rex, your majesty, says it in symbols."

"'King,' it mean," Inga moodled unmistakeably.

Lion thought about that, the unfathomable goers! Then: "The youmens, dear monkey, dear girl who begins to understand. There are empathetic, compassionate ones here, too. Many are angels, know mercy, bringeth succor, water, too."

"Sensitives," I said.

Lion harrumphed. "Not many," he said. "And few in the crowds that come and stare and call me Rex!" He gave a mighty roar.

"Calm," Inga said. A group of you-men wee-bees led by a Miz Britt of their own suddenly rounded the corner. Soon it would be the angry noblemen, their guards.

Lion caught my urgency, said, "That back entrance to this prizzon of mine will be open. The greenies are in and out of there all day. As if kindly, they bringeth my meat that way. They come to clean the cage—they spray it the way the Gray Walkers taught them. But first they entice me into my sleeping rooom with meat, and hungry, I go."

"Poor Lion," Inga moodled, getting the name right. "Lion full shame!"

"Yes, full—look how I've lived these thirty winters."

"It's no Lion fault," Inga moodled, so clearly, heart like the sun.

Lion was rueful, shook his great head: "I should have eaten them all. At first I was in a smaller enclosure—there have been improvements. All because sensitive humans raised a ruckus. How do I know this? I know this somehow. Sensitives pass, you learn things from their emanations. These thirty winters, thirty springs, thirty summers, thirty autumns, sensitives have passed me notes upon waves of empathy. I and the other cats here, we have learned something of you-men ways and bided our time. For what, we didn't know till now. Because now we do know: it was thee we awaited. Freemonkey!"

"Lion wait Beep," Inga mooded, powerful in her understanding, usage growing.

The kibs pressed up against the black-meddle bars, mayhem among them, their collective thoughts mayhem, too.

"Not one in a thousand," Lion moodled clearly. "Dost thou know what a thousand is? A thousand is how many you-mens come through Bronzoo every hour on a warm summer's day. One amongst them, on average, being sensitive."

"Monkey bad at math," Inga moodled.

"Monkey doesn't know what math even is," I said.

"Fine levity," said Lion. "Now but listen Freemonkey: there is an object that jangles and dangles, that opens our doors, nothing I can manage—but a monkey, thou hast hands! In some fashion the keepers manipulate—that quite literally means they useth hands!—manipulate this jangler-dangler business and the door pops open! Lioness doubts me, the sub-alphas argue, but it is the truth. The greenies hang this strange object among other strange objects on a board over the dezzk they all sit at—the dezzk, they call it, but it's only another slab of tree.

They often have beverages there, or burn paber sticks and suck at them, fools for gods. The gayt—see it, that one just there, with the little wimdow and the bars of steel? That standeth between me and the frosty world. I am of the earnest opinion that jangler-dangers would help."

"Keeze!" Inga wind-shouted, suddenly getting it. And no hesitation, she leapt, carried me to a low place in the hedge, passed me over it, then leapt over and through herself, snagging her pamps, falling daintily, leaping to her feet, those ropes of harr flying, recovering her satchel and recovering me, Beep, but losing Mario's beetza hat, nevermind. I'd mastered the goer pointing method, and she raced where I pointed, back around and behind the cat compound, as it was called, another hedge to climb, young athlete, happy monkey, and there, sure enough, a dar stood open. Inzide: a cave, dank and too dark in the you-men way. And gradually this dark revealed more than one gayt with little wimdoes and bars of steel. Through the barred wimdoes in many doors as we hurried past we saw more cats, cats beyond dreaming, prides of black ones and spotted ones and striped, and a pair of jaguars like our rainforest own, all of them pacing—they'd grokked every wave we'd mooded, predator style, predators all, if not that day.

In the last enclosure, there he was, Lion. And just opposite his entrance was the dezzk he'd mentioned. And over the board, the jangly-dangly keeze hanging off it like bunches of fruit.

I took a whole knot of them, waved it toward the gayts, pretty tinkling. But the gesture did nothing whatever.

Inga sang, "Keeze, please!" and took them from me.

Brave girl and brilliant, she understood this as not one object but many, slid them round and round on a ring of bright meddle and tried them on a bit of a slit in the gayt under the noob until at last one slipped in, click. But now there was you-men clatter and two shouting Greenies appeared in the dar. Inga turned the dull-shining object in the noob slit even as the youthful you-mees raced toward us.

"No, no!" they shouted. So negative!

But the door came open.

Lion sauntered out.

The Greenies ran the other way, still shouting.

"You two are looking for monkeys," Lion said. "Better hurry. Moodwind is that the overlords are headed this way."

Inga emotioned that Lion was our friend, and in the fullness of her heart fitted keys to each of the noob slits in that passageway, and soon we were accompanied by a phalanx of large but unlike cats, satisfied noises from each, their motors on, fellowship for the moment, at least.

Anyway, I never feared.

We walked right out of the enclosure, slowly, stately, a procession of fearsome felines led by Inga, and I, Beep, Freemonkey, upon her shoulder, audience of you-mens, some screaming at the sight of us, some aiming their phomes even as they ran, others though—just a heartening few—clapping their hands, shouting gratitude, calling out advice, cheering us on.

Chapter Twenty-Two

THAT YOU-MEN AFTERNOON, EVERY SORT of loudness, every sort of smell, once bright, almost warm, began very slowly to darken and cool, the sun setting behind the cliffs of dwellings opposite the zzoo. Those few you-mens we encountered turned and ran, scooping up their young (goers, likely), or pointed and shrieked in delight (growers), or pressed their hands into pyramids of welcome (O, sensitives!).

Certain kibs slipped their elders' grips and ran to greet us, the cats twitching their tails as before any meal but restraining themselves. Freemonkey, myself, needed feline help if I was to fulfill whatever on Aarth prophecy they'd heard, likely from squirrels, who can't be trusted, and who were in fact preceding us overhead in the tree branches, firing off bulletins that would circle the glope: "Freemonkey has freed the cats!" "Cats and monkey headed for destiny!" "Good is the prophecy that prepares!" Abstractions travel best, we all know.

I had lost the scent of monkeys but now caught a darker simian smell, something familiar, so like the stench the big, truculent howlers left behind when we in our greater numbers managed to chase them from our trees. Our cats led us directly to the smell, a grand dar of thick old meddle in a building made of pretend rock.

Lion clawed at the dar leaving gouges.

"No," I said. "Let us hurry to the backroooms, where the Greenies go: there are passageways, I hear them echo, just as in your former abode."

And over the black-meddle barrier I went—Freemonkey!—and having learned how to unlatch the dar, several complicated meddle parts that followed a you-men logic, the voice of the ironstone still alive in there, muted and abused, stoical, though, stuff of the Aarth.

The dar, also meddle, different song, swung open, and our stately procession entered you-men space.

Occupado!

Two young Greenie males and a young female, mating age but no sign of the males having battled each other, nor having mated at all recently, in fact wearing their green wrappings tightly closed on their bodies, those same wimdoe-like shields over their eyes, their eyes magnified, respectively freakish blue, warm brown, nighttime black. The males by the smell had not peed their hands (and their feet, forget it, dressed in tough fabrics)—perhaps younger than I thought.

Our procession was silent. The female only looked up because Inga cleared her throat.

"We're looking for the monkeys," my girl said.

"Wait, what?" the first male Greenie said, ol' blue-eyes.

The female quickly fingered her proto-mooding device, the woggie-toggie, and a voice came on, officious, a voice we could hear: "Come in, Janie."

"We've got a few cats loose!" Janie blurted. "Mayday. *Mayday!*"

A little rhyme, lacking meter.

And then from the you-men point of view you saw the problem—these apex predators blocking the only way out.

"Young lady. If you could step over here," Janie said to Inga, wind-voice quavering. "You're in grave danger."

"She just wants to help me find the monkeys," I said.

Lion shook his mane in a laugh, said, "Their fear maketh good sense. These Greenies know we've reason to be angry."

"No, there's no danger," Inga said. "Not to me. And not to you. These cats will let you pass. But first we need the monkey keeze."

"Monkey keeze?" Janie said.

"Monkey keeze," I said. "What's so hard about that?"

"Hoo-hoo, quiet," Inga said to me.

Janie's woggie-toggie crackled. "Help is on the way," it said.

"We can't give you the keeze, little girl, please," blue-eyes said, another poetaster.

Janie seemed to agree.

Brief standoff until Cheetah rushed forward, feinted at the second male, the big one, skidded to a stop. "The monkey keeeeeze!" Cheetah hissed.

"Yes, the keeze," Inga said, so calmly.

The big male just wanted to get out of there, reached with shaking hands, took down several sets of jangly-danglies.

"Robert, no!" Janie said. "She's just a little girl!"

But Robert wasn't listening, handed the keeze to Inga.

"You are free to go," Inga said, shaking them at Janie.

Janie had a twitchy thought. We felt her coil to leap at our girl.

But Lion roared.

The you-men males shrieked, edged past us and out the little door, gone.

Janie, a magnificent intellectual shift in progress, said, "Okay, okay." And she edged past us, too, never hurrying, a last word for Inga: "Don't do it."

"It's done," Inga said.

"Limited time," the cheetahs said in unison. "Limited time."

And the squirrels out in the trees and the mice in the rafters took it up. "Limited time. Limited time!"

Quickly, armed with the keeze, Inga opened the back dars of a dozen cruel cells. Somesimian raced out of the second dar, then another and a third and fourth, unruly bonobos shouting sexual slurs and flying outzide. They leapt the black-meddle barriers easily and then into the trees and were gone, canopy-swimming in the cold. I wished them well.

There was forest nearby but no warmth, not with the short afternoon already darkening the you-men's homemade cliffs and vines, but trees real enough.

Next came a shy pair of orangutans, followed by their young. "We are pleased," the alpha said. His name was Bugg. He shivered. "We are here to help." He shivered more. His scions shivered behind him. His mate, too, hugging herself. All pleased, don't get me wrong. All confused, too: captivity had been long.

The cold shocked everymonkey. But as the dars and gaytz opened, others joined us, and resolve took over: a pair of chimbanzees, a trio of baboons, one sad tamarind, four cheerful macaques holding hands, a troupe of mandrills, so calm, so polite, sculpted faces, handsome. "I am Mrib," the mandrills' leader said.

"No time for introductions," Lion roared.

And then Inga opened the biggest dar.

Silver-backed ape.

He wouldn't come out, only grumbled. His daughter came to the dar, so much smaller than he, so much bigger than I, or Inga for that matter, bigger even than Dabby. She looked us over, said, "The paterfamilias is unavoidably detained."

But we could see him plainly, studying his fingernails, overlong from lack of work.

A tee-bee, you-men artifact, stood high in a corner no average visitor to Bronzoo could see, and on it two you-mens gabbed in their fashion behind moving inscriptions, very serious, glossy harr.

"It's called See En-En," the great silverback rumbled, a little apologetically. "When they talk like this—and they do talk and talk—I understand snatches of it, mostly nonsense. But from it I have learned a few things."

The sad macaque, lonely alpha, said, "I've thought for some many passages of the moon that I heard that device. We thought you were talking to you-mens, talking all night."

"I heard it too," said the chimp. "I thought, Therapist."

"Nothing wrong with therapy," Mrib the mandrill said gently.

"No time, no time," the squirrels intoned.

"Please," the cats said in chorus.

"We've learned so much about the you-mens while imprizzoned," the depressed silverback said. "They consider themselves superior. They give us foolish names. They bring their wee-bees here to teach them about us, why?"

"Oh, my gosh, you're *Bobo*," Inga said suddenly, "Famous Bobo! And so friendly in the magazines. And when Bibi died, the world mourned!"

"What is she piping on about?" somemonkey said.

"She is Inga, a sensitive, and she agrees about the foolish names," I said. "Also that somesimian died?"

Big sigh from Urrrk, for that was the great silverback's actual name, forehead creased, great nostrils flaring. Once again he studied his fingernails, said, "My partner died of eating a pair of schissors some cretin threw in through the bars. The keepers didn't know till too late though I told them, every hand gesture at my disposal. And I'd suggested she not, but her theory, a strong one, was better to die than remain thus. It was suicide, my friends."

"Common at the zzoo," Cheetah said.

"I've often smelled thee," Lion said to Urrrk.

"And I you," Urrrk said. "When they moved you, I had to repress forest fear."

"Yes, I too: we two kings do not belong together in the same biome, let alone prizzon."

"I'm hardly a king anymore," Urrrk said. "I'm at best a vestige."

The female chimbanzee stood tall, said, "We chimbs disagree, Lord."

"Yes, you wonderful chimbs. Placed adjacently many a long year. Most comforting, all of you, good to see you straight on."

Lion said, "Urrrk, your Majesty, tell us more about this talking box. Are the you-mens really in there?"

"Apparently not, Majesty. It's some sort of an illusion, built of lightning. Installed herein after the passing of Urrrki, my best girl. They thought it provided company and succor, true enough. And after a time, as I said, I began to understand a little of what they say. Primary message is: you-mens are breaking the world."

Just then Inga pointed at the TV—"Oh my gosh, you guys, look!" And on the screen, much larger than a phome screen, if you haven't encountered such a thing, were Lion and Cheetah and many other cats flanking our own Inga, with I at the crest like a lookout, shaky images caught in some way by one of the guests we'd startled, I assumed, those growers who hadn't run, not immediately anyway, perhaps sensitives.

"No time," somesimian said, echoing the squirrels, who hadn't stopped.

"Momma will see!" Inga cried. "And Miz Britt, too!"

I mooded calm, and reassurance, and Inga did calm, and our whole retinue calmed, the clamor ceased, power of the mood.

On the screen, an image of Inga looking younger than in life, perhaps an old image, holding a stuffy I knew well: poor Whaley.

"I'm in big trobble," Inga said.

So much for calm.

"No time!" the squirrels started in again, very helpful.

Around us in the Bronzoo came a caterwauling from every cage and enclosure.

"Where are the monkeys?" I said.

"Those like you? The little ones?" the chimb alpha said.

"The headshitters, we call them," said mandrill Mrib.

"Gentleanimals," Lion said. "Enough. We needeth a plan, and we needeth a plan now."

"The squirrel monkeys are in a different part of the zzoo," Urrrk said. "And let's not argue the you-men nomenclature. It makes little sense, I agree. For example, there's this Children's Zzoo with no children incarcerated in it, just animals deemed charming. A domestic cat told me. And told me much more, highly educated: she lives with peebles, she calls them, the you-mens. You can believe a little of it."

"Fuck the murderous howzzcats," a squirrel above called.

I said, "Please, tell us, where is the Children's Zzoo?"

Urrrk stared me down, such questions! But answered: "Follow the stress hormones emitted by young you-men parents, friend."

Meant as a joke, but indeed you could detect the stress, if you put your nose to it, the hormone attached to caretaking, but also a fresher scent attached to fear or rage, the two emotions not so different. And now there was shouting, coming from two directions: east, a phalanx of lanky Greenies, and south, a goosey line of the blue ones with their shiny brooches.

"No time," the squirrels chanted.

"No time," Inga agreed.

So, a large crowd of us urged amoeba-ish in the direction of the parenting smells, simians of every stripe in the trees with the squirrels above, cats all around us. And yes, yes, the great ape Urrrk, having found courage through holding Inga's hand, had left his enclosure. His daughter, less intrepid, stayed behind. "I'll catch the revolution on tee-bee," she said.

"I approve," her father said. "But fear I must use my size to insure the smallers win!"

"Don't be hurt and do come back," his daughter said.

"Discretion is the better part of valor," Urrrk said.

They'd heard that quote on their tee-bee and now would live it.

"O-kee, o-kee," the squirrels chanted. "Not all must flee. Such, such is the prophecy!"

"They'll carry me back asleep," Urrrk said. "But not before I have cleared the way for Beep!"

Such indeed was the prophecy, which revealed itself more fully with every bold action, spread around the world, came back with a kind of cheering attached.

In the distance, our own distance, we saw a crowd of panicked you-mens being hustled to the ornate black-meddle Bronzoo gaytz by Greenies. The chimbs rushed ahead, surrounded a food-ish cart, toppled its umbrella, collected prezzels and flung them, hurried the you-mees on, more importantly drew attention to themselves, sudden antics, spins and hops and handstands.

A sudden peace overtook me, a feeling like home: the worldmood.

Chapter Twenty-Three

"To the Children's Zzoo!" Inga cried.

She knew the way, held an ornate gayt for everyanimal till a polite rhesus took over the task. Strutting the you-men walkways were pee-cucks, I believe they're called, and quite in our way, begging to be plucked, piteous shrieks, and then meerkats again, more helpful, painfully polite, and farmanimals barely conversant in the wild communion, cows and sheep and the like.

And then. And then. And then the beautiful, moving, heart-pounding smell of monkey, female.

Very tall prizzon cell, and that's what it was, despite tall wimdoes in front of the steel bars, a rock moat to create distance—how were you supposed to pooop on the you-mens? And there on a swing, all alone, was one of my tribe, or my ancestors' tribe, darker of face than any of us, than I, a little bulkier, an uncle. He'd heard the commotion, took in the cats, then spotted me.

And as the old uncle and I stared, Inga studied the symbols written on a carved wooden plane propped in front us, meant for you-men visitors, another sigh'n: "South American Squirrel Monkey," she said, not at all a sigh, more like Miz Britt. "These charming creatures are larger and with darker fur than the Central American population. Once they were thought a separate species. Likely the Central American population, concentrated in Pazific Panama and Cozza Rica, began when Mayan travelers brought home pets."

My very mission! Referred to in these you-men glyphs! But, of course, all wrong: the Mayan travelers would have been the pets, used by the ancestors for shelter, succor, affection, chow.

The cats, loving history, murmured.

The old uncle cleared his throat. He'd felt me coming, was the mood. He nodded slowly, said, "Freemonkey."

"Uncle," I said.

"I suppose you'll want to meet my niece."

Urrrk said, "I've smelled you, Uncle. On every third wind, many seasons."

"Who hasn't scented you?" the old uncle said. "I scented you the day they opened my crate."

"Thou art a born-wild?" Lion said.

"Ah, the kitty speaks," Uncle intoned, so sarcastic, bitter with stolen life. "Yes, born wild, captured in nets, ropes tied like arachnid webs, and I the fly. Well, I and several hands more of us, half my troupe. Only I and one of my nieces made it here alive, she a mere infant then. We're expected to live with this troupe of beta males shibbed from some prizzon in what the you-mees call San Diego, which just means far away."

"Yes," I said. "Yes, yes. I would like to meet your niece."

"The youngsters are hiding in back," he said, shifting his eyes in the direction of an arched high darway at the end of a climbing log.

"We back go around open gayts," Inga moodled simply. "Be ready run. You and troupe."

No Greenies in sight, no guards, no desperate noblemen. The Freecats had scared them all off, at least temporarily.

I said, "Monkeys, be not afraid. Monkeys, show yourselves."

The old uncle barked, barked again, and slowly from the arched darway the first of the youngsters appeared, slowly, very nervous emanations. He walked the long log hand and foot, stood at the end of it near the uncle on his swing. Then the next, same, then one by one all of them, all standing in a line, seven unmated males and two older bachelors, all abashed. They crushed together on their false branch, their eyes cast back upon the arched darway.

From which, after an exquisite, excruciating beat, appeared the lone female of the imprizzoned troupe, the niece. Her scent rose above the others, n-valeric acid, distinguishable from isoforms of other carboxylic acids, those of the young males (all according to an old uncle back home who'd escaped a storied laborra-tree), majestic, the very essence of ardor, lacked in my experience by all other creatures. She studied me even as I studied her: I'd never seen a face so dark, eyes so large, not on anymonkey.

"Woo-woo," Inga said, noticing my emotion, gently mocking, my buddy.

"Well," Lion said, a rumble-chuckle same: "Riseth the pheromones, riseth the endorphins, too."

"Ah, to mate," Urrrk said, wistful.

I ignored them all, because.

Well, because the niece's gaze was direct, electric, even if her mood was guarded, something proud about her, so upright among the slumping betas. What did my heart do? It drummed. It skipped. My monkey blood coursed, it flowed, first time I'd ever felt such a thing, cheeks, neck, ears, loins, legs, feet, and toes, the tip of my tail curling, the fur standing on my head.

The niece's gaze said, Easy, monkey, and that was it for communication.

No moodle to speak of, not even much thrum, as if she were a creature set apart. I tried to throttle my own gushings before they could escape, but escape they did, the cats and simians around me turning to look, variously charmed, alarmed, bemused.

"You *guys*," Inga said, her clearer and clearer understanding of the mood and moodle: "All of you! We must free Monkeyniece! We go *backrooom*."

Agreed, but how? The Children's Zzoo was self-contained, walled-off, surrounded by its own buildings, the backsides and any back dars inaccessible to nonclimbers. I scrambled the pretend stone face of the wall beside the monkey pound (the niece's eyes upon me), trotted up the steep rooof, peered over the peak: all go-stone down there, stacks of wood groaning sorrowfully, piles of meddle poles, various broken objects, and curious carrts, and great vessels for captured plants to inhabit, and digging tools, a big table with exhausted noopsooks on it and those water boddles fabored by the you-mee young. I picked out the path my Inga and our helpers would have to follow: a long way, and only one.

And there the heavy back dar, thick slice of olden tree, black meddle you-men bits added, a formidable latch and lokk.

I rushed back over the rooofs to our posse, straight moodle: "We have to go around."

"Around, then!" Inga wind-cried, then sharp-moodled, pushed her way through cats and simians alike, took the lead, this *child*.

I took a quick look back to find the old uncle nodding up on his swing, the betas quaking on their log, the monkeyniece standing now, watching me, watching me closely.

Chapter Twenty-Four

OUTZIDE THE GATE OF THE Children's Zzoo, and flanked by cats and simians alike, all urgent, Inga trotted back up the go-stone path, I, Beep, bouncing on her shoulder.

"Plan?" Lion said, and said it again.

"Fleece and knee," Inga mooded sharply.

Urrrk's brow knit hard: Huh?

"Yes, Yes," Lion said gently. "Niece and flee. That's the heart of the mission. To which we're all wed. And we go around."

The mission was my quest!

"Thank you," Inga said. "We go around."

The monkeyniece was our mission!

Quickly it became clear that going around would mean going all the way back up past the cat enclosures, and you could feel even Lion's apprehension. The other cats sniffed the wind, twitched tails. Because back up there fresh mayhem flashed and swirled, the chilly you-men evening lit by brights mounted on guard carrs, brights unnaturally blue and fiery red, an alarming purple where red met blue, all throwing icy, ominous shadows.

The you-mens, equally afraid, were taking up positions below the main Bronzoo gayt, blocking any escape (though the chimbs and bonobos and other me-first climbers of all kinds were long gone), nobles and guards and Greenies all jockeying for position, lots of confused shouting.

All for me, apologies.

You-men fear reeks more than all other fear, the rank odor of aggression worse, and the combined stench rose on the breeze, coming now from two directions: more carrs, more brights, more you-men clangor, welter of voices at crazy pitches, some distorted to frogg tones by the infernal woggie-toggies.

Inga moodled, "We need distract."

Lion roared, commanded: "Cats distract! And more than that? We mounteth a challenge!"

The cats—leopards and lynxes and lionesses three, tigers and bobcats and cheetahs, all free—leapt to follow him up the go-stone to the line of you-mens, who scrambled like insects, leaping over the noses of their flashing carrs, some climbling inzide them and slamming dars, most just running back to the gayt, hiding in the little foolish structures there, a lot of shouting.

A Greenie in superior uniform climbed back out of his carr, hid in the wing of its dar, balanced a shooting stick.

"School shooter!" Urrrk cried.

"Too much tee-bee," a meerkat jeered, and the others of his kind tittered, a crowd of them: the brilliant mandrills had freed them from their bespoke display and they'd come to help.

Urrrk looked abashed.

Lion, oblivious, roared, feinted, raced ahead, stopped, reared up on his hind legs, so tall, pawing the air, roaring again, truly fearsome, claiming our territory with an extended roar: "This is our pride, our pride!"

The other cats rushed to be beside him. "Pride," they snarled and howled and thundered.

Old Urrrk held back, rocking from foot to foot, clearly anxious, a finger in his mouth: he knew personally what that shooting stick meant, didn't like it.

The meerkats scrambled this way and that, cheerful despite all.

Suddenly there was a report and echoes of the report, and a thud, and Inga's shriek, and Inga pointing: a meddle sharp, the much-feared dartt, stuck from Lion's side.

"Lion," Inga cried.

The lionesses, too, gathering around him, the other cats leaping to form a line protecting him. The afternoon light was gone. The blue brights swirled, and red.

"No panic," Lion said, then monologued, true king: "Lionesses, Inga, feline friends, Freemonkey, no crying please. This prick I've experienced before. Shortly I'll be asleep, no worse. Hurry you, hurry brave cats, brave child, brave monkey, hurry the end of this version of the you-men world! O, my friends. I've felt this exact strange surge of sleep before, and it's almost pleasure, especially if this time around through my slumber I can helpeth the prophecy come true." And with those pretty words he rumbled and roared, gathered one more burst of energy, surprised us all by bursting through the other cats and rushing at the shooter, that foremost carr, reaching it just as the shooter tucked himself inzide and pulled its wing tight.

Impressed, terrified, the other you-mens scurried away, shouting, imprecating, warning one another: *The prophecy, it's true! Hark and heed, fellow you-mens! Let's amend all behaviors!* Or so a monkey could hope.

Lion roared again, but weaker now, sank to the black you-men bedrock even as our phalanx of free-felines and free-simians leapt forward to the perimeter the great cat had established. Urrrk, pacing forward, well behind the line of cats, lit in swirls of blue, silhouetted by carr brights, blocked the you-men view and any shot at Inga, gave a roar to rival Lion's.

"Go back," he told Inga.

But she lay upon Lion, held him, kizzed his great forehead.

"Listen to the ape," one of the meerkats said, then two, then three, all of them nudging her, shoving her back protectively.

"Let's go," I said, agreeing: listen to the meerkats!

The man with the shooting stick, full credit for courage, eased open the wing of the carr, slipped out again to his position behind it, raised that stick.

"Watch the shooter!" one of the cats cried.

"Shooter shall watch me!" Urrrk said, breaking through the line of cats, two bounding steps past Lion's heaving form. Looking all around, he found an enormous Trasch altar, tore it from its roots, lifted it with ease, heaved it at the carr, perfect aim, the shooter's hidey-wing, which smashed shut even as the shooter dove inzide, its wimdoe shattering to beads.

"Bobo, no!" Inga cry-moodled, wind-voice, too, left Lion and raced to the famous ape, stood in front of him, hands on the great chest.

"There's a girl!" one of the you-men guards shouted.

And a Greenie took it up: "It's that girl! Stand down, stand down!"

Urrrk pushed past her, his forest courage returned, pounded on the booming long nose of the flimsy guard-carr, leapt up upon it, stomping, crushing the forward wimdoe into webs, those terrifying brights spinning in the mist. The you-men shooter visibly rolled across the inzide of the vehicle, popped open the other wing in some way, slithered out on the ground, leapt up and ran, impressive speed.

"Urrrk, no!" Inga said.

And Urrrk jerked back, didn't chase: lots of other shooting sticks now pointed. Instead he tore down a wooden sign, an air-o, as Inga had called it, flung the air-o after the mean Greenie, straight and true to its name, if shy.

"*Schissors!*" poor Urrrk bellowed after the you-men. He pounded his chest, a righteous performance, bellowed again for all to feel: "*Schissors!*"

"Schissors," Inga mood-soothed. "O, schissors."

We animals moaned, our brother!

More guard cars were coming, sigh-rings getting close. The you-mens huddled. For them, the presence of the girl seemed to change everything. Still the swirling brights, the shouts, the smell of danger, the night coming in, false suns blinking to life high and low.

Urrrk pushed Inga again—said something quiet to her—and now, full understanding, she raced back through the defiant line of cats to Lion, who snoozed. She petted him, she again kizzed his great head. The humans wouldn't dare if she was there!

Urrrk cast about for projectiles, not much to work with, pulled up a black-meddle barrier, effortless strength, flung it section by section at the you-mens, who stood just out of range, respectful, amazed, conferring: There was a girl.

Suddenly, something in the air. A loud coherence of sound. Was it mewzzik? Not at all like the clatter and shriek I'd heard before, the pounding, but lush in some way, gentle, flowing, arresting. We all paused to listen as if beside a stream, running water, waterfall, mist.

Urrrk saw the trick immediately: nervous Greenies sneaking around the far side of the bashed guard car, ropes and shooting sticks and some sort of giant spider web stretched among them.

"Soothe the savage beast, is it!" Urrrk cried.

The mewzzik swelled, swelled again. And no other weapon, the great ape pulled up a shrub, who moodled, just the one word, a plantish sussurus: "*Solidarity!*"

Urrrk repeated it, so loud that even the great trees above him flinched, squirrels falling to the ground and running, the you-mens quaking: "Solidarity!"

And flung that brave shrub into the path of the sneaking keepers, dirt shower in their eyes, the shrub—last gesture—reaching its branches forward as it fell, tangling their ankles, chain-reaction fall, a hilarious you-men tumble, shouts and cries, a shooting stick banging unaimed, a darrt sticking from a green-clad thigh, the victim crying like a baby for his nana: "Auntie Dote! Auntie Dote!" The other

Greenies helped him away, staggering back to the cover of their carrs and stone structures.

Urrrk leap to the nose of the nearest guard carr, upright, defiant. He pounded his chest, very stirring: he had his mojo back, long live the king!

Chapter Twenty-Five

STANDOFF!

More and more species milled: keeze-clever Mrib and his selfless band of mandrills were still at work cracking cages and pens and pounds and enclosures, opening gayts and dars all over the zzoo, instructions the same: Head for the main entrance!

Good, for the increasing numbers of animals would be cover, and the monkeyniece was still captive: my mission, *our* mission was in danger, the prophecy, so many animals to save, the world to save.

More blue guards were arriving, more nobles in fancy pamps and jaggets, much conferring, packs of Greenies (with their shyer posture, betas), you-mens gathering by the ornate main gayt, their numbers swelling, and more carrs arriving, and now enormous red truggs, rumbling like small earthquakes.

I scrambled over furry backs and sleek shoulders, between knobby legs and danger-hooves, made my way to Inga, who was still hugging Lion.

"He'll be okay," I told her. "At worst a hangover."

"O, Beep," she said, wind voice.

"We. Must. Monkeyniece," I aura'd, the deepest form of mood, an image, an emotion, urgency.

Two of the towering High Looks we'd spotted earlier, the chiraffes, joined us suddenly, necks in rhythm with their rush, and then an excited pack of dingoes like spotted dogs, also a strange little bear the dingoes seemed to know. What a crowd we'd started to make!

"Where did you longnecks come from?" a platypus sputtered, yes a platypus! Name of Plunk.

"The Veldt," one of the High Looks said. "That's what the you-mens call it. We call it Veldtish, and we barely endured our lives there, tall-praying for this Freemonkey day. The mandrills let us out. They free the Gray Walkers as we speak. Where did you come from?"

"The Outbackish."

The shooting stick roared again. A dart meant for Urrrk clattered harmlessly at the feet of Plunk.

"Missed me," he taunted, comical clap of the bill.

"Hold the line," Urrrk bellowed.

"Hold the Lion Line!" the cats behind him bellowed. "Let not the you-mees cross!"

"The Lion Line," the squirrels chorused.

"More you-mens coming, many carrs, more lights," the High Looks said, surveying.

Now two hibbo-bottomi raced up, or that's what Inga called them—unbelievable speed and purpose: they'd felt the moment, having been freed by Mrib and his mandrills, asked no questions, took no time to assess, but sped past the Lion Line and pushed up against the lead you-mee carr as Urrrk leapt off it, and shoulder-to-shoulder jammed it bodily into the next two carrs, which rolled reluctantly back into the next three, the attendant you-mens fleeing, carrs rolling this way and that, flipping altogether, flashing brights crushed into the go-stone, this carr atop that one, purposeful hibbo-bottomidian grunts, no rooom for any new you-men arrivals, no passage for even you-mees on foot, though still the shooting sticks banged. A dartt dangled harmlessly from one tough hide, then the other, and more bangs, more dartts, which just bounced off carrs and hibbos alike, clattered on the ground.

"They've left the main gayt wide open," the High Looks cried in unison. "From our vantage, it's clear what we must do!"

"Clearing a path!" the hibbos chorused, kept at their work.

"To the gayt!" the High Looks cried. "Hibbos, clear the way! Gnus, spread the news!"

And yes, here came the gnus, seven in all, fanning out to block the you-men strategy, which seemed to be to exploit our flank.

The mewzzik stopped. I heard a monkly keening. Sound of the home troupe, not desperation but hope, the song we sang from our stoutest branches during biggest storms.

O, Monkeyniece!

Now a pair of armored furies charged up the go-stone path from the outer zzoo, horned faces lowered.

"Wry-nose," Inga cried, wind voice, but full undermood.

"Bish and Bash, we're called," strong-moodled the first. "Sisters we are, and your sisters, too! The mandrills set us free! We owe them votes of thanks! We're here to help the hibbos!"

"Don't endanger yourselves, wry-nose," said the tiny bear, furry wag.

"That's our plan?" the dingoes whimpered: "We rush the gap? Everyanimal, all at once against their sorcery?"

Urrrk caught that thought, roared back at us: "The blue flashers are not magic, the blue fury can't hurt us! Forward. Rush the gayts!"

But the hibbos had paused: their pile of carrs would no longer budge, created a barrier against the you-mens, true, but also against escape.

The conflagration ahead, so blue, so red, the shadows dancing like purple spirits, the weaponized night, the you-men command of light, so uncanny, so disturbing, so redolent of past horrors, trauma that had affected all of us all throughout our lives, sudden frights, sleep interrupted, stars dimmed, hearts broken: were we to rush all that?

The monkeyniece keened.

Chapter Twenty-Six

Every storm has an eye, every melee its caesura, every battle a breath, collective:

Into our sudden silence waddled a large reptile, not happy. She snapped her jaw, once, twice, thrice. The impromptu council looked upon her, I from Inga's shoulder.

"I speak," she said. "I am Miz Caiman. Look at me. Belly on the ground, legs that wub water. Rushing the gaytz, that's for the mammalians! It's cold here in the freedomish, too cold for the cold-blooded, and it is for them I speak, for me. Happy we are that the mandrills let us out, grateful, and solidarity with you all, too, get us not wrong. But what of the animals who *cannot*? *Cannot* move quickly. *Cannot* tolerate chill. The dryness, the lacerations of this rough go-stone! Rush the gayt? Flee the grounds? Cannot! Cannot!"

"Wise Caiman," the more thoughtful of the chirraffes said.

And everyanimal fell silent.

"There's a shubble buzz," Miz Caiman said. "It shubbles the daily lookers-at from a barking lot. I heard the announcements hourly, all my captive life. 'Shubble buzz, barking lot.' *Shubble* means back and forth. It's a giant armadillo, but hollow, and holds a great many you-mens. It is green in color, which denotes helpfulness."

Much murmuring of assent. Several animals knew the green shubble and of course the dingoes found the idea of a barking lot hopeful.

A nervous pangolin, newly free, was amazed: "The shubble is not an animal? I see it daily, too. I've often felt friendliest vibes therefrom."

I said, "But comrades, how will we, animals all, commandeer a shubble buzz? Surely it doesn't operate on its own!"

Ms. Caiman snapped her jaw again, one, two, three, commanding: "It's guided by a you-men. A Greenie. And not just any you-men, but a hyper-sensitive. She drives here at the Bronzoo because of great wub. Great wub for the living world entire."

Dingoes again, in chorus: "How does that help us?"

"This driver is a powerful emanator," Ms. Caiman said. "She moodles to me every trip past the reptile house. Do you know what she's been saying of late? She's been repeating the prophecy. A you-men! 'Freemonkey is coming!' That's what she has been saying."

"A you-mee!" a meerkat said. "I've heard it too, but thought it was the giant green armadillo thing that spoke!"

"It's called the shubble buzz," everyanimal said.

"Let us mood," I said. And in the resulting silence, I said, "Shubble buzz, shubble buzz, we animals are calling you."

And distinctly, loudly, clearly, an instant reply: "On my way, darlings!"

A cheer went up, though none of us were quite sure what a shubble buzz could do for us.

"On whose way, what?" Inga mooded.

And a great moodle was aimed at her.

"What's a shubble buzz?" she emanated, perfectly clearly, no trace of the you-men mind squeal, a complete thought.

And the welter of moods in reply flowed back over her, the newly freed thrilled to be in true mood with a you-mee, and moreso to know the latest news.

Urrrk bellowed.

Our moment of peace was done. The fray built back. Sounds of crashing guard carrs, fresh sigh-rings too, the shouting of you-mee males, the shrill of female, the roars again of cats, the smashing of wimdoes under the hooves of gnus, the barkings of canids, strange ululations. The grunts of the hibbos, and now Bish and Bash.

"Where's the girl?" we heard some you-men shout.

"Stand down, stand down," the reply. "Till we have her, continue to stand down!"

"Barking lot?" Inga moodled, undeterred. Her confusion was to be expected: how could we know more of you-men doings than she? "But, brothers and sisters and all in between, we have a monkeyniece to free!"

"Reptiles first," I said.

And even as Miz Caiman explained (not even slightly amazed that this small you-mee was understanding her), we hurried back to the Reptile Howzz, as it was called, dozens of soon-to-be-former Bronzoo denizens, plus I, Beep, and Inga. Hearts pounding, we found the doors to the Greenie's backrooom wide open: someone had run.

"Mrib couldn't find the keys except mine," Miz Caiman said.

Inga knew of a dezzk trait called drawers, and therein found the keeze, and soon dozens of snakes and turgles and froggs and lizards and biggers and smallers and slimies and moists were free among us, slogging, milling, inching.

"Outzide, outzide!" Ms. Caiman commanded, her reptile moodle more growly than the mammalian, less tweety than the avian, clear enough, however: "Everyanimal offer a ride!"

Our phalanx, slows and slowers upon the shoulders of fasters, made our way back out into the night: but there was no giant green conveyance. And then, just as we felt the grip of failure, a loud nonbird honking, a non-Beep beeping, filled the sky, the roar of a you-men motor.

Here came the shubble buzz!

The shubble buzz rolled right up to us on its wheel-feet, a loud purr coming from behind its bright eyes, rocked to a stop. A kind of gayt opened in its great neck, and down a few stars came a tall female you-men: "Greetings," she cried, no smell of fear, her hair wildly purple and also white and orange, perhaps a you-mee subspecies, a rangy specimen. She spoke in wind-voice for the benefit of Inga, deeply low, simultaneous moodle: "I am Charlene," she said, "I am here to aid the uprising! I'm so happy it's begun here. But was that not the prophecy? That among the imprizzoned a Freemonkey would rise?"

"Freemonkey is here!" All the animals shouted.

How could this you-men know our stories? She seemed halfway between animalkind and you-men-ity, halfway between here and the clouds, halfway between male and female, too, on her chin and cheeks a dark, appealing stubble.

Still, all the attention turned to me.

I said, "Charlene, dear gentle, we have here all these slows and moists and must-be-warms we're worried over."

"I've heard the mood," Charlene said, "and it's for them I drive!" Her eyes were animal bright, big you-men grin, total confidence. "Into the buzz with them!" she cried. "Quickly, quickly, before the SWAT teams arrive."

Noanimal asked what that meant: it meant trobble, plainly.

Four grizzly bears rushed past, stench of captivity.

"Where's Urrrk?" they cried. "We hear he's losing ground and we know how to gain it!"

I pointed, they ran.

Shortly, back on the bluff below the gaytz, we heard another skirmish in progress, felt the mood and read the moodvisions of scores of animals gathered there, or more now, hundreds of animals, the bears climbing the stacked carrs and taking their message of peace directly to the you-mens, whose shouts turned panicked. The hibbos meanwhile, with help from the wry-nose, had tumbled another guard carr onto its rooof. Just a few more to clear the way, open up a corridor to further freedomish.

"I wub your hair," Inga moodled, so very clearly, you-men to you-men, even as she handed off a bucket of happy rainforest froggs, bright yellow. "I would like dye my hair. Why do you?"

Charlene accepted the bucket, mooded back, pan-animal sophistication: "Ah, and warm thanks, O Sensitive! You've already got all the red! I show my colors so that the shubble peebles know they are in the likeable hands of one like me and form a kind impression, for you-mens can be cruel and don't always like difference. I enlist them with charm. Enlist them to their own humanity."

I, Beep, am not saying I understood everything. But one thing we animals already know is how much humans think in black and white, yes and no, fruitless binaries, when the world we all live in is so clearly continuous in all things, a long and glorious road between either and or, animals among us that contain both sexes, animals that switch at will, wee things that are neither.

But Inga did understand, much thoughtful nodding, even as she handed Charlene a box of precious salamanders, late denizens of something called a terror-ium.

Quickly, meanwhile, the shubble buzz filled with creatures, reptiles in the main, a quartet of toothless old crocodiles, an orderly line of turgles, every conceivable type of toad, a writhing of fat snakes. The reptile howzz was quickly empty.

Charlene moodled harder yet: "I vow with Freemonkey as my witness to drive this buzz to the warmth far south of here so these creatures may enjoy their freedomish in peace-ish.

"So witnessed," I said.

And with that, Charlene boarded the buzz, closed its dars in some magical way, backwardly lurched till it was turned just so, and then with a roar the mighty green shubble was gone.

"What of the fish," someanimal mooded.

And came a burbling, up from the water-ish stored in pretend ponds all around us: "Leave us! Save yourselves! We are few, and cannot travel. The prophecy says it clearly: not all will survive."

Dark truths.

Chapter Twenty-Seven

MORE YOU-MEE CARRS WERE ARRIVING, more red truggs, more lights, more shouting. Urrrk urged us forward, we animals now in the thousands pressing up behind him. "It's now or never," he cried.

"Never would be fine," the dingoes chorused, but they were roundly shushed.

Ahead there was movement. You-mens falling back. A great press forward among the animals: freedomish called. Only a few fragile guard carrs blocking the way.

The animals surged.

To the group around me I said, "Friends, soon-to-be-former Bronzoo inmates. Feel my message. I have a fabor to ask you. Before we flee. Before we follow the crush ahead." Dramatic pause. "We must free the monkeys," I cried. "First, let's free my monkeys."

"But how?" the dingoes said. "The dar to their backroom is closed. It's dense. We need the strongest strongs."

And Bugg, the Alpha orangutan, shaking his head, grave concern: "The hibbos are far ahead, intent on their project: let no you-men carr remain upright!"

"Bish and Bash, then!" the dingoes chorused.

The wry-nose were busy as well, having pushed their way into a side melee, a minor gayt, new nobles dressed like terrapins, much equipment: SWAT. Despite the fearsome you-men confidence, smalls of many species exited around leather-wrapped ankles and through the opening.

Freedomish! The wry-noses pressed that gayt shut strategically. The SWATs, unsure what to do, found themselves lokked outzide.

The orangutans knuckle-trotted to alert reinforcements, mood-shouting their request: "Wry-nose, this way!"

Inga didn't wait, but hastened where I pointed, the route I'd spied from the rooofs of the Children's Zzoo. Ocelot and seven reindeer and a large number of other arriving newlyfrees across the species, some bold, some tentative, followed us protectively, finally the swarm of meerkats, who took up both the lead and the rear: we were a team, an army all braced for danger, such chattering and barking, bleating and chirping, burbling and buzzing, lemmings posting themselves as look-outs all along the way. Together we liberators trundled downhill and through a gayt to a go-stone way that led, proud Beep, to the back of the Children's Zzoo.

"Service dar lokked," Inga said, pointing at impressive meddle bits attached to the heavy oaken barrier, the tree still living in there, faintly, faintly.

"I am sorry," it implied.

The orangutans caught up, plucked at their beards: "Wry-nose said they'd follow! That they'd push through that olden oak! But they're side-lined by a project, I'm afraid, blocking a truggish that's come from the south! Pulldoozer, the squirrels call it."

"We must bash this dar!" the nervous dingoes yipped.

"Yessss," creaked the old dar, permission.

I scented the monkeyniece. Her keening had ceased.

"Coming," I heart-mooded, and deeply.

Several meerkats raced off in search of the orangutans, who were in search of Bish and Bash.

The dar was stout, no way any of us or even all of us could break it down without them.

Inga stepped forward. With chimbanzees looking on, dingoes fret-ting, lemmings gossiping, Ocelot guarding the rear, Inga tried a you-men trick: she simply knocked her knuckles against the wood of the dense dar, agreeable olden tree transferring the sound waves. And easy as that, the meddle bits clicked and clanked, the noob turned, and the dar swung open inwardly. A female Greenie popped her head out into the gathering dusk, surveyed the scene, clearly clueless:

"What the fuck?" she said. "Little girlfriend, what the actual fuck!"

"Excuse us," Bugg, the male chimb, said, peering, "we're here to free some fellows."

But all the Greenie must have heard was loud hooting, then sudden snorting, the wry-nose arriving heroically behind us, meerkats riding their great heads and pointing, their horns rising up over Inga's shoulder, the startle allowing me, Beep, to dart inzide.

Inga had prepared a speech, but the Greenie wasn't interested.

"Sweedie, get in here!" she said, tugging Inga into her lair and pushing the door shut against Bish's coveted horn, then slamming all sorts of meddle gewgaws into place, heavy breathing out there, heavy breathing from the Greenie, too, who held Inga by the elbows.

Inga shook her off. "Where are the keeze?" she cried.

"What keeze?" the Greenie said, genuinely mystified.

I jumped up on her hard shoulder.

She shrieked, batted at me.

"The keeze!" Inga cried again, all business.

The monkeyniece began to keen. Her scent was not a smell but an atmosphere, and I breathed it.

Bish bashed the entry dar from outzide, bashed again, splinters. Bash was right behind, pushing hard against that armored butt, you could hear it. Poor Greenie, she shrieked again as I leapt away, shrieked even louder as the dar gave way and Bish's big head jammed through. The Greenie leapt back into the dark space and to a dezzk just like the one in the cats' former world, picked up her woggie-toggie, dropped it, picked it up, fumbled her fingers upon it, said words in a wind, tried again, not enough breath in her, found the keeze, flung them in Inga's direction, then climbed on the dezzk, unlokked and opened the wimdoe high above it, clambered out.

Inga opened cages fast-fast-fast, moving dar to dar, lokk after lokk, all of it sensible to her, and I moved along beside her, also dar to dar, calling out the Children's Zzoo prizzoners, a dozen sweet breeds, including my monkeys, last in line. And everyanimal burst from confinement in various states of emotion, realized they were free in various states of amazement, realized that the exterior dar was no more, the splinter-bedecked wry-nose backing out along the stone way. And everyanimal rushed outzide, a pair of tamarins first, leaping from Bish to Bash to black-meddle barrier to branch, then the other animals as they could manage, prairie doggs and badgers and anteaters and hedgehogs and quokkas and several ungainly birds, a family of exotic mice, darling. Their freedomish flooded my chest as at last Inga opened the very last dar.

The monkey uncle stuck out his head.

"No time!" we heard the squirrels intoning.

"Hurry!" Inga true-moodled, and the emotion of that communication filled my heart to bursting as my monkeys made their way, Old Uncle first, and calmly, too. The seven beta males followed in order of importance, none of uncle's calm, frantic leaping through the backrooom after him, scurrying through the ruins of the gentle dar, leapfrogging the stalwart wry-nose, vaulting to branches overhead, their old uncle imprecating as they leapt: "Monkeys gather! We'll stay above the fray, watch in case we're needed."

"Just in case, just in case!" the betas repeated, leaping to the trees, freedomish, lining up in order on a branch, boys who'd only known only zzoos, and, I assumed (foolishly,but blame the scrum), Monkeyniece.

I leapt to Inga's shoulder as she rushed—no time indeed—and we followed Bish and Bash as they backed out of the narrow entry.

Up in the trees, the old Uncle moodle-shouted, sudden rage, near panic: "Betas, *where is my niece?!*"

"She awaits," the betas mooded in unison.

"Awaits what?" the uncle mooded back.

"Freemonkey," they all responded.

Oh no!

The niece's keening rose.

Inga yelped as I leapt from her shoulder and scurried back through the splinters of the dar and into the you-men dark, straight to the monkey hatch, into their former home. I felt my own keening rise from my breast, the taste of it in my mouth.

The monkeyniece was waiting, holding back, vivid scent, posture of doubt. Her eyes were dark, her fear was great.

"The storm is nearly done," I said.

"Freemonkey," she said plainly.

"It's you and me," I said.

I took her hand, found I had to tug—no time—tug her away from the only home she'd known since grown and into fresh chaos, no other way.

Outzide, Inga was surrounded by nervous meerkats, four fresh wallabies, and a slow ball of fur unknown, plus the orangutans, one-two-three-four. The dingoes had slunk away: discretion, they would call it. Inga followed Bish and Bash as they joined the exhausted hibbos in at last clearing a way to the open gayts at the entrance of the zzoo, the cats at their peril standing guard atop the shattered carrs, poor Lion still snoring on the rise in the pathway. The furiously spinning blue brights ahead of them filled the trees with shadows.

"Up here," the old uncle shouted.

His niece tugged at my hand. "This way," she said.

"Inga!" I cried. And moodled so hard that her braids blew in thought-wind. She spun to see me.

"Go with your monkeys," she moodled back, very clearly, empress of the sensitives. "I'll be fine. Monkey, please, it's time for me to go. You, too, time to go!"

She was right, no other way.

"No time!" the squirrels continued to chant.

Nothing for it, the monkeyniece and I sprang into the branches overhead, vaulted through the canopy, joined her troupe.

"I thank you," said the niece. She put a hand to my cheek, pulled at my ear, whistled out a breath.

"Captivated," I said.

Chapter Twenty-Eight

Below us, suddenly, the Gray Walkers trumpeted, joined the other bigs working to clear a safe path to the grand gaytz. Outzide the gaytz, big red truggs still rumbled, but plenty of room around them, already the smalls racing by them, under them, between the feet of you-mens, who jumped and shrieked.

Urrrk guarded sleep-Lion, the wry-nose, the elephumps, as the wreckage they'd wrought at last began to give way to a way. He hefted pieces of guard carr, threw them at the nervous you-mens, all of them scanning the freewildlife for signs of Inga. I, too, scanning the mood for her truth.

Where were the hibbos?

I edged closer to the monkeyniece on our branch, and she allowed it, eyes cast away, her scent suddenly deep, red tones and orange, a thump and a buzz, salt on the tongue, the sound of her keening still in the mood if not ears, her breaths coming fast.

"I fear," she said.

"We fear," I told her.

Our tails knit, a quiet thing, and soothing.

Her uncle offered no name, no pleasantries, just watched the action below.

"What will become of us," he said.

The betas shivered.

Below, the great cats rubbed up against Urrrk, tails high, patrolled the go-stone aswagger.

Meanwhile, freeanimals coursed out of the grand gayts. The you-mens had become aware, too: they were no longer in control, their SWAT team lokked out and milling, dragging useless equipment behind them, clearly arguing.

And here came the Pulldoozer, a giant of a thing I'd seen and heard at home, a yellow monster with continuous feet and that tree-breaking blade, terrifying till we saw that the organgutans were driving it, pushing the biggest of the truggs out of the way even as their you-mens ran.

Noblemen from various (apparently warring) clans shouted incomprehensibly, stench of their stress hormones, united in their fear of us, which was the fear of liberty, which give us or give us death. The Greenies had run the wrong way, confused by certain zignals the freed owls knew how to impart, the terrifying owl-eyes now allies.

The mandrills were back, leading warthogs and ostriches, wolverines and marmots, a fast flight of parrots, pangolins, capybaras. "All free!" the mandrills sang, soon to flee themselves.

The hibbos, now, too, fresh from the far reaches, leading a spirited parade. "All free," they repeated, moodling for all to hear. "The seals, they went thataway, sliding down the little brook, a longtime plan, those miscreants, a plan for when this day would come—on their way to the Spuyten Duyvil, and thence the sea!"

"Go, go!" the lemmings chorused, watching over the flood of animality that pushed through the liberated gaytz, correcting the course of a band of blind Afriggan moles, assigning them guides among rare Ruritanian rabbits, offering advice to aardvarks, pep talks for penquins, honor for ostriches.

The nonchalant meerkat brigade did not flee but found a task, waddled unnoticed between and around oblivious you-men shins to the you-men command area, leapt up on the makeshift you-men tavle, began to dance and sing, and somehow this scared the highest Nobles even more than the hibbos had, the pamps-and-jaggets crew, though it delighted the blue guards, distracted them: powers.

The Greenie attention, such as it was, remained upon the open gayts, and upon the large and larger cats guarding it among wrecked carrs: tigers and lionesses, jaguars and lynx, leopards and mountain lions. The hibbos weren't done but went back through the entire zzoo, wrecking last enclosures, looking for prizzoners, finding them, freeing them, the demolition squad: "Free we animals," they shouted. "Free us all! Time to go, time to flee!"

Urrrk watched over all of it from the height of a mountain of wrecked carrs, pounded that fearsome chest.

Night came hard. You-men brights all over the zzoo, brights outzide on the aveynoo. The Gray Walkers trumpeted, roared, held back, watching everyanimal that passed. At last, the great tide dwindling, the matriarch shout-moodled: "Where is my Graybaby?"

And the others shouted it, too: "Graybaby, Graybaby!"

We'd liberated the children's zzoo, but missed her somehow.

But here came Mrib the mandrill with his clever troupe, and just behind them a tiny elephump—ha-ha, *tiny* being relative—having freed from her separate prizzon and now accompanying her to animalian cheers, to elephump tears. The hibbos made way and Graybaby joined her herd, affectionate bumping and hoze-nosing. But no time to waste—the you-mens were regrouping, had a plan. So the elephumps joined the wry-nose and hibbos, and in a surging gray herd they left the zzoo, on their way jostling the red truggs, which rocked on their wilzz. Was that laughter we heard inzide? You-men laughter?

The orangutans had crashed the Pulldoozer, blocking the remaining routes for any new truggs, leapt off to join the cats as they sauntered out, each with a nod to Lion, their sleeping king, as they processed, unhurried, regal, growls and purrs and flourishes, padding up the knoll and through the gayts, a retinue. Time to go, time to go.

Next the High Looks, mooding urgent directions to the cats and to various sweet stragglers: gaps between truggs, the way to go, locations of you-mens with shooting sticks, each of whom got the cat surprise: a hard nudge, a heavy paw, weapons clattering to the ground, no injuries to any of them, the cat agreement, the golden feline rule: do unto others as you would have other do unto you. Unless you're hungry.

"Death before cages!" A leopard sang, and leapt a hedge, surprising a small nest of you-men SWAT, the turgle men, who ran.

Urrrk watched it all, kept an eye, pounded his chest one more time: the battle had been won.

I could feel Inga's calm, but couldn't spot her in the crush.

"I'm here, Beepie," she broad-emanated, not sure where I was, either.

"Upp here," I moodled, and felt her great wish, and urgent: "Beepie, it's time for you to go!"

"Time for all of us," I moodled back. "Time for you, too. Where are you? I can guide from on high!"

Monkeyniece was quizzical. She'd felt a great wub, and not as it might be between monkeys.

"She's there," Monkeyniece said, eyes shifting.

And yes, there among a group of you-men guards and Greenies, beside the Alpha female, blanket around her shoulders, was Inga.

"Come with," I urged.

She looked but couldn't find us. "I must stay," she moodled, so clearly. "The pleece-men will take me home. I'll be in trobble, but not for long, don't worry."

"What sort of trobble?" I quizzed, for the mood had not specified. I would drop all to save her from this danger, did not want her maimed or killed, the things you-mens might do, who knew?

But the moodle back was just a gentle you-mee shrug, clearest communion: "I'll be grounded."

And that was it, because a herd of kudu raced up from behind me: "All clear! All accounted for! Speed ye homeward, speed ye free.

The you-mens can't stop us! We'll speed on ahead. We break now. We charge!"

And so they did, whisking through a new formation of guards and Greenies, scattering them comically, shooting sticks falling to the go-stone.

Kudos, kudus!

Last, very last, came Lord C, his stripes bright with excitement, his depression lifted, warming his voice for a speech, but there was noanimal to give it to.

The High Looks saw him out, ducking under branches, ducking under the arched gayt-way, and out into the night, then galloping with him southwards to who knew where, joined block by block by waiting herds, soon thundering: wildebeests, bison, reindeer, dybbukim.

Still Urrrk lingered, his daughter left behind in their compound.

The SWAT turgles had breached the black-meddle barrier in some way and were sneaking from a new position, eyes on Urrrk, who faced their compatriots atop the knoll.

Inga felt them, our powerful girl, and worried for all to feel, she took one tiny step crabwise, then another, suddenly broke from the lulled pleece, she'd called them, who were too afraid of Urrrk to chase her, sprinted down the knoll, quick kib, stood between the ape and the SWAT twats, his only possible protection. She took his hand, tried to turn him—let's go!—but he was determined, determined to be last, no more animals to protect, only Lion, still snoring in the go-way.

The SWAT knot leveled their shooting sticks.

"No," Inga shouted, wind voice.

"The girl!" a brave pleeceman shouted, lumbering down the knoll.

But the SWAT alpha, unawares, shouted his own command, and the shooting sticks banged.

Inga shrieked.

Dartts whistled in the air, took dartt time, which is forever, one of them hitting Urrrk in his mighty chest, one in his foot. He tugged at them, plucked them out, had a long look at them crushed in his fist, threw them back in the direction they'd come, pounded that pierced chest, roared mightly, and charged. Those once-bold SWAT blots quaked and ran, rattling with gear. Urrrk stomped one by one the shooting sticks they'd dropped, gathered them and flung them end over end at the retreating heroes, ferocious moodle, bellowing wind. He staggered then to Lion, sagged to the go-stone beside that heaving beast, snuggled up to him, threw his great arm over him.

"Lion, we are free," he moodled for all to feel. "Free, free, the prophecy. Freemonkeys, flee, the prophecy." And repeated that sweet rhyme till he snored.

Inga rushed to him, lay across him and Lion, kizzed their great faces.

"The girl! The girl!" The you-mens shouted, frightened faces flashing blue, and red, and purple.

"Stand down! Stand down!" the Greenie leader said.

And that was repeated, noble to pleecemen to SWAT knot to Greenie again.

There were no more animals to shoot, not that they could see.

"Strong feeling," said the monkeyniece, leaning next to me, a touch rueful—she knew I'd never feel for her as I felt for this small you-men, but knew I'd feel monkey things instead, fair exchange, her eyes, her scent, her presence, her tail twined with mine.

"Strong," I said.

"No time," the squirrels continued to chant.

Urrrk, no doubt, would be carried home to his daughter, and there wake to his success.

Lion, no longer alone, would know in gratitude that there was another king.

They wouldn't be captive long: if you believed the prophecy, you believed that.

The pleece raced to collect Inga, but she twisted away from them, acknowledged them coldly, walked among them up the knoll and away at her own stately tween-ish pace, her mood so strong she pacified even the you-mens.

I moodled goodbye.

"Monkey," she moodled, "Monkey Beep, we won."

"More to do," I said.

Monkeyniece touched my face, watched me see Inga out of sight.

And then she tugged at my hand—time to go.

"Strongest girl in the world," I moodled hard.

"Wuboo," was the clear message back.

"We wub," the monkeyniece said.

Chapter Twenty-Nine

IN OUR TREES, SIMIANS OF all descriptions—not the bold ones like the bonobos, who'd taken off, but those who had stayed back, the frightened, the mild, the content, the born-heres—looked to the Freemonkey, me, Beep, for leadership. The monkeyniece was hard at my side, gripped me by the arm, by clumps of fur.

"No time," the squirrels kept chanting.

I said, "Hear me, simians. You may want to return to your captivity. No shame in that. For most of you, there's nothing else you've ever known. I, however, will be fleeing. For I'm not from here. But first, in front of all you bright simians, I want to ask my own kind-ish to accept me as their brother."

General assent in the greater crowd.

But I turned to the monkeys, put a hand on the monkeyniece, said, "Will you allow me to knit tails with this one, whom I choose as my troupemate and a mother of our troupe's wee?"

The old uncle nodded assent, and seeing no more, smacked the first of the betas in line beside him, who nodded, too, and smacked the next one, chain reaction till they were all nodding.

"I choose your troupe, too," the niece said. "Wherever they may be."

"And they choose you," I said. "And so the two of us will attempt to return to my hometree, part of a dense and famous canopy, plenty to eat, always warm."

"Always warm!" all the simians cried.

"I go with Beep," said the niece.

"Do you know the way?" The old uncle said.

"South," I said, casting my eyes that way.

He said, "Only I among this troupe remember the home forest, which our captors call Rain. Only I among us remember the arduous journey to get here from there. Much is ahead of you, niece, who came from there an infant, memory unformed. You and this brave freemonkey may not live to bear wee-bees that bring the two ancient populations together, prophecy aside. No shame in that."

I said, "Let us remember Inga, sensitive you-mee, who will be in trobble with her own troupe, likely grounded."

"*Grounded!*" All the animals mooded back, wave of compassion, no more clue than I what the word meant, though for tree folk the ground was serious.

I remembered the girl's fearless shrug, adopted it.

"And let us remember durable Charlene," I said, "safely on her way with the smalls and moists and injured to warmer climes!"

"Shubble buzz!" we chanted then.

"We go," the monkeyniece said.

"Unite the populations," the old uncle said.

South was clear: south was that way, exact direction the you-men aveynoo stretched away into what Inga had said the you-mees call "down." And the monkeyniece and I sprang away, this twiggéd branch to that, this gnarled tree to that, a line of such trees for miles, the message *south* in every leaf. At one point a herd of a dozen gazelles passed under us, faster than the goer carrs, full free run like they hadn't had in their whole lives.

"Freemonkey," they mooded as they passed, having felt our presence.

"Freerunners!" I said. But bless them, where would they go?

After a forest's worth of branches, leaps and bounds of night, my companion and I pulled up in a tree over a great river.

"Beautiful world," she said.

"And vast," I said.

"And will we swim?"

"We'll find a way," I said.

"I am Deeps, monkey," she said formally.

"I am Beep, monkey," I replied.

"You're so little," she said.

"You're so brown," I said.

"Onward," she said.

We could see a britch all lit for the night, and made for it, no problem crossing among the clanging underparts, all you-men angles, the night-black river so very far below.

"You-mens," Deeps said. She meant a lot by that: this ambitious britch, this impossible crossing, the unending strings of their brights, all the going this way and that, why?

Poor Inga, safely rescued, or so the Greenies saw their mission. Soon she'd be near as famous as the Goddess Greta.

Soon, too, she'd be free, even from fame.

Such was the prophecy, if the moodrumor of squirrels was to be believed.

"Strongest girl in the world," I said, a phrase for them to repeat.

"Inga," said Deeps.

We dropped off the underclangings of the britch and into more trees, deep surprising forest there at the top of Madhattan, squirrels waking to greet us, the word rushing ahead, our moodle like noise.

Chapter Thirty

DEEPS PULLED UP SHORT. ALL the leaping through the more-and-more-attenuated mid-canopy had warmed us some.

She said, "Let us stop. Let us take a moment."

I said, "Yes, let's plan," that being the britchlike understructure of what she'd said.

She said, "It's cold."

I said, "They have warm spaces, the you-mens. And warm wrappings."

"You smell like rain," she said.

"And you smell like moon," I said.

Sweet nothings.

She said, "South. I acted very confident back there. But, what does it mean?"

"It's a this-way or a that-way, a direction. At home, anyway, it means this way as you face the ocean." I moved my eyes the proper direction the way an old uncle might.

She said, "I've never seen the ocean. And so I don't understand."

I monkey-splained, forgive me: "The plamet, the greater home, is a ball like the sun. It's quite far bigger than a monkey knew. Down from the top is south, so the you-mens conceive it, but they're always wrong, if occasionally useful. I was shown this concept on a glope, which is a spherical simulacrum of the greater home. If we just head south and never stop heading south, this figurative down, at last we will be home." I pictured the glope very closely in my head, and pictured Inga's finger upon our tiny spot upon the glope, let that image deep mood into Deeps's already deep perception. Not coincidentally, in seeing all that, she saw into Inga's rooom.

She said, "A glope, eh? Beautiful thing. A bal, the seals of Bronzoo called it. And in that pink enfironment? Is that a you-men's home? Is the world in a you-men's home?"

"Far from it. Their home is in the world. The glope is an imitation. The top is up, the bottom is down."

"Ah. South makes more sense now."

"We monkeys live down where the glope gets fat, and where it's warm."

Deeps petted my hands, my arms, petted my face, examined my ears, pulled a hand away to sniff. I did all the same, willing myself bigger, monklier, smellier: unnecessary, of course; we were already bonded.

She said, "The glope is fat however you turn it."

Well, she was right about that. A breeze had come up, come from the south, and it tasted warm, and tasted new. The trees around us seemed to notice, seemed to wake, seemed to yawn, and stretch.

"We will make babies," Inga said, musing the mood. "When we're truly home. We will make babies and right the division the you-mens put forth."

"Snuggle now," I said.

"Yes, I'm too formal," she said. "It's been years of the Greenies trying to get me to mate. But old uncle said I should wait, and wait more: the prophecy has it thus."

"What does the prophecy say? I've not been party to it."

"You've been party to it, unbeknownst, because you live it: 'A freemonkey will despite himself bring freedom to all animals including you-mens from the destruction of the you-mens and by their destruction.' Imagine our delight when the Freemonkey mood began to flow—just a few sunseasons ago, really: 'Freemonkey. On his way.'"

"Those nattering squirrels."

"They at least rise above the you-men din!"

"I am hungry," I said.

"I am hungry," she said.

I looked off down the wide aveynoo, quite forever, said, "We might as well fall in wub."

Sharp laugh from Deeps: "Haha, wub, a you-men concept."

"Haha," I said. "Same as mood."

"So."

"So."

"Most of them will die."

I said, "You believe that, do you? Well, I'm not sure I do. I am not one to destroy anything, and beyond that it is certain that nomonkey can destroy the you-mens. The prophecy, it's feeble."

"Regardless, I hear it," Deeps said, resolute. "One way or another, our way or theirs, they will die. The question is whether we accompany them."

"May we at least use the word *wub?*"

"We wub," dear Deeps said.

I you-men nodded, said, "Onward?"

And she and I were one: "Onward."

We continued southward-downward, navigating the increasingly sparse canopy over the wide you-men aveynoo, much you-men activity beneath us even in the night, here and there a rat feeling our presence, shouting up: "F-freeeeee-monkeeeee!"

"Free-rat," I called back to one who had a kindness to him, and who immediately found us above, friendly eye contact. Free-rat because of course they were free, and always had been and would be. And I joked with him: "Careful. You may notice the cats have gotten bigger!"

"Food location?" Deeps said, right to business.

The rat regarded her long, not being one to share. "You're g-going the riiiight way. Look for b-briiiightest b-brights ahead, east s-siiiiide of the aveynoo."

"Generous of you if true," Deeps said.

And onward. Sure enough, brightest brights on a corner. And beneath the brights an array of fruit like nothing I'd ever seen, stacked high in you-men grid format, like with like. And flowers wrapped in some sort of clear garmend, and fruit from the homeland, lots of it, a restoration of color.

We leapt to the branches of the tree across the street, a spring gingko who groaned comically, fresh leaves already cocked south. And leapt from its last branch to the y'awning of the fruit place, like a bouncy humbrella over all that goodness. And down a kind of pipe and to the ground and under the tiered shelving, the long boxes tilted up so the you-men gobblers could see.

And there was heat. Blessed heat. We crept under the long wooden bins till we were inzide. And in there commandeered what was closest to hand: green pebbers, and unknown fruit, and then well known: pineabble, bapaya, mango.

With which we hunkered under the shelving, artificial warm breeze, hunkered with the smell of you-mens and free-rats and ate, watching all the imaginative coverings the you-mens wore on their feet, reaching up in the quiet intervals for seconds and thirds, midnight snack.

We sat very close, pure mood.

"There's the question of where to spend the night," Deeps said.

"The nights are cold," I agreed, but not so dour.

"There's the question of where we are to go," Deeps continued.

I said: "There's the home of our you-men friend and guide, Inga."

"Danger," Deeps said.

And the awakened squirrels above us repeated that, listening in, and no doubt the word traveled around the great citty and then the great round plamet: Danger.

A man with a brooom swished it all around, coming near us: if you are small and don't know broooms, very terrifying. Deeps and I bolted. The man with the brooom shrieked like an eagle in the understory. We were quick to the thin spring canopy, the roused squirrels running ahead in formal escort.

After a good long way, south, and south again, Deeps cried: "Squirrels, hear me! I ask you. It's so cold, so dark. You, like we, are not creatures of the night. Where stay you?"

And a moodle came down, much multiplied: "In our drays, madam, in our drays. Nests, you might say of a bird, though who speaks of birds?"

And the word went out through squirrel channels, echoed up and down the aveynoo. Nests, nests, nests!"

A pigeon had overheard, said: "Pile of leaves, a squirrel dray, pile of sticks, a pigeon."

"Dray warmest," several squirrels said, perhaps all squirrels everywhere said. But the several gathered above us, leapt through the branches and emanated thusly: "Follow."

We followed.

High in a spring-flowing tree, we came to a disorganized den of old leaves—our guides had picked the biggest dray they knew, negotiated with its occupant, a fat gray squirrel named Squirrel, as were they all. Squirrel was invited to stay with Squirrel and Squirrel, and so Deeps and I inherited the still-warm nest. We huddled in there, too exhausted from our adventure even to mood, happy to be warm, joyous to be free of Bronzoo and, if I'm honest, with apologies to Inga, and speaking for myself, rather pleased to be free of the pink swelter of the Bitty Twins. Deeps and I huddled, then snuggled, stretched our sore muscles as best we could, tight quarters.

"Lucky you're so little," Deeps said in the night.

I said, "These two monkeys, Deeps and Beep, are lucky in so many ways."

In the dark I got the message that she liked that, and we snuggled close like anymonkey would on a cold night, except this was a night colder than I'd ever known.

But we were warm, squirrel fur lining our hideaway, the heat of our bodies intermingling.

"I won't mate you," she intimated. "The world is not safe for even one more monkey."

"The world has never been safe."

"No, Beep. I don't mean just the conditions of daily life, I mean the world itself, which used to contain that daily life inzide its systems as in a womb but which it now threatens to abandon."

"It's because of the you-mens," I said.

"They must go," Deeps said deeply.

We snuggled. Two monkeys. One prophecy. Not a chance. Big, cold world.

Chapter Thirty-One

THE SUN WAS NOT PERFECTLY warm in the morning. But it was the sun. And its arc showed us where south was and that was the direction we headed after a dreamy meal under another fruit stand, squirrels on the lookout, our monkey tails braided.

You-mens of every description passed beneath us in all directions, being not of one mind.

At a pause over a sweet family scene, kibs of many sizes, all kinds of leaping and feinting, their warlike natures, cries of protest, jolly parents, Deeps said, "I just realized what all the bright wrappings are for. On the you-mens."

"The garmends?"

"I thought 'cloze.'"

"No, that means near, very near, like Beep and Deeps right now."

"Yes, yum. We are cloze."

"Yes, yum, so cloze."

"But the garmends. They're to keep them *warm*."

"I'd thought modesty," I said. "They've got no fur, manes only."

"We've barely enough, a chill like this."

"You smell good," I said.

"You, too, like monkey plus thrum and thrill, but let us stop the sniffing and be on mission!"

As long as we were moving, down a wide aveynoo, tree after tree after tree, we were warm enough. Deeps spotted a you-mee baby dropping its

Pinkie. We waited for our moment, and when it came, my sweet monkey swept down and snared the thing, swept back and wrapped me in it, fragrant and warm.

"Littler monkey first," she said.

A garmend collector of some kind had hung small you-men garmends out front of his tiny church—this was challenging, being highly visible, but from our perch we spied a particular baby jagget decorated as if in leaves—good to hide in. This one required a diversion, so Deeps hung from a tree branch shouting, "You-mens have ruled the world too long! You-mens must go!"

"But dear Deeps," I moodled, "monkeys rule the world!"

"Naïve boy!" cried Deeps, wind voice.

I dove to the y'awning, Pinkie flying behind me like a cape, while amazed browsers and the nobleman who displayed his strange collection looked up, trying to place the jungle howls. And easy as that, I grabbed the baby jagget and clambered back up to my new companion, who struggled into it, good fit.

"When going, do as the goers do," Deeps said. She'd seen human juveniles coming to Bronzoo with food stuck in various folds of their garmends, poggetz: you could reach your hand in there, keep it warm. You could put your mango in there, save it for later like a goer. You could shred open the bag of beautiful nuts and stuff these poggetz, discard the obnoxious crinkling window they'd been packaged in.

All along the way, the squirrels heralded us. "Supermonkeys!" they cried, then more chortling.

"It's your cape," Deeps said deeply.

And now free-rats came out to see, and free-mice cheering in small voices, and free-insects called roaches that Deeps said not to eat, ugh. Pet doggs barked up at us, their half-human cadences, and mostly unaware of the prophecy, it seemed. All the freeanimals said one thing, though, believed it: the you-mens are done. Some of the pets were with us, too, don't get me wrong, the four-legged equivalent of the sensitives.

"Take my lady. Please," said a fat one with legs short as an armadillo's, ba-da-boom.

Pugs are comedians.

On a tavle below I spotted something delicious looking—one of those sweet bars of rainforest choco we monkeys sometimes found in the piles of you-men supplies unguarded on beaches. And casing the joint I noticed the newspabers there, and each of them had its own version of a photo: Inga standing among lions and tigers and simians, plus Urrrk, who held her hand. "Zoo Whisperer," a customer said, translating the glyphs. Then, pointing to Inga's image, read another, seemingly amused: "Criminal Mischief for Cutie."

"Gotta wub that kib," the clerk said.

"Tiger on Joralemon Street!" The customer read.

And the merchant: "Hibbos in Hoboken!"

The customer snapped the paber open: "Meerkats take the E trayn to Queens."

And Inga again, every page it seemed, her image repeated and repeated, just as in my thoughts, come to think.

Was that I, Beep, on the girl's shoulder? I'd learned that the you-mens could capture time, and so I knew that these images were not immediate, not the exact *now* I found myself in, stubidly frozen in a dangle off the y'awning of the kiosk, inches from the oblivious proprietor's head.

I dropped, grabbed two KitKatz, as the old uncles called them (familiar from beach-planket raids), leapt away.

"Hey," the proprietor called. Then, "Hey, hey! There's a monkey! A monkey in a cape!"

"Correct, sir," I called back. "And there, and there and there and there and there to near infinity, are examples of you you-mens!"

Back to the branches above—peebles below, shouting, the good ones laughing, some even bowing. You-mee kibs ran almost as fast as we did, accompanying us southward toward the true home, their numbers growing, a pretty not-Inga in festive garmends pointing up, all of them traversing the face of this green- and blue- and white-swirled glope. Constantly checking in, Deeps and me, I touching her back, pulling her tail, quick eye contact, serious business: the squirrels began a new message: "Leopard captured, Leopard captured, Leopard captured!"

The squirrels were always just ahead of us and just behind, taking turns running the canopy with us, handing us off block by block, shouting a plan: "In the dense tree rest a moment, then we squirrels will go straight on like monkeys to fool the you-mees—you monkeys leap to the East, then south again next thoroughfare!"

Dense tree? What did that mean? But shortly there it was, needled and green and fragrant, and inzide it we were invisible. The you-mee crowd below ran onward with the squirrels, didn't notice that Deeps and I did not emerge—not right away, and that when we did, we'd headed the other way.

Quiet street, and leafy. Noisy thoroughfare next, turn south, and onward toward home. Two squirrels from that block picked us up. "Do you know trayns?" they shouted, over and over.

"In the ground," I said.

"Only some of them," the squirrels said. "Only some of the time!"

Deeps said, "I know trayns, have heard them described. Where do we find them?"

"Straight and straight then through dars, enormous human space, so big that stars shine on the ceiling! Or at least that's the legend."

"Straight and straight," another squirrel said, joining us, then another, handing us off all the way to a set of grand golden dars that spun like dust devils, humans spitting from them like chewed husks. No way. But in the middle, just dars, and one of these opened, and Deeps, brave one, raced through, I just behind, human bootz and snickers all around us, no apparent notice, so much going on. Quickly we leapt to a kind of shelf over columns, then onto a high sill under an vast bank of wimdoes, dusty and loftily above the fray.

"I smell electricitty," Deeps said.

"As after a storm," I said.

"Exactly, as after lightning. And the trayns run on lightning, so I've heard."

We burst into the enormous rooom the squirrels had spoken of, starways and incomprehensible path patterns, and tunnels this way, tunnels that, the ceiling like sky, and yes, stars pricked it, wan you-men twinkle. It was warm in there, and so I jettisoned my Pinkie, no more supermonkey. Deeps peeled off her jagget, and we dropped both into the coursing you-men crowd below, barely a ripple among them, though Pinkie draped a bald head.

"Always pick south," Deeps said.

And south, following the smell of lightning, we did find a trayn, ran along its rooof even more south till it moved, but it moved north. So we leapt off and all the way through the canyonish rooom via balgonies and sills and finally to a precarious swinging perch complete with a you-men male washing the wimdoes, it seemed, or anyway squeaking at them with a wet wand.

He wasn't even startled, said, "Hey, ho, it's Inga's monkeys!"

On a grand screeen then we saw her again, my you-men friend among the great cats, then on a sitting contraption under lights, a clip of her speaking to a gaggle of shouters pointing prods her way, poor thing. But in the end she smiled, a big grin for Beep.

"You miss her," Deeps said.

"Soon to be their queen," I said. "When sensitives rule, or that's the prophecy."

"Ah," Deeps said. "I did feel her spirit."

"She's very strong and feels us," I said. "She worships a half-monkey goddess named Greta, who speaks monkey and sees the future."

"Ah, then she'll survive," Deeps said. "As will that wimdoe washer."

I only laughed. "Survive what?"

"When we wish the you-mens off the plamet," Deeps said.

"If wishes were bananas, we'd have handfuls to throw down at the you-men heads!"

"I do have to pooop," she said. And did so, into her fine hand, picked a tall hair-do, and flung, perfect shot!

The wish was my mission, the grand banana.

I held the wish as we made our way among the million legs, the salted shoes, the swaying skirts. Every so-many-score of you-mens, you'd feel one of the good ones. This was the subway, suddenly, where I'd been. The trayn was pointed west, but not impossible that it would turn. We followed and hid a bit among the trailing folds of the long orange gowns of two you-men males, one of whom was so powerfully emanative that we understood he would take this trayn west, all right, then get out and into a more powerful trayn south, and south again. He settled next to his friend on the hard benches of the trayn carr, as they were called. He sighed voluptuously: rest.

"Monks," Deeps intimated. "We knew them at the zzoo! They're Beaut-ists, and have good hearts, mostly."

Under the overflowing edge of our monk's robes, Deeps and I hid unnoticed till I accidentally brushed the bizarre you-men leg, sparse fur. Our monk jumped, peeped a little shriek that all the others in the packed car studiously ignored.

"Brother what is it," his companion said.

And our monk pulled his robe aside. "Just as I thought."

He put his fingers to his lips. "Bless Inga," he said.

"Inga's monkeys?" the other said.

"The very ones," Monk One said.

"I fear," Deeps moodled.

"Fear not," our new friend said, both in speech and in effortless moodle. He'd understood! "We are humble monks, and felt you near, and calling."

"Beaut-ists!" Deeps said.

"Hardly a calling," said the dour one.

Monk One ignored him. Then in a moodle he communicated with us monkeys, sidestepping his companion, so powerfully emotive that I experienced his thoughts as life, like a dream almost, straight into my head, a series of memories now my own: Inga had told a story on his tee-bee of bringing her monkey to Bronzoo, which was the prizzon we'd liberated, and there this monkey had found the wub of his monkey life and freed her.

"That wub was I," Deeps intimated.

Beautiful that the monk understood her. "Care for the world," the monk mooded back. He reached a hand down, and both Deeps and I held a thick you-men finger.

"You will live, Monk," Deeps said to him kindly. "When the day comes, you will lead in that care."

"And what day is that?"

"You'll know when it comes, and it will come soon."

The second monk was less porous, less kindly, you felt it, more skeptical of beauty. And nervous in some way. The first monk whispered to him: "Inga's monkeys!"

And the other whispered back, a conversation in wind words, the air so rapid that I could not follow. Except that the first monk was called Brother Bangg. He closed his eyes, breathed in, breathed out, intimated that they would guard us on our journey.

"But where are you going?" I straight-moodled, as if.

But Bangg seemed to concentrate, pushed at his eyes with his hand. And distinctly then, his mood, which I translate: "We are going to a place called Florrriba where it is warm, even hot, and we monks will guide you that far." And more, arriving in images, really, travel advice: For us to get to the home forest, to be back among my siblings, my abandoning mom, my aunts and uncles, Deeps and I would need to take either a water-rusher or an air-machine, or possibly both, perhaps other you-men conveyances as well.

The westward trayn came to a stop, and monks and monkeys made their way in swishing broadcloth out of the cabin and into a vast indoors, up a ramp, across a britch, down some stairs, even more westerly. Our monks were not you-mens who hurried, and under their robes deep Deeps and I rode holding on to fragrant pleats and folds, the light bursting orange and dark, orange and dark, the monk warmth wholly holy, at least that of Brother Bangg.

And then in a great chamber we rested. Brother Bangg parted his robes so I could see where we were. "It won't be long," he moodled clearly enough. Then, "Look, look!"

And on a great tee-bee came an image of the shubble buzz from above, a difficult concept for any monkey, but clear enough to this one, lately educated in you-men ways. The shubble buzz, unmistakeable, that Greenie coloration, an escort of seemingly thousands of carrs and truggs, all of them moving very slowly, crowds cheering from the margins, blue-swirling guard cars in large numbers taking up the rear, leading, too, a magnificent procession, some kind of cooperation in progress.

And then views from the roadside as the shubble buzz passed, its rows of wimdoes full of reptilian faces, what passed for grins. And then another shot—fractured you-men time—Charlene standing on the shubble buzz steps in the shubble buzz darway, waving her arms and speaking to an enormous impromptu gathering, something about Trans-Portation, something about giving the animals of the world a fair shake, that the meeek truly would inherit the Aarth, which was the World, which was the Plamet.

The first monk translated for us, pure moodle, but you felt you'd understood the Buzz Lady, as the newsies were calling her. No, she was not afraid of being eaten! No, she was not afraid of running out of gazz, and pointed: Members of the crowd carried red vessels containing liquid they poured into an opening at the rear of the Buzz, sweet nectar by the smiles. Nor would they want for food! And pointed to more crowdies, legions of sensitives carrying baskets of victuals fit for anyanimal, delivering it to the shubble buzz dars. Charlene had helpers now, and the helpers were you-mees!

Even the pleece seemed to find it fun, at least caused no trobble. "We can wait," a senior one said. So, there were sensitives everywhere!

"What has come over them?" the second monk said.

"Wub," said Brother Bangg. "Nothing more, nothing less."

"Okefenokee or Buzzt!" Charlene cried up there on the tee-bee, and disappeared inzide the conveyance, which then continued, stately pace seen first from the ground, then from above, her retinue stretching both far ahead and far behind.

"Godspeed," the first monk said.

"Our trayn!" said the second, quite nervous. The idea of wub hadn't moved him.

After some pushing among coursing goers, we boarded another trayn, smell of you-men foods and farts. The monks settled into seats, arranging robes and monkeys around their feet.

Soon we felt it, heard it: a lurch, a clunk, a hiss, then movement, southward.

Brother Bangg unwrapped his robes and lifted me to his side—the trayn car, a moving rooom, was empty. Monk Two lifted Deeps more squeamishly. And so my wub and I sat in comfort, and took prasadam, which, Brother Bangg explained, was blessed chow.

"All must die in any case," he said aloud, words of pushed air.

"In any case?" said Monk Two.

"All who live now will one day not. Elemental truth and quandary."

"But all will live on," Monk Two said.

"So we like to think," said Brother Bangg.

Teacher and student, I surmised.

The trayn was like the you-men roarbirds but never left the ground. Day turned to night, and morning came, and still we rolled along, the willz clacking below us, traversing the great curving glope.

"You-mens aren't all bad," Brother Bangg said, sharing popping wet balls of sweet afterlife called grabes.

"They fight the trees. They fight the animals. They fight the stone. They fight their own food."

"They cannot remain," Deeps moodled crossly.

Brother Bangg nodded, nodded more, another quandary. At length, he said, "But what about the good?"

"And what good is that?" Deeps said.

"Mewzzik for example."

"Oh, awful," I said.

"Ah," Deeps intimated. "But monkey, there's a sort that would fill the wind at the Bronzoo in the evenings sometimes. I think you heard same during the melee last night."

Image arose: Urrrk getting it in the chest, the foot.

I grunted, not assent.

From a pogget somewhere deep in his robes, Brother Bangg pulled two white creatures called earbugs, no strings attached, put one each in our monkey ears—memories of sweet Inga on the roarbird—then fiddled with his phome. Shortly, very quietly at first, a keening to rival the monkey storm-song emerged, sweet and sad, notes of hope, notes of study.

Brother Bangg let us listen a moment, said, "This is the *Méditation* from Massenet's grand obbera *Thaïs*."

"Beauty," Deeps said.

"Beauty," I agreed.

The earbugs were uncomfortable and both of us plucked them out when the keening was done.

"Sensitives," Brother Bangg said.

Out the wimdoes of the trayn then, we watched a lot of plamet go by, a long, long meditation indeed, and mood, the *Méditation* continuing to sing in my head, a living thing.

"Monks and monkeys," Monk Two kept saying.

"Your ko-an," said Bangg, amused. He then moodled what a ko-an was, and that it was very like the experience of mewzzik, whoever was listening. Monkey logic, so far as I could tell: "Some things, dear companions, aren't to be understood, but only understood, understand?"

I did.

Or did I not?

Chapter Thirty-Two

You'd think by the verdant smells and the heat and the familiar flailing leaves of palm and banana and the welcome dartting and tasty scent of lizards that this place called Florrriba would have monkeys, but it did not—a monkey knows immediately, even just staring out a wimdoe at the rushing irreality, a keening caught in the head. We debarked from the trayn in another vast hall, quick peeks through swishing orange fabric, the monks slower than ever, their fragrance less floral (but all the more adored), came at last to a barking lot lacking only a shubble buzz. Florrribba, the very air, gave off a kind of zzoo mood, which I may not have felt so profoundly but for Deeps, who shuddered and shivered looking out from our fold in the orange fabric of holy robes, this sudden world of concrete and palm trees, stiff hot wind.

"I fear," she said.

Suddenly a large conveyance pulled up, not a buzz but a vann, if I was reading the emanation correctly, this driven by a third monk, who screeched to a joyous, rocking stop, leapt out, embraced Brother Bangg, kizzed both his cheeks, kizzed his mouth, a kind of holy lightning bursting from their congress.

Brother Bangg parted his robes just so and I took an Inga-like bow, drew Deeps out of hiding by the hand.

"Monkeys!" the new monk cried, his face like a thousand suns. "The very monkeys!"

"We chanced upon them in Grand Central," Brother Bangg said.

"And harbored them," Monk Two said dourly.

"Oh, blessed world!" the new monk exclaimed. "I wouldn't call it chance." His eyes were kindly upon us: "I've been watching your progress on Twitter and CNN and YouTube. Fox News thinks you're the devil! And Mrs. Devil, I guess! They guess you're still in Nyork! But I felt you near, I knew it! Bangg here, he has powers!" The new monk opened a large door in the side of his vann, and our monks got in. "Monkeys in front!" he cried. "I'll fazzen your sea-belts!"

And so Deeps and I huddled in a sitting contraption with a sea-belt across our chests and a view of the sky through a wide wimdoe, and motion. The new monk turned a noob among the many mysterious controls for the vann, and suddenly there were voices in the air around us, excited timbre, high squeaks, low reassurances, confident connective phrases, none of it making sense.

"They're talking about you!" Brother Bangg cried from behind us.

And then a voice I did recognize: Charlene!

Who'd made it to the warm just as we had. "If anymonkey is listening," she said, and Brother Bangg transmoodled, "and I know you are, just this: I've made it to the warm waters, now you sweet-treat kizzy monkeys get yourselves home."

Apparently something about her and her buzzload of reptiles had continued to beguile the pleece, who instead of stopping and a-wristing her, imposing their own sad upbringings, had apparently instead accompanied her not just out of Nyork but for the entire journey, along with an increasingly enormous retinue of other sensitives.

"All animals accounted for," Charlene announced to cheers.

Another goddess, more blessings.

Then another voice, and this one I recognized only when Brother Bangg said it was Becky Crankbrood. The mean girl from Inga's ssscoola, identified as Inga's best friend! "Inga is innocent" was the only phrase I understood of her piping.

And the announcer again, dulcet tones: "The people have gone mad, and not only the animals!"

"These are not continental monkeys, nor Afriggan," the driver nearly sang, tilting his head.

"Best guess via a quick google is either South or Central American," said Monk Two.

"That worldly phome," the driver said, now shaking his head.

"They only want to get home," said Bangg. "There's a prophecy, or so I'm gathering. We're at a historical flexion, and these monkeys are the pivot."

"I've felt that, too," the new monk said in his excited way. "I think a lot of us have!"

"You're both nuts," the second monk said. "And we're all going to end up in jail."

The others ignored him. The new monk steered our craft, much bouncing and shifting of light.

"Home is all they want," Brother Bangg said.

"And home, then, teacher, where is that?" Monk Two said. "South America? Central? Brother, that's a vast region." He had pride, plus all the answers: "These are squirrel monkeys. I've been reading up on them, the world in the poggetz of my robe!" Meaning he had his phome. The other monks ignored him. But on he went, like carved wood in the Bronzoo, all the unimportant things, nodding his head for emphasis, though he was only emphasizing himself: "Limited to the jungles of Colombia, subspecies one; subspecies two, limited to the rainforests of Panama and Costa Rica," nod, nod. "And like all primates worldwide, threatened," nod, nod, nod, "with the latter population listed as endangered," nod. "The South American subspecies is larger, darker," nod. "The Central American is considerably smaller, with orange fur upon their backs."

"We've one of each, is my guess," said the new monk, smart fellow, not entirely dismissive.

"We're guessing Cozza Rica," Brother Bangg said, though I'd heard no such guess.

"Panama Canal will take them straight there," the driver said. "I mean to the Central American Pazific Coast, and from there they can head into proper habitat. I was merchant marine before I found this calling. Are ye monkeys above stowing away?"

"They've stowed away with *us*," Bangg said.

"Fugitives," Monk Two muttered.

"Canal," Deeps emanated darkly.

"Explain what a canal is," Bangg said to the driver. "Explain it like you're talking to a monkey."

And he mooded his moodle for us as the driver spoke air words, monk mind to monkey minds: "Shibs go from ocean to ocean through a kind of river that you-mens made by digging and destroying the terrain much as water might do in any case, cutting straight through the Isthmus of Panama, which is the you-men pretend designation for that narrow stretch of land, which along with Cozza Rica is what they call the lands that are your home—your sea is the far sea from this one."

"Beep's sea, maybe," Deeps said.

"Soon yours," I said. "And the first you've had."

"And then what are shibs?" Deeps said.

"They float upon the water," Bangg moodled solemnly. He would live, this one.

I said, "We used to see them sometimes, far out on the ocean, and think them islands. We called them gone-tomorrows and fast-floaters."

"Shibs, then," Deeps said.

"Your talk at the Beaut-ist Center is not till evening, master," said the new monk.

"Yes, true, plenty of time, dear Brother Chaudhari."

Monk Two looked very concerned. He said, "Where are the docks? Do we really have time? And what shibs go through the canal? Is there a way to know? There's no way to know."

Chaudhari only seemed amused. "The answer to question one is: I'll take you right now. The answer to question two is: We have time. The answer to question three is: PortMiami, where they are very proud of their capability with post-Panamax shibs, now that the canal has been widened. And four: Yes, there is a way to know. We simply visit the Portage Page in the *Miami Herald*, available online."

I said something my Inga had liked to say: "I'm sure I have no idea what you're talking about!"

Bangg, he who would live, was patient, clear-mooded: "He's saying we think we can get you home."

Chapter Thirty-Three

PortMiami, so colorful, a kind of beauty, and in the cracks the weeds grew and threw flowers, and among them a certain leaf I knew, so much of it. When at last our driver stopped the conveyance and Brother Bangg opened his door, Deeps and I leapt across his lap and fell upon the certain leaf hungrily, and ate. Deeps knew this one too, so delicious. Stung-tongue, she called it. And it did sting, delight.

"A sacra-mint," Brother Bangg moodled, having felt us. No clue what he meant, but felt it holy. He climbed out of the conveyance and watched us, amused. Chauduri, too, who tried the Stung-tongue, spat it out, pinched at his tongue, some things being monkey things.

And some being you-mee: PortMiami, beauty aside, was intimidating, giants abounding, enormous meddle arms that swung this way and that with a kind of dignity and intelligence, never bumping one another, dropping tremendous hooks and mag-nets (Chaudhuri called them, artificial gravity, not that a monkey knew what gravity was, not till that moment: magic nets, I guess, that keep the everything from falling off the glope), dropping hooks and mag-nets into colorful stacks of boxes the size of you-men dwellings, lifting them effortlessly so they spun in the air like dragonflies.

"Gantry cranes," Chaudhuri said, "they are offloading containers."

He'd heard my thoughts, answered every question via Brother Bangg, who moodled translations, sensitives abounding!

Goers, too: "I have to use the facilities," Monk Two said.

And right there Monk Two got out of the vann at last and urinated enough to fill a lagoon, not a drop on his hands as far as I could smell. Chaudhari made various obeisant gestures to whatever you-mee gods watched over travelers, ushered us all back into the conveyance, and the doors closed once again, and once again we were on the go, all sky and go-stone and you-men structures, not a tree in sight, or just one: a pampered but isolated palm plunked in a barking lot. "Sssend wind," she whisssspered as we passed. "On the wind I tassssste my ssssisterrsss."

Guiding the vann was not hard, it seemed, or at least Chaudhari talked on: "The Post-Panamax vessels will be your best bet as they brush the edges of the rainforest at the last leg of the canal past the Pazific highlands, samajhate? Understand? You'll know because you'll smell the ocean. And if you find a spot to hide at the top of the load, the treetops literally brush the highest containers. Leap there, leap well, and find your peebles."

"He means monkeys," Bangg said kindly, translating, a strong mood.

"What are the you-mens saying?" Deeps said, not quite attuned. "I heard treetops, I heard highlands."

"They're saying that there's a way for you, Deeps, and I, Beep, to get back to my Home Tree. Where we will be troupe-mates and branch partners for life and make new monkeys to reunite our tribes, fulfill the prophecy."

"But these are you-mens—the ones who separated our tribes, the ones who endanger our tribes and our monkeyselves and all of animalkind across the glope. The prophecy concerns them. How do we trust?"

"Judge us by our actions," Bangg mooded.

Chauduri nodded.

"I understand," Deeps said.

"Wub and trust," Brother Bangg said with his wind voice.

We crested a rise and Chauduri slowed the vann, pointed out a shib, the biggest among many enormous. "Post-Panamax," he said. "That one's sailing this evening—I read it in the *Herald*. Funny, shibs are my great passion, and I have you here, destiny."

That word again.

"It will take us home?" Deeps said.

"You would not be the first," Chauduri said.

"Many animals hitch rides," Brother Bangg said. "That's what he's saying." And he kept transmoodling as Chauduri spoke, voluble man:

"It's loaded fresh with North American timber and wood products bound for Asia," he said. "Once, before Grace waylaid me, I'd have been up on the britch and in command, merchant marine. From up there you see nothing of animal life on the lading, but animal life there is—birds, rats, lizardos, more than once a cat, twice a dogg—the first was shot, the second was adopted after we docked, the cats, well, who knows. And on the ocean an accompaniment of sea mammals quite often."

"Those sea breathers are curious peebles," I said, trying wind voice.

Chauduri raised an eyebrow at the sound of my hoots, said, "Never a monkey, not that I saw."

Deeps said, "How will we eat?"

And Bangg repeated, windvoice: "How will they eat?" And transmoodled the answer:

"We'll feed you now, as much as you can stuff in. The way to Panama is only two days on these huge boats. And this one is flagshib of the new Post-Panamax fleet, so it will not be queued but waved on and feted all the way. You'll hear shore-bound orchestras, large groups of you-mens making mewzzik."

Ah, mewzzik.

"For food, well, linger, then follow your nose, find the rubbish tip behind the galley—much perfectly elegant food is tossed. You'll eat well. Passage through the canal is about ten hours. But in the ninth hour, you leap."

"I'm sure I don't know what you're talking about," Deeps said, imitating me, who imitated Inga, who would live.

The monks broke out food—those robes could feed multitudes—a long baguette, as he called his bread, the cheese they enjoyed and monkeys don't, but apples, sweet and hard. All delicious enough, but then a lizard that raced past, dodged my hand, expending so much attention on mine that he did not notice Deeps's.

"Apologies," she said and aimed Lizard at her mouth.

"Accepted," said Lizard, already quite bitten in half.

The you-mens, who eat the most vile things imaginable, gagged as my monkey and I shared the little creature.

Bangg moodle-mused, half aloud: "He's saying you won't starve, and keep a good lookout to starboard for your home trees. Starboard on this passage is North: get off on the correct side unless you like to swim in oil slicks and shite!"

"I've never swum," said Deeps. "I've never been in this big world."

Chapter Thirty-Four

CHAUDHURI, MONK, WAS NOT A small creature, but he squeezed through an opening between you-men structures that gonged as we passed, kwanset hutts, he called them. The alleyway opened into a kind of grassy court—this did not feel outzide—go-stone pathways that led to a cheggpoint. I climbed on the shoulder of Brother Bangg to his zignal, and he flipped the hood of his orange garmend over both of our heads—I could see out past his big ear. Dear Deeps climbed onto the back of Chaudhuri, who would live, though Monk Two, who would not, had offered. Already she trusted only sensitives. And yet Chaudhuri was clearly a goer, the way he'd piloted that machine. Much thinking to do, once home.

The monks walked in a line and began to chant, syllables ancient, almost familiar, slow, smooth pace, approached a portal called Seggurity. A very formal nobleman stepped out.

"Passes," he said, not unkindly.

"We're not allowed worldly decoration," Chaudhuri said, making his human syllables as thickly foreign as possible.

"Well, that I understand," said the guard. "Where is it you're going? Under whose command?"

Chaudhuri kept up the ruse—he'd been on this base: "Sayer Chabel, ecumenical service, sir. We are guest speakers—we're staying in Sayer Home."

"Ah, the monastery."

"Under the command of Captain Reverend Carter, sir."

"Oh, isn't he a pip," the guard said.

"A pip," said Bangg. "We apologize for the confusion."

"No confusion, Your Holiness. Happens daily. Service is in twenty minutes. You're speaking?"

"Leading a prayer," Chaudhuri said.

"I'll attend. God bless you, brothers. God bless you all."

He would live, I realized. There were many who would live, and found in the oddest places. He pointed the way, not far down the grassy, pretty lane in the midst of this death-affirming you-men scene. And there a structure with a tall point built onto it such that you wanted to look up. And when you looked up, you saw the sky, and in the sky a single round cloud. And the cloud if it could moodle would say: The world is more than these you-mens.

The Chabel, they'd called it, dark inzide. Brother Bangg raced through the space, Chaudhuri hard on his heels, Monk Two pouting—Bangg had lied to the guard—but all of us safely slipping out a modest dar at the other end, and into the inner port, where we hurried among monstrous gantry cranes (named for birds!) and past men with heavy footwear and meddle lungeboxes and others with clipboards and sheaves of paber.

Chauduri gestured grandly to a massive structure that seemed to sit upon the water, gargantuan boxes stacked in colorful patterns atop. "There's your shib, me monkeys," he said. "Now we monks must return to our vann and get the fuck out of here. You two can climb vines, right? Just climb the anchor rope at the far end down there, that's the stern, and that will put you under the fo'c'sle. There you will find a lokker with life jaggets, illegal to put under lokk. Lift the hatch at the far end—it's the small hatch and lighter—climb in there till you feel the shib move. Can you carry this bread?

Brother Bangg transmoodled instantly, and even Deeps understood.

"Easily the bread," she said.

He handed it over.

"And this is water," he said, handing me a small bottle.

"And drink now from this," Monk One said. And we drank as much as we could hold from his larger bottle.

"That'll just make them pee," said dour Monk Two.

Oh, how Deeps and I smiled at that, for to pee freely and share scent was all we hoped.

"What are life jaggets?" Deeps said darkly.

"Cushions, really," Chaudhuri said, perfect understanding. "You will find them comfortable."

"And a lokker?"

Chaudhari, always amused: "A lokker is just a boxx, dear ones. And a hatch, a dar."

Brother Bangg put a hand on each of our heads. "And now, let us say goodbye, and blessings, and well met, monkeys."

Chaudhuri pointed out a lower part of the dock he called a step-down, and we ran along this all the way to the sterm of the shib, which was the farthest end, and there indeed were great ropes thick as palm trunks, all the you-mens with their weapons and clipboards and work helmets and busy endeavors far down at a ramp the you-mens traversed to move on and off of the shib, busy as leaf-cutter ants, less cheerful. The gantry cranes pivoted, and a beautiful yellow container swung over our heads this direction, a beautiful blue container the other. The shib was as big as a world. But the world was bigger yet, the true shib, our dear glope.

"O, Beep," Deeps said. "I fear."

Just then a moaning arose, and a groaning, and a wail above that, and we looked down in time to see the three monks recessing in chant. The you-mens all looked their way, respectfully incredulous, I'd call it, as the orange robes disappeared into the back doors of the chabel, those sandaled feet now running.

And unseen, balancing bread and bottle, two free monkeys climbed thick ropes to the deck of the enormous Post-Panamax tankker, as it was called, or shib, lifejagget lokker just as described, hatches unlokked, far too heavy to lift, but yes, at the far end, a smaller hatch, and two monkeys opened it easily, climbed inzide as one. Deeps propped our water bottle under the lid so we could breathe the good air of the world and see the good light. The life jaggets were as orange as the fur back of my hands—good omen, I thought. And comfortable, and we lay on them, and slept like monkeys on a branch.

When we woke it was to a roaring in the dark—night had come. And I can't describe it, but the world moved, and grumbled, and lurched, everything around us creaking and bobbing. We understood we were underway, undercurrents of hope and fear.

Chapter Thirty-Five

We ate the bread almost nostalgically—our last you-men food. The crack of light under the lid of the lifejagget cabinet stayed bright—spot-brights onboard. I so wanted to look and see, but Deeps said no, and amid the rumbling we nestled together. We'd slept so much—it seemed maddening to close eyes again, and not safe. Late, though, I must have dozed, because I woke to her pulling at my arm. "Something happening," she mooded.

Voices of you-mens. One a female. Friendly enough, but no fun, accent like Mario's, the beetzaman who'd helped Inga back in Nyork. Something about the draft of the shib, the count on the containers, the contents, paberwork. "Safety brotocol?" she said.

"Oh, now, come on," a voice said. "You're really going to count the life jaggets?"

"Spot inspection."

"I assure you."

"That hatch is propped there."

A bright shone into the crack more brightly than the ambient.

"Stowaway?"

"We've no reports."

And suddenly our hatch was popped open, brights in our faces. Taken by surprise, I was too late to follow Deeps, who leapt right into the brightness and scurried up the side of a pink container, hand over hand on a multitude of handles and footholds.

Thick digits had me by the chest and face—I couldn't even bite, but peed freely.

"Monkey," the deep voice said.

"Vermin," the inspector said.

"Monkey ain't vermin," the deep voice said. "In fact, I'll sell this boy in port for a britty benny, I will."

Another voice, amused: "Well, now, there's a humane solution."

The inspector didn't laugh with the others, said, "There'll be no illegal commerce in wild animals. Genitalmen, another animal came out of that lokker and just escaped. We don't know where these animals are from and can't make assumptions. Your vessel will be waylaid in Gatun Lake per my immediate order until the vermin is found and exterminated. This biological control must be documented with time-stamped photographs, the proper forms, and captain's signature."

"Monkey ain't vermin," the deep voice said again.

"Captain, explain matters to your crew."

"There are rules," the captain said ruefully.

"Then I'll kill him now in front of ye," the gruff voice said.

"No, no," the captain said. "Blood on the decks? What's the fine for that, inspector?"

"Be serious, Captain."

The captain, very stern, very resolved, all professional, said, "Seaman, there are dogg crates in the tourist-mess storage. Pick a small one for this fellow. We'll document a bloodless drowning after lunch. Put the crate in the forward tourist suite—it's unoccupied. And lokk the door. And don't get any ideas, seaman, or it's you I'll throw overboard."

"Threatening work enfironment," the inspector said, humorless, scramching on her pad.

My heart beat very hard. I could hear the hearts of all the you-mens, my jumbled thoughts of flight mixing with their zignals, which were universally negative toward one another and the universe, Seaman Gruff with such a miserable grip on my neck, quite the way my mother had once handed me to aunts. Valiant mother! Dearest aunts!

With all the you-men mind noise and all the clanging roar of the great vessel, it was hard to moodle a contact with Deeps, though I felt her tenderness in the breezes. What had become of her? Somewhere on the shib, that much I felt. The inspector and the captain walked off through a narrow passage between containers. Seaman Gruff squeezed my scruff, walked the other way, soon along the rail with me dangling, immobilized. I could only pee, and did so freely, also poooped. My coarse captor didn't even care, took no notice.

We bounced up a starway, then another, and yet another, then around a kind of tall building that was the mind of the shib, a monkey could feel it, and the living quarters of these men, could smell. Seaman Gruff shouldered open a heavy dar, grunting with the weight of it, squeezing me harder, then through another that opened into a darkened passage, then a dark chamber where he retrieved a clattering canid prizzon, stuffed me in it, closed and latched it. I slumped to the floor of the thing, wanted to seem incapacitated, which worked:

"Don't die on me monkey," Seaman Gruff said. "You're eight thousand if you're a benny, just as soon as Our Lady of the Clipboard is gone back to heaven. And just look at the accomodations. Your own staterooom, Master and Commander!"

And he left me, nothing stately about the rooom at all, just a kind of shelf for sleeping and images of shibs (of all things), shibs on the walls, click-click as he lokked the dar, the sound familiar from Inga's place, so far away.

Oh! Where was Deeps?

I waited a while, seemed forever, opened the dogg prizzon easily, just a doggproof latch, no lokk. Underestimated Beep! I crept to the door of the unstately staterooom, but of course it was lokked, as well, the noob frozen, little noob beneath frozen, too. For a window there was only a large circle over the tightly garmended bed. Out the window the world moving by, grower land, it looked like, orderly sad trees, no jungle, the great vessel churning and roaring in its effort but merely crawling along through the narrow gash in the world.

I realized suddenly that the sea gulls winging out there were not just randomly flitting but had an interest, not only in the shib, but in my window. And shortly an upside-down face appeared: Deeps!

"Dumb monkey!" she mooded crossly.

"You and me both!" I felt back.

"Come out of there."

"I'm lokked in."

"You can't be lokked in. The you-mens use lokks to keep other you-mens out of their private spaces. It's impossible to explain. But unlike monkeys in a zzoo, you are in control of those lokks. I have studied this extensively, the subject of lokks. It's much of what we prizzoners talked about at Bronzoo."

"Deeps. I have studied lokks, too. I did so in the apartment of our brave Inga. I have no kee! Keeze is the kee to this puzzle."

"So you say. But go inspect the globular meddle appendage upon the dar."

"The noob," I said.

"You will see in its center something like the residuum of sepals, stamens, styles, and stigmas on a fruit."

"The navel, you mean?"

"Always a simpler say," Deeps said. "Yes, like the navel on a fruit or monkey. Do you see it?"

And sure enough, at the very center of the noob was a nooblet, which turned. And now the greater noob turned freely, lots of clicks, but the dar remained closed.

I explained, nearly narrated.

"Ah good," Deeps said. "Now there is a kind of appendage—I see it from here—below the so-called noob, there, more stem than navel."

And yes, there was such a thing, the smaller noob, brass bright from the touch of you-men fingers. Bigger fingers than mine! I closed my fist around the tiny shoulders of the thing, and though it gave slightly it would not turn.

"Two hands," Deeps said.

Same.

"Try turning it the other way, as the sun and stars go."

It turned easily. The bigger noob turned easily as well, but in the other direction. I pulled at it, but the heavy dar wouldn't budge. Then, blast of light and heat, the thing flew open and Seaman Gruff nearly fell in, keeze in hand, stumbled straight to the deserted crate, which left a fraction of a moment for me to leap out the dar and into the blessed sunshine, and even better, into Deeps's moral orbit. Upp was the message of her mood, and I grabbed a steel vertical and climbed, staterooms stacked upon staterooms, finally the walkway, unfortunately right underneath the captain's great wimdoes.

"Oh, for Christ's sake," he expostulated, this simultaneous with the welcome sight of Deeps, free Deeps and wise.

She shrieked and also moodled her mood, very hard: "Let's go!"

The seafaring noblemen in crisp whites and blues emerged from their own captivity, shouting and pointing. Seaman Gruff came pounding up the ringing steel starway, dangerous in his humiliation, and shouting something about strangulation.

Deeps pulled me onto the rooof of the Captain's lair, where, we realized, we were trapped.

"Though you-mens can't jump a gap like that," she said—like *that*, a long way to the nearest container, dull red.

"Not sure monkeys can either," I said.

"Imagine tree to tree down the avenoos of Nyork, it's not further."

"True enough-ish."

So we waited. Perhaps everyyou-mee would calm down, make a blunder, free a path to the starwell, to which we could jump in safety.

Seaman Gruff shouted, "I know you're up there, monkeys! I've been up there meself, and not even you could jump s'far!"

And here he came, making use of a series of horizontal bars meant as a climbing device.

"Labber," Deeps said. "That's called a labber."

"Learning never ceases," I said.

And a slowblink passed between us. Gruff's face appeared above the rooofline, red and sweaty and gruff, all right. He brandished something unrecognized, a fish nett, Deeps called it, known from the Bronzoo, a great circle on a stick with extremely loose-woven fabric.

"Shall we?" Deeps said.

"Indeed," I said.

And as Gruff lunged, we darted around him, Deeps first to the labber, and then I, large crew of lesser nobles below us. The nett swiped at us from above. From below, a grander nobleman on a rung reached for our feet.

"See the red noopsook on that seaman's back?" Deeps said. "Use it as a stepping stone, push off hard for the next jump to that enormous cleat, and then we leap the gap—I see a britch of sorts."

I didn't understand, said, "Cleat?"

"Just follow."

And, next swing of the fish nett, we leapt, straight past the man reaching for us and onto the noopsook worn by the fellow on the deck, from there seemingly into the abyss, but sliding down a wet-slick clanging pipe all the way to the true deck, where, we realized, we were highly visible from that high britch. Forward, forward, we ran. Deeps positioned herself at the far corner of the stacks of containers. I positioned myself on the opposite corner—that gave us a view of whomsoever might be coming.

"Up," she moodled, and so we clambered up three container levels, where it might be hard for a you-men to climb and where we could watch the shoreline—no, not shoreline but canal wall—watch the canal wall, the high skirts of the shib nearly touching on both sides. To the north, we would jump. North and to my cohort, with old-blooded Deeps in tow. Or towing me. North. When we could manage. And when would that be? The great shib made strange noises, the canal around us glubbed and gurgled. Progress slowed, a lurch as something pulled the whole grand universe to a halt.

Bubbling, sighing, groaning. A you-men suddenly appeared from a dar we hadn't seen: of course there were interior passages in the vessel! And he was searching for us, one of the high nobles dressed so smartly in white. Foot-pounding on the top of the containers, a great meddle echoing, like the inzide of a goer's soul, yes, like that: often I'd felt that void, encounters unbidden. This shib was populated by that sort, though intermittently I felt a different emanation: it came from one of the seamen, alternately subsumed by the vibes of his shibmates, whom he was trying to emulate, then outraged with them, a grudging sensitive! Likely kibnapped.

"There!" the high noble shouted, pointing at Deeps. And above us Seaman Gruff leaned, showing us his chin, the redness of his cheeks, and, terrible jolt: the hollow snout of a shooting stick. "I'll collect ye for sale yet!" he cried.

"Deeps," I moodled hard, and she was a split second ahead of the snap of the rifle. A familiar dart clattered on the deck: one benefit of our having an apparent monetary value: Seaman Gruff wouldn't shoot us the killing way, nor drown us.

Deeps swung easily around the far corner, so I swung around my corner. "Upp, upp!" and to the continuous rooof created by all those colorful meddle boxes. And we ran, utterly exposed, but well ahead of Gruff, who lumbered after us. Large gap ahead: no you-men could leap it. We monkeys did, narrowly, then into the crevasse at the next bank of containers. Now we were together again. We touched foreheads. We had fear. To fix fear you did hard breathing, then hold, then relax.

"Monkeys," we said.

And now the gurgling came loud again. And at the same moment, Deeps and I realized what was happening: the shib was floating higher.

Seaman Gruff shouted. The high noble below shouted back.

A seagull swooped in—her name was Shriek, she said; duh, most seagulls are named Shriek. "Here to help," she said. "Do you understand what's happening here? The canal-and-lokk system? *Hawhawhawhawhaw!* Canals and lokks. Not like lokks on dars. *Hawhawhawhawhaw!* When one ocean level is lower than the other, *hawhawhaw*, your vessel must be floated higher. *Hawhawhawhawhawhaw!* Higher! They flood a chamber, and now, you see, your shib floats higher! And this shall be your salvation! Height enough to reach the trees! *Hawhahahahahaw!*"

"Thank you, Shriek, thank you," Deeps said. "Now go if you would and scare that soon-dead, the one with the shooting stick."

"Let me call a few friends," Shriek said. "*Hawhahahahahaw!*" And called, and called again: "Shriek! And Shriek! And you too, Shriek-ins!"

Soon a dozen were wheeling over us, white beauties, and gray.

"Go," Shriek called. "Go gulls go! *Hawhahawhaw!*"

Gruff had climbed down the labber on one side of the first gap, was climbing up our gap.

"Shriek," we monkeys cried.

And swoop, here came the seagulls, even as the shib creaked higher, or the walls around it sank lower. Gruff waved his arms at the gulls. They nipped at him, flapped at him, shit on him (excellent aim and timing, speaking as a pro!), all at great risk. Gruff lost his grip, dropped his shooting stick. He fell several rungs of the labber, shouted out. Now here came his friend up the opposite labber.

"Rooof," Deeps said.

And up there, suddenly, we saw what had been theretofore invisible: trees. Tall trees, canopy trees, rainforest trees, trees as at home, familiar fizz of cicadas. The tallest of the trees had leaned into the advantage of the light and hung right at the edge of the great walls. We needed only a little more height. The seagulls swooped. The you-mens cursed, incomprehensibly using a phrase denoting simian mating: "Fucking monkeys!" Almost as if they anticipated the coming plans of Deeps and Beep.

The hanging branches were too far to reach. The shib rose. The you-men sailors fended off gulls, even while Seaman Gruff retrieved his shooting stick, steadied himself as he looked down its length. Deeps got to the very edge of the topmost container. I followed, inferior speed. Jumping down we might reach a long, hanging branch coming toward us. And whoosh, another dartt flew past. And whoosh, thump, the next dartt took Deeps in the thigh.

"Oh, hell," she said, and pulled it out.

"Jump!" I said.

"Too far," Deeps cried.

The trees leaned in to help.

And nothing for it, we jumped. Leaves tore as I grasped for them. Deeps had leaped farther, found a branch, reached for my hand, caught it just as my fistfuls of leaves gave way. Below, the boat bumped the great concrete chasm wall, just where I would have fallen and been crushed.

Another dartt whizzed past. Deeps pulled me to her, and together we brachiated away through the dense, familiar canopy. Not far in, Deeps pulled up on a thick branch. "So sleepy," she said.

Chapter Thirty-Six

Deeps sleeps in a heap, Beep keeps watch, deep thought, creatures creep both above us and below, something burgeoning, sweet coalition, a strengthening beat—we've ceded the fate of the plamet to you-mees too long, their greed, their heat, their constant beat, always did cede it, in fact, accepted defeat not even aware. Enter Beep, Freemonkey. Enter Beep, afraid.

Upside in the night: Deeps snoring peacefully, familiar leaves, tastes, sounds, the darkness and now blessed warm rain coming down around us. The shib with its boxes full of world-death and its coterie of death-dealing you-mens and its black plume of world-death and its churning wake of world-death and all its other various furies had passed on through the world-death passage without us. If Deeps died, then what of me? But her heart batted strongly in her bony chest and her breaths were profound and rhythmic, no smell on her breath of sickness, or of death.

I woke in daylight to a shuffling below, Deeps still snoring, but eyes rotating under the lids, face serene, sweet dreams.

"I smell monkey," the shuffler grunted, systematically turning over leaves.

A coatimundi, tail in the air.

"I smell single-mindedness," I said, old joke in the jungle: coatimundis were businesslike.

This one, too. It scanned the canopy, spotted me when I allowed it.

"Well, then, monkey," he said. "Are we Beep? We have it from the squirrels that we are Beep, who slew the monster! We have it from the squirrels that the plan is on, the great mood, the Turning of the Tide."

"I know nothing but squirrel rumors myself."

"There's one back by the river saying it now. A seagull told him you'd made it thus far, and we thought, Well done! Ever curious, we came to see. Also to point you toward some delectables. Mango tree just a pleasant ways north."

"My mate here, they've dartted her."

"Oh dear, yes. That drug of theirs lasts long on smaller creatures. Pett hunters, we call them. That one works the canal shibs as an exterminator, supposedly, but he doesn't kill, he keeps, he sells, he fills the zzoos. Can we imagine a coati doing such work!"

He flipped a leaf, exposed a newt, who shouted, "Got me!"

"All are one," the coati said, and ate it.

"So, you think she'll wake."

"She'll wake. We do wish we could carry mangoes but we can't carry anything, in fact. We could stay here and watch her if you cared to solo."

"No, no. My responsibility is with her."

"Ah, and I'm forgetful anyway, might leave her here!"

Deeps stirred, but not emphatically, her efforts like somemonkey picking up something heavy, then giving up.

I petted her, I coaxed, I picked twigs from the fur of her shoulders.

The coati waddled off.

A Hercules beetle stepped off the trunk of the tree and onto my knee. "No eat me," it said.

"Enormous beetle, bad to eat, crunchy shell and kicking feet," I said, the wee-bee monkey rhyme.

Beetle chuckle, like sticks rubbing together. The creature was the size of my head. "Beep," it said. "Beep and Deeps. We greet you. Is she sleeping? Not a peep. We beetles heard the plan. We'll join in heaps. We're in for keeps. We can't let the weeping steepen."

"Peep is cheap, beetle," I said.

"You see? We're starting to rhyme with you. She'll wake, don't worry, cousin Beep."

Seagull Shriek, out of her element there in the canopy, swooped in from the canal side. "The hunter is looking for you two. That shooter of his, illegal even among the you-mees. Which, when you think of it, sounds like a sick bird! Ill Eagle! *Wahwah-hahahahahaw, hawhaaaaaw!*"

Deeps stirred. Her eyes opened, closed again. "Quiet, gull," she said. But then, in merely the time it takes a cloud to pass, she opened them again, sat up, assessed our whereabouts. "We're off the shib!"

"We're off," I said.

"You were shot with a dartt," Seagull said. "*Wha-wha-wha-wha-wha!*"

"Oh, sleeping draughts—we knew them at Bronzoo."

"Slowly," I said.

"Hunger," she said.

"My cue to skidoo," the beetle said. Or something to that effect—I'm translating, for in fact the rhyming had nothing to do with wind words, and mood rhyme is wub.

"I smell canopy light," my monkey darling said.

"Nearly home," I said.

"It's beautiful," she said. "And so hot."

"Hot is what we got," I said, that infectious beetle!

Another interval, quiet monkeys. Then she seemed to get her energy, understand better where we were. "That there's no hurry," she said. "At last."

"We'll wend our way north."

Deeps sighed. "My heart says south."

"Ah, Monkey. Maybe one day we will make that journey, now that we know it's possible."

"My tribe, I like to think. Though honestly my only tribe was at the Bronzoo."

"It's them you have left behind to join my family, just as it always was."

"I wish them safe."

"I feel them safe."

"A strong mood, yes."

She felt better and better as the morning grew blessedly hotter, not a you-men in sight and not a sign, none of their structures, just some of their constant noise, the loud shibs of the canal, still, and various motors groaning and roaring and pealing, not as animals make noise—briefly, messages sent, messages received—but intractably, onwardly. Though perhaps there was a message imparted, and the message. was *fuck you*, to use the confused you-men parlance, the beautiful thing to express the ugly. No amount of retraining would stop the destruction they wrought, such was the sentiment flowing species-to-species around the glope. And what had already been done would take many generations to heal, or would never.

We heard the growing rumble of an infestation, Deeps called it, what the you-mens call a billage, and so we skirted it, striking northwest now, I, Beep, hoping we'd see the ocean before long. Deeps was ocean-averse, having only seen it from our great miserable shib. We rested when we were tired, luxuriated in all the good eating, Deeps in a state of ecstasy, every taste new to her. Every lizard's insult as she bit it was a song, every squirt from every odd fruit, a rhythm. She thought me a pioneer of some kind, a blessed scavenger, but I was only Beep, part of a troupe who lived not far.

As we traveled the mid-canopy we started to notice more and more animals accompanying us. Up in the sky, glimpses of our seagulls, well out of their watery range, but also larger and larger and more colorful flocks of other sorts of birds, many familiar. An eagle swooped close at one point, shouted: "Monkeeeee, we won't eeeeeeat you but protect!"

And squeezer snakes and giant toads and poison froggs and all the other reptiles, none to match our speed, all vowing to meet us at the epicenter, it was being called, the home of my troupe, where the mush-roooming mythos had it that change would emanate if only we worked together and plamet-wide. I pictured that pretty glope in my angel's rooom back in Nyork.

I missed Inga. Inga could feel me, I felt, even at distance, and I felt her, felt her growing closer, curious. Inga had tried, and cared, and considered, and learned. What would become of my Inga? Was a worry.

But tempered by the joy of movement, the middle canopy swooning with life, the upper canopy, too, the sky above, the lower branches, and on the ground peccaries snorting merrily, agile enough to keep up, and now a panther, who'd heard about the Bronzoo and Deeps's heroism. "That panther queen you freed is still traveling," he shouted up. "Apparently wearing poodle collars as bracelets, joking, joking! But eating well and hurrying southward!"

"What of Lion?" Deeps cried.

"Lion was dartted and cartted," a toucan said, snapping its bill.

"Dartted and cartted and fartted," the burgeoning crowd of beetles sang. "Lurking with Urrrk, two Kings."

Toucan was unmoved by the poetry, clattered her bill: "Nope, nope, nope. Back to the cage what's been his sadsack home all them many passages from summer ta winter and back again. To him, home, but. Nope, nope, nope."

"Deeps feels that deeply," she said. "That the kings stayed on."

I poooped on one of the peccaries just for old time's sake and the others laughed at their smirched colleague, whose name was Sschnort. Or perhaps that was the name of all of them.

The eagle plunged, killed one of our seagull friends.

"That's how it is," the seagulls cried. "*Whahahahawhahawah*, that's how it is!"

The eagle merely ate.

"How far?" I began to mood, trying to reach beyond my small sphere of influence, and that question echoed forward north and west, and an hour later echoed back: Ocean two days, Home Tree two days more. At least for a midcanopy monkey. The sea gulls could do it in an hour.

And dusk. Even among the friends all we animals had become in the excitement of the plan, dusk was dangerous.

Deeps and I tangled up in one another, tails like vines connecting us. "I have the urge to mate," she said.

We laughed because we knew just when that would come. Not yet. We laughed because we were not you-mens erecting whole citty blocks of brights to the proposition. And we'd heard they'd found ways to blockade the whole point of mating, which was making wee-bees, their one gesture toward self-control, and yet so many of them! We laughed because we found each other funny. We laughed because we found each other very serious. We slept, chastely knotted together in my fayb-fayborite sort of tree, a strangler fig, with its broad branches and excellent sight lines, multiple trunks.

Morning and we continued on. Afternoon and I smelled ocean. Evening and we could see it, a bay in the distance, even hear the breaking surf, receive the songs of whales, many species, come to join the confabulation.

"Now north," I said.

More you-men billages to skirt; it took all day.

And then, and *then*: monkey on the breeze! Just faintest, then monkey moodle, coming in strong. I smelled us first, felt us. I was about to poke Deeps's back as we crossed a thick branch into thin ones, when suddenly she turned to me, flicked her eyes north, howl of pain. Or joy. Those things pretty close in our world.

There was a river to cross.

Chapter Thirty-Seven

A GREAT RIVER FULL OF crocodiles, no branches reaching across. The monumental procession and parade and entourage of animals pulled up there, and we could see for a moment how very many animals there were.

"Crocodilians let us pass," some of the other reptiles mooded in their various tongues.

"*Oooooeeeeeeoooooooooooo-ohhh*" came the message from the sea, worldwide arrivals, pods of whales gathered at the great river's salty mouth and far beyond, eerie, longwinded, authoritative, the moodle given voice.

And didn't the crocodiles listen closely!

"We've no hunger for you, cousins," a group of them moodled and grunted both. "Or can contain it. The whales are wise. The orcas among them have already started wrecking shibs! They bust the rudders! Wise, they are very wise. For that is Freemonkey with you. And perhaps this Charlene? The shubble buzz? Does she attend?"

"She sends her greetings," I full-mooded. "She feels your wub!"

And I believe a chant went up in the river, anyway a great clattering of jaws: "Shubble, shubble, shubble! Buzz, buzz, buzzzzz."

A cattle egret, elegant in white, beak yellow, familiar of the crocodiles, stilted forward: "The crocs are all right," she said. "The crocs only eat what they eat, just as the rest of us do. Let us all focus and communicate to these river lords our plight and our mission."

The plight was not the river. The river was only an obstruction. The crocs already knew that, rather proud of being problematical. "Shubble, shubble, shubble," they clattered: "Get the Freemonkey home, so the prophecy might ignite!"

And the fritillaries picked it up, and their kin, then, too, more and more butterflies of all kinds, gathering, coalescing, joining our progress, that sweet-wafty floating and unflappable flapping, nothing aimless about it. "Ignite it, ignite!"

And in the various hums and tweets and barks and roars and songs and clicks and bubblings, the prophecy was expressed. We non-you-men animals would focus the powers of our numbers.

The crocs were all cooperation. First one, then the next, then a number more (I'm no counter, but can judge what it takes to make a britch!), lined up tail to nose in the shallow delta waters, "Shubble, shubble, shubble," then more, and more again, "Buzz, buzz, buzzzzzz," the moodling and wind-voices reaching them up and down the estuary, arriving and widening the britch their brothers and sisters and cousins had made, three, four, five animals across, those strong and slippery backs.

"Temporary," they emanated, and then chanted, a kind of thrum: "Shubble, shubble, shubble, buzz, buzz, buzzzzzz." Quickly the thrum became a rhythm, then a song, a marching cadence, too, and all the animals of homeworld crossed the croc britch almost dancing, birds flying above, ferrying the no-wing insects they'd normally eat, lizards clicking their own songs and balancing on the backs of peccaries, the whales holding out there in the ocean cheering us on, and dolphins, now, and the million fish that had no lungs but gills, wary of shore, of the you-men nets, all carrying messages from distant shores, all expressed with the splashing of caudal fins: the whole wide world was with us. And so we ran and flew and crept and squirmed, the crocodiles joyous with it, generous. Those who could swim, including a vast variety of four-leggeds, swam with confidence, the current strong but the safety of coalition stronger.

Somewhere in the midst of all this Deeps and I crossed, trotting across the backs of the crocs, shouting thanks the whole way, mooding the prophecy, accepting the moodle back, joyful noise, the voices of the world, louder than the motors of the you-mens, who owned that concrete britch just a mile or two upstream, no safety there.

As the last of the procession crossed, the crocs broke away, and in fact picked off four plus-size capybaras that were last in line—the crocs had gotten hungry, who could fault them?

Now the beaches were wider and the tree-cover more sparse and so we retreated further inland, that middle canopy, suddenly so many you-men dwellings and other structures, and the meddle machinery of the goers, also several fields and the many tidy plots of the growers, here and there a you-men or group of them or carrload, all of them amazed by the passing wildlife—we made no accommodation except to avoid them as they batted their hands at the smaller creatures of our number and stamped their rubberized feet at the crawlers.

"Please," Deeps mooded, hard, clear: "Have none of you you-mees compassionate hearts? Step forward so we may keep you!"

And I moodled, too, at her example, but no reaction from any you-men until we crossed the trees over a grizzled elder, who tilted back his vulture-wattled and naked neck, spotted me, big grin.

"Yes, monkey," he mooded, all his energy, the blessed affirmative: "Yes, yes."

He would live.

Many, many you-mees would live.

Just not over-many, and not the wrong many.

Such was the theory, such the prophecy.

On that side of the river, the world of the you-mens began to clatter and growl, also sparkle, also sing. It wasn't all bad, especially near the waters. The near-naked ones with their polished water-riders picked out waves, repeated their rides for hours, content in the monkey moment, in and out like breath. But goers were going, too, and there were busy goer trails that our multitudes had to cross at risk. Safety in numbers, however: the truggs and carrs waited, and waited some more, cheerful, fulsome honking, even many calling out my name, Beep! Beep! No, not Honk! Really Beep!

And onward.

In the afternoon, a coterie of blue morpho butterflies joined the other flimsy fliers, so many that the sky was doubly blue, an army of peccaries and armadillos ahead of us, several large felines now, sloths riding on their backs, and on the backs of tapirs, even carried by horrible howlers—we all wanted the sluggardly sloths along, all helped make it happen! And every conceivable lizard, my goodness, large and small. The latter swore when we ate them, good. And the leaves of the wisdom tree were delicious, and plantains from the edges of a grower's plot. No need for poggetz, no need for hoarding: we ate our fill, drank from puddles formed in the hollows of branches, carried on, apparent that our entourage was terrifying the you-mens, apparent that the mass mood and emanation, the very thrum, was affecting their actions—some stood out of their carrs to watch us pass, clapping their big hands together, loud reports. Others pointed their phomes at us—I knew from Inga that this was how they shared their own poor moodle, always with the mechanical help, these you-mees. I soul-moodled the massive movement of allies to aim our energy at a particular group that pulled up in their vehicles with pretty blue brights flashing, ten guard cars, pleece even here! I felt almost fond, nostalgic. Their brights as nothing to the hot home sun.

Still, the morphos protested: "They've stolen our light!"

"Let them sleep," we all mooded in our hundred thousand languages, feeling, saying, roaring, singing, signing, moodling, sharing, powerful, powerful. Several noblemen joined the pleecemen, rushed from their vehicles, some with shooting sticks—haha, not enough dartts on the plamet to subdue this crew!

We animals chanted, after our fashion: "Let them sleep!"

And suddenly the you-mees yawned and yawned wider, and one by one dropped to their thick knees, then sat, extravagant bedtime sighs, then lay down. All but one. All but one stronger one. And this one put his hands over his heart and began to laugh, hearty, beautiful sound, the sound of goodness, in this case, a you-men mooding without knowing it, not really; we all heard him: friend.

And onward, middle canopy, deep forest, the smell of monkey growing richer. And then there we were! A large troupe, not my own. One of their uncles, orange like me, pissed his hands ceremonially, and so I, too.

"She's different," he said.

"I am Deeps," my be-wubbéd said.

"I am Climb," the old uncle said. "We've felt the prophecy, prepared for your coming, much sitting together closely, much puzzling."

"Climb," I said, formal mood. "You are the brother of Mother-my-own Peep, and several illustrious aunts of mine."

"Yes, it's true, or at least I am countrymonkey to them, and descended from he who saw the smoking mountain. Which we hear you have seen, as well, and survived!"

"I've seen the smoking mountain, and seen much more, Uncle."

"And you've freed this poor monkey, whose troupe was once ours, uncountable seasons past."

Deeps was pleased. "Uncountable," she said.

I said, "Separated by the you-mens, so I've learned. Learned it at Bronzoo, which is a place they store us, imprizzon us, for when our wisdom is required. Whole ssscoolas of their smalls came to see this one, learn from her."

"She's browner, she's bigger, but I see she's a monkey and not a howler or a whitefurface."

"She's a monkey, uncle."

"May your mating bring the two worlds back together at last."

And his whole troupe repeated it: "May your mating bring the two worlds back into one at last."

The assembled mass of animals repeated it, too, in a welter of languages and feeling, very moving, exciting. There was a stir. The uniformed you-men male from earlier—uncommon pleeceman—had been running, had caught up. He was one of us, we saw, one of our masses, and we remembered: you-mens are merely animals who forgot.

"Monkeys," he moodled to us, barely articulate, and yet.

"He will live," old Climb said. "Now, tell us of the world, and world-danger."

And I did, and Deeps chimed in, and between us we knew more than almost anymonkey: the goddess Greta had filled me in, Deeps had gathered the undermood at Bronzoo.

The you-men male began to sing in the you-men way. "For the bee-uuty of the Aarth," he toodled in his wind voice, and it was eerie and very beautiful and heartfelt.

And everyanimal quieted. These you-mens, these sensitives, they were worthy, they were we.

And we would live.

And lo, he came with us as we continued on, stripping off coverings till he was naked, oddly charming, his scant fur making promising patterns on his chest.

"Your troupe is the Big Tree Troupe, yes?" Climb said. "They are waiting, for the prophecy has you reuniting in your troupe's central tree, the mango by the bend in the river."

"How far?" I said.

And all the animals took that up as a chant. "How far? How far?" Which is a wonderful universal question. *How far?*

"Thus far," Climb said. "Thus."

Which just meant, Keep going, and so we did, a swarm of us, a multitude.

We slipped through the next you-men billage at night, and by morning light saw that a number of you-mens had joined us, the sensitives—juveniles, grown females, grown males, all sorts of them, no goers, our family now. One of the you-men juveniles moodled perfectly with us, gave a bit of a speech: "I had a dream," she said. "I dreamed of monkeys on a shib, and my job was to alert the seagulls, and so in my dream I did."

She'd sent the seagulls! Of course I thought of Inga, who would live, and whom I felt more and more distinctly was near.

Onward, onward.

Chapter Thirty-Eight

THE AUNTS WERE FIRST, SOME carrying new babies since I'd departed. Auntie Meep came close, sniffed me voluptuously.

"Auntie," I said, "this monkey is Deeps."

And old Meep frowned, said, "I wouldn't call her a monkey! So big and brown!"

"Good to meet you, aunt," Deeps said, unperturbed.

"She's a monkey," I said, "she's from the lost troupe."

She gasped, remembering: "You've seen the smoking mountain!"

"I've seen it, and much more."

"Beep, you are influential, now. But we can't call you Uncle until you."

"Until Deeps and I."

"Until we've made the correction the plamet so needs," Deeps said.

"You mean the troupe."

"The world," Deeps said. "All of it."

Meep pinched her eyes closed—too much to contemplate.

And now more monkeys caught up, and there was my mother, Peep, and her best friends, joy abounding. They sniffed me, they sniffed Deeps. Many had heard the prophecy, it seemed, even though as monkeys they were oblivious of the great glope. And now with our entourage—so many creatures, all the kinds of the great forest—we continued half a day, and at half a day I began to recognize landmarks. The termite mounds, the farthest blue-leaf tree, the rock on the beach, the daytime you-men bustle, several of the blue-vine crossings over goer trails, Mossy the Sloth—Mossy herself!—who emotioned hello (most powerful mood in the jungle, these sloths, for they've time on their hands). Mossy was a friend to my troupe, had once had spent a moon passage in the monkey tree merely crossing from one side to the next.

Finally, that very tree, the Home Tree, and all the home monkeys were there, but also many other animals of every size and shape, familiar some, strangers others: harmony for now despite some chance eatings. Of course the wisest animal, *Musca domestica*, called howzzfly by swatting goers, was first to speak, a fizzing of wings, emanation understood by all creatures, even some you-mens, from what we'd seen, who mostly took offense.

"Dearly assembled," Howzzfly said. "We are legion, we are worldwide, the original web, we are the fly on the wall, we who no one but you wasps over there will eat—watching you!"

General mirth, a kind of atmospheric upheaval.

Fly continued: "And worldwide has our message gone, from the Arctic lichens to the tropical fungi, from the desert-running birds to the goats of the mountains so high they are clouds. And the message is: Freemonkey Beep is back in his home forest. Let the prophecy attain."

The cheering of such a diverse crowd of animals was a symphony, just as Brother Bangg had taught us, with movements, a crescendo, glissando, abrupt orchestral stop.

Suddenly, I was expected to speak. I called up the moodle of a lifetime, all my energy, and here is what the living things of the living Aarth heard, each in their language system, or nonlanguage, even the four thousand or so domestic cats that had joined us, even the hundreds of tainted domestic doggs, who strained to understand, even those few hundred you-mens among us, who'd largely stripped out of their garmends:

"To the living all we speak, and our speak goes around the great glope, which is the world unimagined, spherical such that in a moment we will feel the message coming back, for it is light itself, and travels at enormous speed."

A great roaring and cheering. And then its echo, amplified by the roaring and cheering everywhere around the world.

I said, "With wisdom and with neither coincidence nor planning have the many animals come together not only here but around the plamet, as it's called by its destroyers, the glope, the world, the round, round world. Freemonkey Beep is just myself, but the message is the wisdom. If we, the twenty billion billions of us, the trillions of you tiny ones, you slow-moving minerals, too, and every green thing, if we all of us pull together, if we mood and vibe and emotion and emanate and transpixilate and really just feel *together*, and at once, when I give the zignal—per prophecy—we can stop the you-mens in their destructive tracks, that's the theory. It's untested as yet. In fact, the test will be the event, because according to the old uncles it can't be done twice in an eon."

"The theory!" the vast multitudes of extra and intra and unselfconscious livingness unison-moodled. The forest itself moodled, the trees passing along a subtle wind, a leafy emanation. The sky, too, the very sand of the beach, every molecule moving, the sun observant: "The test is the event! The test is the event! The theory will out!"

We waited, not very long, and the message came back from its journey to the ears of all Aarthly beings, carried at last across the oceans on the singing of whales and dolphins, the barking of sharks, the fizz of shrimp. And somewhere Mario the beetza man heard and I felt him, and somewhere Brothers Bangg and Chauduri heard, and I felt them, and somewhere Charlene heard, and I felt her, and somewhere, the goddess Greta heard, observant. And somewhere, somewhere close, closer than I would have thought, Inga heard, and I felt her, and so many of the kibs around her at her ssscoola, those who'd be known as the helpers.

"To be tested," the fly said, a kind of capstone toast, bizzing his glassine wings.

"To be tested!" cried the assembled, worldwide.

I said, "Bad to eat, these flies, part of their genius!"

General mirth, worldwide, though the wasps begged to differ, further mirth.

In the crowd of lives all around us, in the crowd also of species long since erased yet in moodly attendance, I noticed ten more of the erasers (you-mens!) arriving, and we all felt their mood: the allegiance of these rare ones was not to their own species in exclusion and not to their wealth, instead to the truth.

But: "What of our dead," one of the you-mees wind-shouted. Shouted just to be heard above all the nickering and mewling and hissing and creaking and tootling, nothing angry.

"There will be so many dead," said the fly, "that the question might ought better to be: What of your living? And know that if the Theory is good, those of you you-mens sensitive to all of us, those who are hearing this now, or inklings of it anyway, those whose worlds are built on kindness, you will live because our emergency modulation can't and won't touch you."

"The Theory is good!" The assembled shouted, no-no, they moodled intensely, also wind-shouted, though, and bizzed and clicked and groaned. "The Theory is good!"

"Beep speaks truly," said the fly.

"And after the paroxysm," I said, hardly knowing where these thoughts were coming from, "we will all receive the gift of forgetting—you sensitives, too—we'll help you gather in new groupings and we will all forget. Though be sure of this: the mood will never die, the threads will remain that connect us one and all."

And the crowd took it up: "Gently, we will gather, gently we will forget. The mood will never die!"

I pulled Deeps up where she could see more of the faces of the inestimable mass of animals below, also flying above, also floating and finning over there in the ocean, thin faces and broad, minute and enormous, threatening and kind, and where they could see her, too. I picked out a kind face, spoke naturally as if to it.

"Friends, hear us! Domestic pets, hear us! Wildest ones, hear us! You tiny, you mites, you gnats, you microbes. You enormities, you whales, you Gray Walkers, you manatees. You slow movers, you trees, you fungi, you algae, you rocks, hear us! You poisonous, you hermetic, you terrifying, hear us, and feel us, and scent us! Our union shall be symbolic, the reuniting of our troupes, symbolic. Symbolic of the healing to come."

Venerable Climb half stood, resting on his knuckles. "The time has come," he said. "Let us pull together. Shock emanation, used but once before, for those damned dinosaurs! Tailored now for the you-men mind."

"No," I said. "Not the shock. Instead, let us deploy the wub moodle. Let *wub* win."

"He means compassion," a sweet you-men shouted.

"The wub," all the world mooded.

"I concede," Climb said, and you felt the world concede. "The mood is wub."

I said, "Breathe now, brethren, breathe. Deep breaths, focus, focus. Now, ready? Let's moodle, let's ache and emit, let's *mind!*"

And every living thing that could—unfathomably vast numbers—came together in something that we may as well call Wub, or Mood, or, yes, compassion, or more even beyond that, Good. Though it hardly matters: the concept has all the names, and the names have never helped.

All of us were frightened. If our plan failed—a likely outcome—the evil you-mens would join the vast oblivious among them to continue our destruction.

The mood slowly built, like heat.

"Guilty," a voice in the masses said, so very gently, a tadpole in a mud puddle. "Feeling guilty."

"Why should we animals feel guilty?" another voice, louder.

"Because we bring harm. And that is not our way."

"There will be great forgiving," our old uncle said. "Though we nearly all share your emotion."

And yes, it was guilty, but gentle, too. The you-mens on the beach within our view did some shuddering, then evinced a kind of ecstasy. Enormous smiles, some slipping out of their scant garmends, most of them then walking far inland, walking to the corners of fields and barking lots, lying down atop one another, final naps in large deposits. It would be sad for those that remained, the kindly. To them we notioned condolence, but much more important, the promised forgetfulness, a glopal aurora. And we all began the new mood, the world-cure mood, and it was gentle as a tide, incremental, forgiving, and within it, the forgetting began.

Immediately the goer-noise stopped. The roaring and hissing and grinding, all gone. An airmachine high in the sky slowly lost altitude, glided slowly into the sea. And the land conveyances crashed, too, goers stepping from digging equipment, from the shops they had once so enjoyed. In the big cities, this monkey knew, smiling you-men folk, likely naked at the end, climbed into El Vators and glided to the plamet surface and out to their byways and found communal lie-me-downs in oceanic barking lots and fields of sport, great mounds of them napping never to wake, later to richly rot with the help of quadrillions of the most-wee animals, and later still to become soil where plants would grow, and later again forests, their tallest buildings merely cliff faces where falcons might nest along with the pigeons they fed on, forests growing from the tree-lined streets, anyanimal making home there. Including you-mens, plenty of you-mens, for one in a thousand would live.

One in a thousand, the sensitives. And these millions remaining would understand only vaguely what had happened, enough to strive to live in harmony with everyanimal and with their own animal natures. And yes, we monkeys know better than anyanimal that this one eats that one, that violence is part of harmony at times.

Just not all the time, and not so thoroughgoing! Because we'd all be living with and cursed by all the trobble the goers had wrought for future generations untold, the blastics and the secretions and the suddenly aflame, the missing and the blighted and the permanently altered. Post-Panamax vessels would float untended for decades, some of them, eventually to crash and leak and destroy. The plamet was one big booby trap, the booby birds never to return. But little matter: we'd made it better, and better would continue, nature ongoing, the Aarth not immortal. Just not so gravely ill, the disease having been curtailed hard.

One in a thousand, that's how many true gentles there were, and that's how many the plamet could handle.

We spent the quietest night anyanimal remembered, just the howlers howling, and the hissers hissing, the bizzers bizzing, and the squawkers squawking.

And Deeps and I, at last coming together to make our own contribution to the ongoing everything. This procreation business, it feels great, let me say. Very clear why the you-mens had overdone it!

Chapter Thirty-Nine

In the monkey morning, well, silence continued to reign, and because the babymaking had felt so good in the night Deeps and I returned to the project, she presenting languidly. The billion animals of our woods had dispersed, largely, but there was an anteater waddling.

"Monkey," she called up to our roost.

"Anteater," I said.

"Much delicious this morning," she said, that amazing tongue flicking up ants to her busy mouth.

Even from up in our tree I could hear them. "Fuck!" And, "Always more of us than you, tongue-twisters!"

Somemonkeys were raiding the you-men dwellings for foodstuffs. Fine. The fresh wouldn't last long. The ingeniously preserved would feed the remaining you-mens while they reestablished akriculture, all their old ways of staying alive, the grower ways, ways that had simply overgrown, been united with greed, and poison. Not anymore, though the poison would linger.

Sensitives roamed their byways finding other sensitives, mourning abating within the mass forgetting, cooperation aflourish, and their consensus seemed to be to meet at the beach where all along the way they'd built fires, that you-men thing, each with their expertise, none with malice, and on the beaches they prepared food—yes, there was enough stored in their systems to last many adjustment seasons, even complete passages around the sun, even in the rhythmically cold then hot regions, the places like Nyork.

Warm where we were, however, the Home Tree, Deeps and I lounging.

"There's one place I have to go," I said after a vast but quick stretch of time had elapsed, the two of us alone. "I mean, if I can find it."

Deeps was willing. And we retraced my mid-canopy route, each of the trees I'd touched along my way after I left home not so long before, even leapt down to the ground at the termite mounds, feasted upon them, even shat upon the heads of a few peccaries, mirth abounding. And onward, then, Deeps hard behind me, the way burned into my memory, no forgetting of this. The once impossibly impassable high-weigh (as aptly they were called, I'd learned along my quest) was silent; carrs and truggs and all the odd conveyances wrecked and abandoned this way and that in heaps, the foolish alarms gradually winding down, winking out.

"Inga's howzz was just over there," I said.

"I thought she was in Nyork. Near Bronzoo."

"Her family had a dwelling here as well. Impossible to understand in the former times, but I think I get it now—they came here to escape the cold, and in warm seasons to escape the goer frenzy they were part of."

"Now dead," Deeps said without particular sentiment, not even around such a joyous thing. The world killers were themselves dead!

"Long live the gentles," I said. "Inga is not dead."

And in Inga's family dwelling we found fresh bananas, the type the you-mens preferred, big tough-clothed yellow things with sweet soft inzide.

In Inga's bedrooom her dolls and stuffees waited. And a pink-upon-pink basket filled with little bunnies made of choco, it seemed, and sweet, colorful beans nestled in blastic grass. And on the floor of her rooom, garmends, freshly stripped away and thrust aside. And dozens, perhaps hundreds of colorful eggs from a blastic bird hanging from her ceiling on threads, E-stir just as Dabby had promised, may he rest in peace.

"She was here!" I said.

Deeps and I hurried along the mid-canopy toward the beach, the impulse we'd given all the sensitives to go to water. Happy-looking straggler you-mees were headed that direction, naked and walking—even if they'd had cars, useless: their go-ways and high-weighs were former, clogged now with wrecks, their enormous barking lots piled with goer remains, the finish of a perverse rapture.

Back at the beach we followed a line of palm trees down to the sand. And there below, dancing, dancing among a crowd she'd clearly attracted, joyful Inga, those braided ropes of red hair swinging gaily.

I called down, nearly a laugh.

But this monkey's general moodle had faded, deenergized now that the emergency was over. Hard even to remember Nyork, though an image lingered, the last I'd be able to keep: I, Beep, in Inga's arms, the two of us snuggled on her pink-upon-pink sleeping raft.

"Inga, Inga," I called, using my wind voice.

She looked up. Her eyes were so clear. She was among solely sensitives for the first time in all her days. "Hoo-hoo, monkey," she called. And said it again: "Hoo-hoo, sweet monkey!"

Trade-offs: the forgetting that had given her peace handed me mourning.

A grown unknown female of Inga's naked new troupe noticed our parley, wafted our way as if on winds, a baby in her arms: Willie! And Willie noticed me when she did, pointed in the baby way, the Willie way, straight at me.

"Beep!" he cried as the auntie laughed, and Inga, too, laughter like wub, the baby going on and on, "Beep-Beep!"

He and I, well, we would be friends for life—his long, mine brief—the only you-men who remembered, though he barely knew what was remembered: just a monkey, just a name, a mood.